MICHAEL ALLEN GEORGE

MARUGE
PUBLISHING

Seeking Refuge

MICHAEL ALLEN GEORGE

This book is for
the forgotten ones
who made the mistake
of getting old

BOOKS BY
MICHAEL GEORGE

THE REFUGE MYSTERY SERIES

Why A Refuge	Book One
Bridge To No Good	Book Two
Grass Was Greener	Book Three
To Save The Refuge	Book Four
Without Refuge	Book Five
Refuge Of Another Kind	Book Six

THE REFUGE MYSTERY SERIES
WRITTEN AS MICHAEL ALLEN GEORGE

Places Of Refuge	Book Seven
Refuge Life And Home	Book Eight
Refuge Rescuers	Book Nine
Walking The Refuge	Book Ten
Lisa's Refuge	Book Eleven
Seeking Refuge	Book Twelve

BOOKS WRITTEN AS MICHAEL GEORGE

Horses Lemons And Pretty Girls
More Horses And Pretty Girls
Finding Peri Gray
Of Rain Barrels And Bridges

BOOKS WRITTEN WITH BUD GEORGE AND DAVID GEORGE

Stories From Three Brothers
More Stories From Three Brothers

PROLOGUE

Jamie Foster was fourteen and had little to no appreciation for the place in the world where he lived. He could see no beauty in the myriad of life forms surrounding him. The narrow country road he walked down was something to escape from, not live by. If it wasn't for his stupid parents, he would still be living in the city where all his friends were. Where there was something to do.

He picked up a rock and threw it at a squirrel, up high in an ancient oak tree. He missed it by enough, so the squirrel barely moved from his perch. He thought about a second rock, but decided it would be too much effort to throw another one.

He was on his way home. He'd walked the three miles from there to the general store, hoping they would have some new video games. They didn't, so he was in a bad mood. As he usually did, he walked with his head down most of the time. After all, there really wasn't anything to see on a country gravel road. Not like the city, where there were people and cars and girls and other stuff.

He had no interest in the wild flowers scattered in the ditches and hedgerows. For him, the small critters constantly scurrying around him were boring and not even worth the effort it took to look at, let alone throw rocks at.

The fresh county air just smelled bad compared to the city streets, where there was a constant scent of human activity. Where it was filled with real life. Here, all there was to see were butterflies and other bugs. On the ground there were only ground squirrels, snakes and rabbits. In the trees there was nothing but some birds and squirrels. For him, even a pair of scarlet tanagers were boring. Nature's colors meant nothing to him.

It all was nothing but boring, until Jamie saw a coyote crawl from under the branches of a weeping willow tree. That alone wouldn't have caught his attention, but the animal had something in its mouth. Something that looked very much like a human hand.

This time, what he saw was enough to inspire him to pick up a rock to throw at the coyote. When he did, something rare happened. He actually hit it, and it dropped what was in its mouth. It took off running, and the boy checked out what was dropped. It was a human hand. Somewhat mutilated, but still a human hand.

His heart skipped a beat when he saw the hand. He made a quick look around him, almost as if he thought someone might be watching him. As he grew aware of the fact that no one was, he turned his attention to the tree. He wondered now, what could be under it. He wanted to look, but was somewhat afraid of what he might find. What if someone dead was under there. What would he do then? He'd never been close to a dead body before.

He stood there, staring at the tree, trying to make up his mind about what to do. It wasn't until it occurred to him that if there was a body, it might have something worth money on it. That thought finally gave him the courage to look. Slowly, he crawled under the tree's low hanging branches.

The body he saw leaning against the tree, wasn't mutilated as bad as he expected. Its eyes were gone, part of a leg was chewed up some, and of course, the hand was missing. The kid stared for a while before he got too close to the body. Even the kid could tell it was an old man when it died.

Very slowly, he started a tentative search of the body. He didn't have to go far to find the letter the old man carried. The kid set it aside, then continued his search of the body. It took a while, but he managed to find the old man's wallet. The kid was delighted when he opened it. He found money there. He counted it. Slightly over a hundred dollars. A small fortune for him.

Now the question was what to do with the money. It was a cinch the old man didn't need it any longer. So he couldn't see any reason why he shouldn't keep it. The problem was, if he told his parents about finding this old man, they would ask him a lot of questions. They would find out about the money. And being the kind of parents they were, they probably wouldn't let him keep it. They would say it belonged to someone else. Like a relative of the old man maybe.

He decided that he didn't like that idea. He just wouldn't tell anyone about what he'd found. There were plenty of places to hide the money around the stupid farm where he now lived. He would keep it until the next time he got the chance to go to the city. He could save some and still have enough to buy some really great video games. He could tell his parents that he bought them with his allowance. They didn't know enough about games to know he had extra money to spend on some better games than those he already owned. To them, one game was the same as the other.

So he stuffed the money in his pockets. As an after thought, he picked up the letter as he crawled out from under the willow tree. He looked at the letter and thought about opening it, but it seemed so thin he was sure there was nothing in the envelope but a letter. It was addressed to someone named Mack Thomas. The only address was Refuge Rescuers, Kingsburg, MN.

He considered throwing it away, but then worried that someone might find it. That might make them wonder where it came from. He pondered the problem as he walked, but found a solution for it as he passed a neighbor's mailbox. The flag was up, telling the postal delivery person that there was mail to pickup. He opened the mailbox and put the letter he held in his hand in the box, leaving it wedged between some other envelopes. That way, the mail person wouldn't notice that the address on the envelope wasn't complete.

Now Jamie was a much happier person than he was before he saw the coyote. The letter would disappear in some post office so no one was ever going to find out about the body. He could keep the money now. As far as the body was concerned, he figured there were worse things that could happen to it then end up under a willow tree.

CHAPTER 1

The new girl at the post office wasn't sure what to do with the letter. The stamp was missing and the address was incomplete. But she had sorted a lot of mail that was sent to the Refuge Rescuers, so she showed it to her boss, the postmaster, Charlene Leaf, who took it from the mail sorter.

"I'll take care of it," she said. "Those are good people at Refuge Rescuers, and Mack Thomas has helped us out more than once. The way they do things, a person might sometimes think of them as more of a social services department than a private detective agency."

She decided then, that instead of following normal procedure, she would bring the letter out to Mack Thomas herself. He was a few years younger than she was, but she loved to flirt with him anyway. Especially since he went along with it. He also had a knack for keeping it light and fun. It was well known that a woman could easily flirt with him, but he never let it go any further than that. The way he felt about his wife, Lisa, had everything to do with how he reacted.

Luck was with Char when she brought him the letter. He was just returning to the office when she got there with it. He smiled when he saw her. He knew from past experiences with her, that whatever her reason for being there, her visit would be a pleasant one.

"What is it, Char," Mack asked, "that brings someone as beautiful and important as yourself all the way out here?"

"A letter addressed to you. The address is incomplete, there's postage due, and there's no return address on it."

"You drove out here for that? Why? Is there something special about it? It cost you more for the gas you burned in your car to get here than the postage amounts to."

She gave her dark eyes an exaggerated blink for him. Her eyes were her best feature on an already very pretty face. "That's not relevant. It gave me an excuse to come and see you." She grinned, and touched his cheek. "I thought I'd check and see if you wanted to sneak out some night soon. I can always tell my husband that I'm working late. He won't miss me for a few hours."

Mack grinned back at her. "Probably not a good idea for me," he told her, "but if I was ever going to sneak out on Lisa, I can't think of anyone I'd want to do it with more than you."

"Damnit, Mack, but you are such a smooth liar. You sure do know how to make a woman feel special. So how have you been otherwise?"

"Good. To damn busy like always, but good. Lisa and I have been talking about a vacation. I think we might actually take one this time. How about you? Is the post office treating you okay?"

"About as good as can be expected." She handed him some mail. "The letter in question is on top."

"How much do I owe you for postage?"

"Don't worry about it. You can maybe buy me coffee sometime when you're in town. I brought it out here, mainly because I like seeing you, and for a break. Once in a while, a break is nice." Without any warning, she gave him a kiss. It wasn't exactly romantic, but it wasn't just friendly either. "When decide you're ready to properly misbehave, call me. I'll make it worth it for you." With a wide grin, she got in her car and left.

Shaking his head, he brought the mail into the office. The fact that she'd pushed the flirting to a new level surprised him. To get his mind back on track, he looked through the mail. The most interesting thing in the pile was the envelope with no postage. So he opened it.

When he pulled out the letter, a key fell out of the envelope. He put it in his pocket so he wouldn't lose it. Then he opened the letter. When he saw who it was from, it was enough of a shock to make him sit down. It was from a man named Jasper Klug. A man he, along with his wife, Lisa, and their friends Dale and Kathy Magee, helped out one night. The whole incident had only covered a few hours. But it left a lasting impression on all four of them.

It began when Mack found Jasper in a bad way, laying next to a hiking trail in the wildlife refuge. He and Lisa had a serious disagreement earlier, and he was in the refuge to cool down. He knew he couldn't safely handle the man alone, so he called Lisa so she could help Mack deal with him. When she came, she brought their friends, Dale and Kathy along to help. The man didn't want to go to a hospital, so they brought him home. With that memory, Mack read the letter. It was hand printed on lined, yellow paper that came on a pad.

It started simple, with just the name, Mack. No dear in front of the name. It was short and directly to the point. It said, "I'm getting close to the end. I can feel it in every part of my body now. I've lived a long life, so it's not a big deal.

I'm writing to you, because I don't think I have anyone left who was part of my life in the past, who would care much about what I'm going to tell you. Or what I'm going to ask of you. I'm hoping that you found the key I put in the envelope. It's for a safe deposit box, which is in the Kingsburg Bank. I've already authorized you to access it. So don't let the bank give you a hard time about it. The package in the box is my story, such as it was. I know it probably isn't worth anything in the way of money, but from what I learned about you in our short time together, I think you might find some value in it.

I want you and Lisa to have it, because of the very uncommon kindness you and your friends showed me during the short time I spent with you. It went way beyond anything I've experienced for many years. Especially what Lisa and Kathy did. It went so far beyond exceptional, that I don't have the right thank you words for them. If you don't know all they did for me, and they don't want to talk about it, just know that it was a kindness done for an old man that went far beyond anything I deserved. No matter what though, don't ever lay any judgments on them. Love them instead. It was an incredibly wondrous moment during a time when the harshness of life seemed endless.

Almost as much, I loved being part of your conversation. You didn't treat me like some homeless bum who couldn't possibly have anything to say that was worth saying. You treated me with respect. Something else that was a long time coming. That's why I want you to have my story.

It's not just my life story. It's as much about the lack of respect for life itself. What we've done to this planet is an atrocity beyond description. And something needs to be done to fix that. But my story is about the way we destroy and throw away people.

I thought, when I started aging, that I still had something to offer. I did a lot of things in my years, so I figured that at least the stories I had to tell might mean something. They didn't. Nor did anything else about me matter. I was old and a burden.

I was determined not to be a burden to anyone though. That's why you found me where you did when you did. I was trying to find a place to rest. Most of society doesn't like to see us homeless types rest. So I try to be out of sight when I do it. As far as you finding me, I'll be grateful to you and Lisa, Kathy, and Dale, as long as I'm alive.

I didn't stay with you because I didn't want to be a burden to you either. It's been a couple of days now, since my time with you. I kind of wish now that I'd stayed longer. Even just a day or two. All four of you seemed to have something burning inside you. A something that went way beyond the day to day just getting by.

It looked to me that you had big dreams of fixing big problems. But you weren't afraid to take the time with small problems. Problems like me. An old man, with no longer a place to go. For that, I again thank you. I thank all four of you. Especially Lisa. She has the softest of hands.

But I'm tired now, Mack. So I'm going to put this in a mailbox somewhere tomorrow maybe, so you get it. I still have enough cash for a stamp.

Lord, but I am feeing tired."

Your, I hope, friend,

Jasper Klug

Mack wasn't sure what to make of the letter. He'd had the feeling when Jasper left them without a goodbye, that they'd all missed something that was valuable. Something told him that Jasper wasn't just an old man who would get in the way. He was a real person who came across as a man who had a lot to say about life and what mattered. But like too many old people, he'd been pushed out of the way, as if he was nothing but a useless old body who did nothing but burden young people. The people who, in their own opinion, were the only ones who mattered.

Jasper was just one more on an endless list of people who committed the sin of getting old. People shuffled aside by an all too busy world. Often into nursing homes. Most of them places that couldn't provide a real home for anyone, no matter how hard they tried. And a lot of them didn't even try. They were simply a warehouse for old, worn out bodies to go to to die. Often of acute loneliness.

So it was with a heavy heart and a deep sense of frustration that Mack walked the short distance home. His wife, Lisa, was in their home office, using their home computer to pay some bills.

She gave him the same smile she always gave him when they saw each other again after being separated any more than an hour or so. Then she saw the grim look on his face and her smile wilted into a frown.

"What is it, Mack. Why do you look so down?"

"Because sometimes life sucks for too many people. I got l strange letter today. I don't think we can solve the problem, but in this case I want to try to do something. If nothing else, learn from it." He handed her the letter. "I'd like for you to read this. Then we'll talk about it."

Lisa read the letter. She was an exceptionally strong women and had seen and felt more of the world's evils and problems than most people. Be they male or female. Even so, tears lightly rolled down her cheeks when she handed it back to Mack.

"I can see by the look on your face, Mack, what you want to do. So do I. I have no idea where it's going to take us as we try to find him and follow his story. But I can't imagine not doing it."

"You're right. We have all the resources we need to do any research or tracking we might need to be done in the company office. I think we should use that vacation we planned on taking to do whatever it takes. I have a feeling there's going to be a lot of travel involved in looking for the answers I already want. I just hope we can find him before he's gone from us permanently. Either way though, I want to follow through on this. We've done a lot of work for a lot of people. Some of it important. I think that this, whatever it turns out to be, will be something that matters to us, too you and me. I don't think it needs to be important to anyone else."

"I can't argue with that, Mack. For me, it's pretty much whatever it takes for us to get it done. Let's talk to everyone about at the breakfast meeting in the morning."

"Good idea. We'll do that."

Mack went into their living room and sat down in his favorite chair. Lisa joined him a few minutes later. She curled up in his lap. They both found comfort in their closeness. It was, they knew, near the best thing they had in their lives. Each other. It was a lot later before they moved off the chair. Even then, they didn't get very far apart.

Because of the lives they'd lived, they knew all too well how fragile life could be. And because of their occupation, their lives were more fragile than most. So they tried to live it the way they thought best. For them, the best was the time they had together. That meant they were careful to never miss a chance to be close.

CHAPTER 2

Every morning, Mack's father, Ben, and his wife, Theresa, cooked breakfast for anyone who managed to be there for it, who was part of the detective agency, Refuge Rescuers. Ben started doing it years before, when Mack came home after several years of chasing rodeo. He was a bull rider.

The shared breakfast grew into a tradition. As time went on, more people were part of it. Now it included everyone from Refuge Rescuers, along with an occasional guest.

Mack and Lisa created a custom of their own. They were nearly always among the last to arrive at Ben and Theresa's for breakfast. Mack's uncle Roy and his wife Wanda, were almost always the first to arrive. Roy, being the kind of person he was, always had a comment or two when Mack and Lisa got there. He especially enjoyed teasing them, because the cause of their tardiness was caused by their continuously acting as if they were newlyweds.

This morning, Roy didn't have too much to say when they got there. They arrived shortly after Roy and Wanda did. "You two look awful serious this morning," was his opening comment. "Is there something serious that we're going to talk about today?"

Mack handed him Jasper's letter. "I want you and Wanda to read this letter. I'm going to have everyone who shows up today read it. Then we'll talk about it. It's something Lisa and I want to follow through on. So it's important, because we will be gone a lot for a while. How long? We have no idea. Whatever it takes I guess."

"That sounds serious," Roy said.

"Probably only to us," Lisa answered this time. "Mack and I aren't quite sure why this is so important to us, but it is. And since we're a few years overdue for a vacation, we thought we'd make this project part of the vacation we want to take anyway."

Roy's wife, Wanda, answered Lisa. "God knows you've earned a long vacation. But why don't you just find a quiet place to rest and maybe do a little fishing?"

"I might be able to do that," Lisa told her, "but Mack wouldn't last more than a couple of days that relaxed. You know how he's always got to be busy."

"Yeah, I remember. Wasn't a day we were in Texas, that he wasn't busy with something."

Mack and Wanda spent some time together on Roy's ranch years before. It was a hard time for Mack, but still filled with a lot of good memories for both of them.

As soon as Roy finished reading the letter, he gave it to Wanda. She was shaking her head when she finished. "It's really sad that people like Jasper have to feel that way. And to be living homeless because he doesn't want to be a burden on his children's lives."

"It is that," Roy agreed. "And Jasper sounds like he's an interesting person. But where did he come from? How do you know him? You've never mentioned him before."

Mack gave Roy a brief description of their time with Jasper. Then said, "We'll talk more about it when more people get here."

It took close to another hour before they were ready to bring the subject of Jasper Klug to a full discussion. Mack gave them all a description of the time they spent with Jasper. Leaving out, of course, what Lisa and Kathy did for him when they put him to bed. Something that was an unusual act of kindness for a very lonely old man.

"So," Roy was the first to ask, "what are your plans for finding that old man?"

Mack answered him. "To start with, check out the safe deposit box, and get the manuscript that's supposed to be there. Then read at least part of it to start. Maybe even all of it right away if it isn't too long. We are also going to purchase two class C RVs. If not new, then late model, depending on what's available in this area. One of them is obviously for Lisa and me to travel in. The other is going to be for everyone else in Refuge Rescuers. As we travel, we are hoping you guys will be able to come visit us now and again. You can come as couples, or whoever is single can come alone, or with whoever you want to bring."

Mack paused a moment to let everyone digest what he'd just said. No one asked Mack about the cost of the RVs. Even though he lived on the scale of the average wage earner, they knew he was rich. Years before he received an unexpected inheritance that ran into millions.

Sue Sartor, the agency's technical expert, was the first one to ask a question. "Are you going to want help while you're out wandering, trying to find that guy?"

"We will. Your help especially. We might even want it when you come visit us, wherever we might be. Can you make a laptop work where there's no WiFi?"

"No problem. We have one that uses cell phone technology. But even with that, there are places where I won't be able to get online. So on those times I come to visit you. you'll want to give me any questions as soon as possible. That way, I can hopefully get you the answers you want when I get there."

"That sounds good," Mack said. "Most of the time, we won't have the same urgency to get answers as we do with most jobs we take on. I'm anxious to find Jasper, but I know that the odds of doing so are pretty slim. But based on what we find at the bank, I'm pretty sure that we'll be wanting to learn as much about him as we can."

"We only knew him a few short hours," Lisa said. "But there was something special about him, that made all of us that were with him that night wish we could have known him better. A lot better, actually. So I for one want to do every thing we can to find him. And if we can't do that, at least learn a lot more about him."

No one disagreed with their plan to try to find Jasper Klug. No one even questioned the validity of the venture. Most of them thought it would be a good thing for them to be doing something, that as far as any of them could see, had no danger or violence connected to it. That lack appealed to Mack and Lisa even more than it did to anyone else. They'd already seen enough violence and been in enough danger to last a lifetime.

So after breakfast, they went to Kingsburg and to the bank. As Jasper said they would be in the letter, they were authorized to get into the safe deposit box. So there was no hassle there. The manuscript was the only thing in the box, so it gave them little to immediately go on as far as finding Jasper.

The manuscript itself was hand printed, rather than typed. The handwriting was clear, and could be read without difficulty. It was a couple of inches thick, but had it been typed, it would have been less than an inch.

When they brought it back to the office, Lisa's sister, Julie, came up with an idea to make the whole procedure work a lot smoother. She was working for Refuge Rescuers, along with Sue, learning how to use technology in ways the average layman would never understand. She was also in training to be a private detective.

Her idea was simple. Enter the manuscript into a computer, using the word processing program called Word. From there, it could be turned into an ebook and put into other computers, tablets, or cell phones. That way, any number of people could be reading it, making it much faster to learn what it was about. Best of all, it made the task of reading it far easier. Once it was set up, whoever was reading it could choose the size of the font, and even the font itself.

They typed the manuscript in one day, by splitting the manuscript into several sections, so several people people could work on it at once. The sections were numbered, so when the typing was completed, all they had to do was merge them in sequence on the computer.

While all that was being done, Mack and Lisa went shopping. First to a RV dealer. Even though they could easily afford them, they found the sticker prices on the machines shocking. They checked out three dealers, and ended up buying the two RVs from the first dealer they went to.

Originally, they planed to buy a larger one for themselves, and a smaller, less fancy one for the others to use. Instead, because that's what was readily available, they purchased two moderately sized and priced RVs that were virtually identical.

As he usually did, Mack dressed in his western style clothes while he shopped. Lisa was dressed simply. She was wearing jeans, a light blouse, and had her hair in a pony tail. So when they completed the deal with the RV salesman, and Lisa sat down to write the check for the full amount, the man was a lot surprised.

He had to ask. "Are you sure you're able to do that. It's a hell of a lot of money, and you two don't strike me as the kind of people who could write a check like that one."

"Well," Mack asked, "would you prefer we go somewhere else? There's plenty of dealers who'd love to get paid in cash for a sale as big as this one. Even if they did lose their kickback on the loan. It's up to you.

Especially since you can make sure the check clears before you deliver the vehicles to us. And that'll be a while, because as soon as we're done here, we'll be going out to buy something to tow behind one of them."

The salesman shook his head. "I apologize. But this is the first time since I started selling RVs that anyone's written a check for so much."

Mack chuckled at his response. "It's okay. It happens to us a lot. Now you do what you have to do to get these things ready to deliver. And make sure that all of the gas tanks are full. We'll be back later with something for you to hook up a towing system to."

Late that afternoon, two class C RVs were driven into a parking area Mack made for them near his house. It didn't take long for most of the people who would at one time or another be using one of them, to come and check them out.

Roy, of course, was the first one of them. "I would have thought you'd have bought one a little bigger, and maybe somewhat fancier, for you and Lisa. There's no difference in the two. Why?"

"Number one, we really liked these two. There weren't a whole lot of them out there the size we wanted. There's no way I want to be driving one of those class A monsters. Besides, whoever it is that uses the other RV is going to be doing and needing the same things as us. They might as well have the same accommodations as we do."

"I guess, but it is pretty generous of you."

"Not really. Not when it comes to all you guys. If Lisa and I were going into this alone, I don't know that we'd do it. The support we'll be getting from all of you will make this whole effort a lot easier."

"I have to agree with you on that, Mack. We're all lucky to be working in a group like we have here at Refuge Rescuers."

Mack smiled. "That explains best, why we bought what we did."

Roy returned his smile. "I like your choice of tow vehicle too. That little Jeep will tow easily, and will take you places you couldn't go with most vehicles."

"That's what we thought. I didn't buy one for the other RV, because what we'll be doing now means that when it's being used, it'll be with us. If we find we need one sometime later, I'll buy another Jeep."

"Well, Mack, it looks like you're all set to go."

"Pretty much, in a day or two. I want to check into the manuscript first. Then decide where to go from there. It might have some hints as to where we might find him."

"I hope it does. We've all gotten to the point that we want to meet him. I think that he, too, will enjoy meeting all of us. From his letter, he sounds pretty lonely. I think that between the bunch of us, we can do something about that."

"Me too, Roy. Me too. So let's hope we can find him in time."

CHAPTER 3

Everyone who looked at the RVs had the same thoughts about them as Roy. They thought Lisa and Mack were especially generous to buy the one for everyone else to use identical to the one they would be camping in.

The general consensus about Jasper Klug was the same as Roy's was too. A universal hope that they could find him before anything bad happened to him. To a large extent, what they had was a fear he would die before he could be found.

The same thought continued to plague Mack as they tried to plan their trip. It was enough to make him stop what they were doing.

"You know, Lisa, I think that before we start any traveling, we need to check close to home to see if we can find any trace of Jasper."

"I agree, Mack, but where the hell do we start?"

"I think the best place might be the post office. If we can find out where his letter was mailed from, then that might give us a clue or two as to where he is."

"I think that's a long shot, but it still sounds like a good place to start."

"Let's do it then. The post office will still be open for a couple of hours yet. If we go now, we might get the chance to talk to someone who remembers where they picked it up."

"I don't think it should be a we that goes there. You should go alone. I'm pretty sure Char will be more willing and a lot quicker to help if you go alone."

"I don't think my being alone will make her any more willing to help than what she would be if you came."

Lisa chuckled at Mack's answer. The way he was so often oblivious to the way women reacted toward him was often difficult to believe. They almost always found him to be someone they enjoyed being around. They loved the way he focused on them, whether it was just a conversation or something more active. With many of them, Char Leaf the postmaster being a perfect example, their reaction to Mack was a lot stronger.

Her reaction to Mack was one of a sexual nature. She was a woman who'd followed the strait and narrow path all her life. She had never had even the slight consideration of cheating on her husband before she met Mack. From that day on, she knew she wouldn't say no if he asked. In fact, she'd reached the point with him that she encouraged him to ask. So Lisa was correct when she said that Mack would get more help alone, than what they'd get together.

"Mack, sometimes I'm not sure if you really are that dense about how woman see you, or if you just act that way so I don't get upset. Either way, it doesn't change the way Char feels about you. She goes way beyond any normal friendship. She's got the hots for you, Mack. Big time. And I'm anxious enough to find Jasper to take advantage of it."

"If she does, as you say, have the hots for me, aren't you worried that I might take advantage of it?"

"No. There was a time I might have, but no more. You and I have been through enough to keep us from doing that. But even if you slipped up and did do something, I know you'd come home to me."

"Okay, I think that's settled now. I also think I'd like to have you along. Your skills in solving this kind of thing are as good as, if not better than, mine."

"That might be true. But in this situation, you will get further to start with going it alone then you will if I'm along. So get the hell out of here and see what you can find out. I can always work on it with you later."

Mack gave up on trying to convince Lisa to go with him then, and drove into town. Postmaster Charlene Leaf was delighted to see him when he got there. Enough so, that he finally realized how accurate Lisa's assessment of Char's feelings were. He knew that without a doubt, it would be a very good idea for him to be careful with her.

After their initial greeting, he told her, "What I'd appreciate help with, Char, is trying to figure out where that no postage letter you brought me came from."

"You mean like, what mailbox it was in when it was picked up?"

"Yes. That might give us some ideas about where to start looking for the man who sent it."

"I take it you don't know the person who sent it that well?"

"I don't. I hardly knew him at all, but from what I do know, I'd very much like to find him and get to know him better." Mack told her what they knew about Jasper.

"Figuring out where it was mailed will depend entirely on the mail carrier who picked it up. Given who was sorting the mail it was mixed with, the letter had to have been picked up from a rural mailbox. She sorts the mail brought in by some of the ones who only deliver to the rural areas. Odds are, given the amount of mail those people handle, whoever picked up the letter won't remember it."

"That I know. We've known from the start that finding the answers we're looking for is a long shot. Even so, it makes more sense to try than it does to do nothing."

The look she gave Mack then was something between a grin and a smirk. "You are so right on that. You're trying to do what you want to do, so I'm going to work on what I want to eventually accomplish. I'll give you all the help I can, if you'll take me out for a drink or two when we're done today."

"If that's what you want to do, I'll be more than happy to take you out for a drink or two. Although, I don't know why you'd want me to do that."

She giggled. For her, his question was so absurd it was the only response she find. "Mack, if you haven't figured that out by now, you plain haven't been paying any attention. The reason I want you to take me out for drinks is because you aren't ready to be convinced to take me where I'd really like to go with you."

Try as hard as he could not to do it, Mack smiled. "I hate to tell you this, Char, but the odds of that happening aren't any better than finding out where the letter came from."

"Well then, I guess we'd better get to work and find out where it came from. And if we do, and you figure out where that man Jasper is, you have to promise me more than just a thank you."

"I will promise you some of what you want," Mack said. "But I can't promise you all of it. Lisa's too important to me to be able to do that."

"Good enough. To get started, since it'll be a while before anyone gets done and comes back here at the end of the day, I'll see if I can get them on their cell phones. Even if they can't answer our questions right away, it'll start them thinking."

On the third call, the mail carrier she connected with remembered the envelope. "Normally, there's no way I'd remember something like that. But I remember that one because of the way it was put in the mailbox. The folk's whose mailbox it was in, had four or five other out going envelopes in the box. That letter was in the middle of the pile, but near half of it was sticking out, like it wasn't really part of the pile. When I looked at it, I saw it was addressed to Refuge Rescuers. So even though there wasn't any postage on it, I kept it with the rest of the mail. Was I wrong in doing that?"

"No," Char answered. "You did the right thing. Do you remember whose mailbox it was in?"

"I sure do," the carrier answered, then gave Char the name of the people and their address.

"Well now," Char said, "that was quick. We now know where to start looking. I think though, it'll be best to wait until tomorrow to go see the folks who had the letter in their mailbox. Because of who they are, I have my doubts that they put it there. It would be my guess, that your friend did it. given that he's homeless, you might find him around there someplace. At least, I hope you do." She laughed softly. "It'll be to my advantage if you do."

Her comments at first gave him hope, then scared the hell out of him. He'd just made a promise that he never would have done if he'd known that there was even the slightest chance he would have to keep it. And now it looked like he might have to, because out and out lying to Char wasn't something he would want to do. He knew then that he'd have to talk to Lisa to find out what the right answer to his problem might be. Even giving Char part of what she wanted, was more than what would be fair to Lisa.

Char called the people who owned the mailbox the letter was found in, and made an appointment with them for mid-morning the next day. She then did something with her computer and left some instructions for the people left working in the office. At the same time, Mack called Lisa.

She was delighted when Mack told her what they'd already learned, and what he and Char would be doing the next day. She laughed hard when he told her that Char wanted to go out for a couple of drinks.

"I shouldn't say I told you so, Mack. But what the hell, I told you so. And it is okay for you to go. Just so long as you don't get too carried away. That would be something very easy to do with a woman as pretty as Char."

"I don't plan on being late, Lisa. I don't plan on doing anything I shouldn't either."

"I'm sure you don't," Lisa agreed, "but the fact that you mentioned that at all, tells me you're thinking about it."

Mack could tell by Lisa's tone of voice that she wasn't upset with him. It was much more that she was teasing him about what was happening, and enjoying his discomfort with the situation.

"I know you're having fun with this, Lisa," he said, "and that's okay." This time he chuckled. "Just keep in mind that I will be taking all of this out on you when I get home."

As soon as he hung up his cell phone, Char took his arm and led him out to his truck. As he opened the door to his pickup he asked, "So you don't want to take your car this time."

"No, I sure don't. It's still working hours, so it's best no one sees my car parked in a bar's parking lot."

"Does that include your husband?"

"It does. Mostly because it would embarrass him if one of his friends noticed it and said something to him. Otherwise, I'm not so sure he'd give much of damn about it."

"That doesn't sound good. If us having a drink tonight is going to cause problems between you and him, maybe it'll be best if we don't do this?"

"It won't. And the thing is, right now, I wouldn't care if it did. Some time alone with you, Mack, is worth what ever trouble it might cause me."

Mack parked in the lot behind the bar, and they went in the back door. He didn't see any sense in advertising the fact that the two of them were having a drink alone together.

Inside the bar, she led him to the booth in the farthest back corner there. She took his hand as she slid into the booth, then pulled him in next to her. She was smiling as she did it.

The waitress came and took their drink order before they had the chance to start a conversation. They didn't say anything to each other until she brought Char her bourbon and water and Mack his usual glass of beer. Char sipped her whiskey, then set it down and turned to Mack. He drank some of his beer and then set his glass down.

The bar was quiet and they were for the most part out of sight from everyone. Char didn't hesitate. She put her hand behind his neck and gently pulled him to her. Their lips met, her tongue slipped out, and he opened his mouth for her. The kiss was long and filled with a scorching heat. She was breathing heavy when they split apart. She let her hand drop high on his leg.

"I think we've gone as far as we're going to go," Mack said. "It's not that I didn't like what we just did. The truth is, I loved it. But I can't let this go any further. You know why."

"I sure do, Mack," she said, moving her hand as far up his leg as she could without getting totally intimate. "But damn, I like kissing you."

"I like kissing you too. But that doesn't change what is."

"I know. It won't either. Until we find that Jasper person you're looking for. Then you'll have to keep your promise."

"Well, even if I do, there'll still be limits to how far we go."

She moved her hand up and down, then around on his leg. "I think that remains to be seen. We go that far, it'll be damn hard to stop it."

"I'm sure it will, but I've faced hard before. We'll somehow do it."

"Facing hard is what I'm looking for. Followed by doing it." She chuckled and moved her hand over him.

He shook his head no, and gently moved her hand. Undefeated, she kissed him again. Rather than try to stop it, he let it happen. He quickly found himself enjoying it way too much.

"I think, Char," he told her, "that if we kiss like that even once more, this time together tonight is going to get cut real short."

"Okay," she said, "I'll behave. Until we find Jasper tomorrow anyway."

She didn't try to kiss him again, but she did slide her hand over him a couple of times before she moved it up on the booth. Once she settled down, Mack found her to be good company. She was intelligent, knowledgable, and could talk about any manner of topics. Mack especially liked the fact that she knew a lot about the environment. They had three drinks before they called it a night. When they got back to the post office, it was closed.

"I want to kiss you goodnight," she told Mack. "But not out here. Come inside with me for a minute."

Against his better judgement he did. They didn't get very far inside before they were locked in a passionate embrace. It lasted far longer than Mack hoped it would. It took a lot of will power for him to break it off.

"Another time and another place, Char. I'm sorry to say though, this isn't the right time or place. You can congratulate yourself on one thing tonight. You did get to me. Big time."

She looked at him, her eyes slightly misty. "Thanks for saying that, Mack. After tonight, I'll be looking for that other time and that other place."

She wasn't crying when he left her, but she was close. Later that night, when she thought about wanting the wrong thing and did cry, her husband didn't notice. Her next thought was, "Mack would have noticed."

CHAPTER 4

Lisa was definitely waiting for him when he got home. He was surprised to find her in his favorite nightgown. She was freshly showered and her hair was combed out, the way she wore it when she dressed up for special occasions. She was wearing the makeup Mack preferred to see on her. Which is to say, she didn't have any on.

As soon as he saw her, he stopped. He stood perfectly still, with only his eyes moving over her. Seeing her this way was something he was having a hard time absorbing. All he could do was wonder how he could be so lucky that he could come home to the woman he was watching.

Finally he said, "I think I'm in the wrong house. There's no way I could be lucky enough to come home to anyone as beautiful as you are. I don't think you're real. You must be an angel or something."

"No, Mack. I'm just your almost forgotten wife, waiting for you to come home. Your supper is going to have to wait tonight. Earlier, you promised that what ever you had to do tonight, you were going to take out on me. So now I expect you to carry me to our bed and do just that very thing. More than once."

When he picked her up the joy of doing it made her feel lighter than a feather. Once they were together on the bed, time floated by them faster than a feather in a strong wind. By the time they left the bed, darkness filled the room. It was so late that all they had for supper was canned soup. Luckily they were so contented by then, that even the soup was gourmet food to them.

Sleep came so late for them that night, that Mack barely got up in time for his meeting with Char. When he got to the post office, she was all business until they were on their way and away from all of her employees.

"I have to tell you, Mack," she said, back in the flirtatious mood, "I had a really good time last night. So I hope that even if we never go to the place I want to go, I'd like it if you and I could just be friends. You know, like the people who have coffee or lunch together now and then. Or maybe even go out for a drink occasionally."

"I'd like that. I had a good time last night too."

"Good. I'm going to count on it." She sighed, sounding as if she'd found some kind of relief from something serious. "Now, about today. I don't know these folks all that well. Only that they're good, church going people, and are likely going to try to help as much as they can, once you tell them what this is all about."

"Sounds good. I'll try to be as laid back as I can when I talk to them. I don't want in any way to spook them."

"I don't think that'll be any problem, Mack. One of the things I and so many other people like so much about you, is the fact that you always come across as who you are. A kind and gentle man, who doesn't need to prove anything by playing the part of some macho male."

Mack didn't know how to answer that, so he did it with a compliment of his own. "You're a lot more than only nice yourself, Char. I consider myself to be a real lucky man to have you as a friend."

They were quiet then, until they reached their destination. The two story farm house appeared to be in near perfect condition. It was freshly painted, and even the roof looked fairly new. The only thing that seemed way out of place was the paved driveway. It was too much of a contrast to the hundred or more years old house, and the ancient looking red barn behind it. Mack thought the place would look better with the original gravel driveway.

The only one home when they got there was the wife. She was a handsome lady, even though she'd added several extra pounds in her fifty years of living. She introduced herself as Mace Nutman. Being a real, old-time country person, she insisted they sit down for a cup of coffee.

As soon as they were settled in with it, Mack explained why they were there. She smiled when he finished. Even before she said anything, her faced was filled with the look of someone very pleased with herself.

"I don't claim to understand why that old man you hardly know is so important to you, but I think I can help. I know who put the envelope in our mailbox. I watched him do it. I thought it was kind of strange, but then Jamie is a bit different."

"If you do," Mack told her, "it's a lot more than I expected to learn today. I sure will appreciate it if you'd tell me who it is."

"I will, if you'll promise me that you won't be hard on him, no matter what his reason for putting it in our mailbox was."

"No problem there. All I want to do is find Jasper. Anything else isn't that important."

Mace turned too Char. "I have to ask you. Can I trust you to tell me the truth? Will Mack treat him fairly."

"More than likely, he will go beyond fair. I've never known Mack to ever intentionally hurt anyone. Other that some evil ones who deserved to be hurt. There's no way Mack would ever consider putting a letter in a mailbox to be doing any kind of evil."

"Sorry I had to do that, Mack," Mace explained. "But the person with the letter was our neighbor. They haven't lived there long. It was a boy who put the letter in our mailbox. His name is Jamie Foster. He's only about fourteen. He seems to be unhappy with his life as it is now. He's a kid from the city, and hasn't taken to country life at all well."

"How far away does he live?"

"Next door." She pointed out which side of her place the kid lived. Her version of next door was a quarter mile down the road.

Mack was in a hurry then, to talk to the kid. But he endured another hour of small talk in order to be polite. He knew there could be a chance he'd need some kind of help from this lady sometime in the future. It only made sense to stay on the good side of her.

Another lady answered the door when Mack and Char knocked on the neighbor's door. Mace had called her, so she knew they were coming. She said she was Lily, but didn't give them her last name. They already knew it was Foster.

Just as Mace did, she insisted they sit down for coffee. Once she had them settled at her kitchen table, she left the room to get her son. When she returned with him, Mack was instantly worried that it might be impossible to get any kind of good answers from the kid. His look was belligerent, scared, and skeptical, all at the same time.

Mack introduced himself, doing his best to keep his voice soft as he talked. He then explained about the letter, and how their only real interest was in finding the man who wrote it.

Jamie was quick to answer Mack. "I don't know nothin'," he claimed. "I found the letter layin' on the road. It was by the Nutman's mailbox. Their flag was up, so I knew they had mail going out. I thought the letter fell out, so I put it back."

Jamie sounded good, for a fourteen year old liar. Mack's experience as a deputy sheriff told him that was exactly what Jamie was. He was sure the kid knew a lot more than he was telling them. The question was, how could he get him to tell the truth?

He looked around the room. The house was a nice enough, but these people obviously didn't have a lot of money too spare. He knew that he could eventually get Jamie to talk, but that it could take hours. At the same time, he didn't think bribing the kid was the best thing for him. He decided on that option anyway.

"I'll tell you what, Jamie. If you'll be more up front with me, and what you tell me helps me find that old man, I'll give you a five hundred dollar reward. If I find him right away because of what you tell me, I'll give you two thousand dollars."

Lily stepped in then. "Now don't go making promises you won't keep," she said. "It wouldn't be fair to Jamie."

Mack took out his checkbook and wrote two checks. One for five hundred. The other for two thousand. He handed them to Lily.

"You can hang on to them. If Jamie tells me what I want to know, you can keep which ever check he's earned." He looked at Jamie. "Is that okay with you?"

"Yeah, it's okay. But if I tell you the stuff you want to know, you got to promise me you won't get mad. Someone's always gettin' mad at me. So you got to promise."

"You've got it. Whatever it is, I won't get mad."

"Okay, but instead of me tellin' you all of it right away, I think it'll be better if we go for a walk first. There's something you need to see. Then I'll tell you what I can."

Jamie took them outside and walked them down the road. Mack was beginning to wonder if Jamie might be playing some kind of game with him. Then they stopped by a particularly beautiful old weeping willow. Jamie refused to look at it. Instead, he just pointed.

"In there," he said. "It's not my fault.'

Really unsure about what was going on now, Mack crawled under the tree. He didn't stay very long. He had tears in his eyes when he crawled out.. He looked at Char. "I owe you," he said, "But I won't be able to pay you today. It'll have to wait." He looked at Jamie. "Keep both checks," Mack told him. "And the money you found in his wallet too. Just don't tell anyone about it."

Char looked under the tree, then went back onto the road. She took out her cell phone and dialed 911. Mack used his to call Lisa. He needed to ask her to wait a minute when she answered. It took him a while before his voice was steady enough to tell her about Jasper Klug.

She said she was on her way there when they hung up. Mack went back under the tree and went through Jasper's billfold. He used his cell phone camera to take pictures of each thing he found in it. He knew that whoever the cops were that got there first, they would want everything that was in the wallet. He also knew that they would then be very reluctant to share the information.

When Lisa got there, Mack suggested that she not look under the tree. Lisa being Lisa, she did anyway. She didn't cry, bad the sadness written all over her face was obvious. Her hold on Mack was strong. They backed away far enough to talk softly to each other.

"You know, Mack, knowing that he died alone the way he did, makes me glad I did for him what I did. If I could do it over, I might give him even more."

"That doesn't surprise me." Mack said. "But don't be too sad that you didn't. What you did for him went way beyond anything he would have ever expected."

"I know. But I still wish…"

"We all wish this would have turned out different. And as sad as it is that it ended this way, we were at least able to give him a few good hours, not too long before he died."

"So now that we know he's gone, and that there's nothing more we can do for him, where do we go from here?"

"First, I think we need to find someone in his family, to find out what they want to do to his body."

"They didn't want him when he was alive, Mack. Why would they want anything to do with his body?"

"Odds are, they won't. We'll take care of it then."

"Just like we so often end up taking care of things." Lisa looked and felt a little lost. "We spent a lot of money on those RVs. Are we still going to take some kind of vacation? Or did it get canceled when you found his body?"

"I definitely still want the vacation. One of the things we can do is read his manuscript, and maybe visit some of the places where he spent some time. Maybe even part of his life. We can go to other places too. Whatever seems to be the right thing at the time. I think we'll have more fun if we don't plan too much."

"I like that idea, Mack. For us, it's the only thing that will work anyway. Regimentation just isn't our long suit."

Knowing that anything between her and Mack was going to have to wait for another day, Char went back to the post office. Mack and Lisa stayed around, waiting for someone from law enforcement to arrive. They were pleased to see Dale when he was in the second official car to arrive.

"You found him then," Dale said. "It sure didn't take you long. How did you manage it?" Mack explained how he did it. "It all makes sense. Char can be a lot of help when she wants to be." Dale gave Mack a wry smile.

"I don't think we need to go there," Mack answered softly. He shook his head. "The fact that she was a lot of help is all we need to say about her."

Once Dale had everything moving smoothly, they decided it was time to go home. Lisa gave Dale a hug just before they got in the truck. They were home and in the house before Mack mentioned what she did to Dale.

"I think you embarrassed him," he told her. "He was on duty."

"Maybe. But he's a friend. I felt like giving him a hug, so I did," she answered.

"I know. It's just that sometimes I get a kick out of the way you're so open with your feelings. I kind of like the fact that you can still care so much about some people in spite of all of the really hard times you've been through."

"Don't you see, Mack. You were there. As long as I have you close, it's easy to trust. Without you, well, I don't know."

CHAPTER 5

Jasper's manuscript was converted into an ebook by the next afternoon. Mack and Lisa both managed to read it in a couple of days. They found it interesting that Jasper had written his own life story like a novel, rather than as a journal. The story was character based, and the general layout of the book tended to feature one or two different people each chapter. So the story constantly moved back and forth in time. It wasn't great literature, but was well written enough to be very easy reading.

The character that caught Mack's attention the most was Jasper's brother. Liam Klug. He was six years younger than Jasper. Even so, they were close from the time Liam was around five, until Jasper went homeless. According to the manuscript, now referred to by everyone as The Book, Jasper's relationship with everyone stopped when he went homeless.

They decided then, to first find and visit the brother, Liam. Dale and Kathy would have been their choice to meet them on this first RV journey, since they were with Lisa and Mack when they helped Jasper. But Kathy had a concert already scheduled for that weekend. So they drew straws and Roy and Wanda won. They would be the first to camp with Mack and Lisa in the new RVs.

Mack and Lisa sat down with Sue and Julie in the Refuge Rescuers' office to research Liam. They wanted to know as much as possible about him before they visited him. After they learned all they could, they checked out the area where he lived for a place to camp. They planned on at least one night, or more, if it turned out to be a decent spot. One of the major things they wanted from this vacation was the time to simply relax. To take the time to kick back and to do as little as possible. The chance to get rid of the normal stress that drove them most of the time.

They found what looked like a perfect spot to camp, not much more than fifteen miles from Liam's home. It had once been a commercial campground, but was now on land owned by the state. Even so, it was still used for camping. According to the description of it, there was only primitive camping available. That was a plus as far as Mack and Lisa were concerned. It meant it should be a lot less crowded, and if it was located in an out of the way place, there might be a good chance for them to see some wildlife while they were there. Something that was always a plus for them.

Finding their first campsite finished up what they needed to do, so they were ready to go. Their plan was to leave right after breakfast the next day. The only problem with that was caused by Ben and Theresa. They wanted to be sure that they made an especially good meal for their travels. It was too good, and all four of them were overfull when they left in the RVs.

They drove directly to the campgrounds, and reached them in the early afternoon. Setting up camp was quick, so Mack and Lisa left to visit Liam right away. Roy and Wanda stayed at the campgrounds. They didn't know the area at all, and the campgrounds were very isolated from the outside world. The only sign of humans that could be seen from the campgrounds was a boat ramp on the other side of the lake the campgrounds were on. They thought it would be best to always have someone with the RVs, at least until they had a better idea of what the traffic on the lakes was like.

Mack and Lisa found Liam's home without any problem. It was a basic three bedroom, two bath rambler on a medium size lot. It was in a typical development at the outskirts of moderate sized town. It's condition was still decent, but was beginning to show telltale signs of neglect.

They knocked on the door three times before it was answered. The man who did, looked similar to Jasper. "What is it you want?" was his greeting to Mack and Lisa when he did. "If you're selling something, I don't need nor do I want whatever it is."

"We aren't here to sell you anything," Lisa answered with the sweetest voice she could produce. "We were friends of your brother's, and we would like to learn more about him. We weren't lucky enough to have known him very long."

"That sounds like him. Did he run out on you too?"

"I think he would have stayed with us a little longer, but he was afraid he'd be too much of a burden on us. And now that it's too late to learn directly from him, we're trying to learn about him this way."

"What do you mean," Liam asked, shock and worry quickly filling his face, "it's too late to learn directly from him?"

Realizing that he didn't know that Jasper had died, Lisa immediately apologized. "I'm sorry. I assumed that you knew. Jasper died."

Liam dropped his head. He didn't make a sound, but tears rolled freely down his face. He didn't do anything to stop them. He just stood there, his body seeming to be hanging loose in the air. It took him a few minutes to recover enough to step back from the door and motion for them to come in.

Liam led them into his living room and motioned for them to sit on his couch. It was well worn, but it was a quality piece of furniture, so worn or not, it was still comfortable. They sat quietly, waiting until he recovered enough to talk. He sat down on a chair facing them.

"When was it?" His first words. "When did he die?"

Mack told him about their search for Jasper and how and where they found him. Liam didn't move or say anything. He sat there, staring at nothing, his face filled with an empty sadness.

"He shouldn't have had to die alone like that," Liam finally said. "He was a good man. Most of his life, he was doing something for someone. A lot of that time, he should have been doing for himself. But no, not Jasper. He almost died the time he pulled me out from under the ice. When it broke under me, he didn't hesitate. Not even for a second. I was only about six. He was a small kid then. When he got my head above the water, he had a real hard time getting me back on the ice. He went under several times, trying to do it. He swallowed a lot of cold water doing it. Got some in his lungs too. He carried me to the cabin. The worst that happened to me was some mild frost bite. He spent a couple of weeks in the hospital. Almost died. He got pneumonia. That's the kind of man my brother was." He went on to tell them several more stories about Jasper.

"Do you know why he ended up homeless?" Lisa asked when Liam paused in his story telling.

"Mostly, I think, because he wanted to take care of himself. Didn't want to get in the way of anyone else's life. The worst part of that was, his kids agreed with him. They didn't want him in their way. They didn't see why there was any way or reason for them to be saddled with an old man."

"We kind of figured that was at least part of it. He told us that he'd tried to live with them, at least for a while. Said he left after they spent all his money."

"That sounds about right," Liam agreed. "He never worried much about it. He always said he considered himself lucky. He had a roof, was warm in the winter, and never went hungry. So how could he complain."

Lisa sighed heavily. "Jasper's story," she said, "is an all too common one. If the world was right, there'd never be another story like it."

"The trouble is," Mack said, "as you and I know all too well, the world getting more distance between compassion and caring and stories like Jasper's everyday. As long as conservative politics and religion rule so much of the world, things are never going to get any better."

"What's wrong with being conservative?" Liam asked. "I'm a conservative. I've voted Republican all my life."

"That's fine," Mack said. "That's what this country is supposed to be about. The freedom to make your own choices. We are lucky to live in a place like this, where the one right we don't have, and shouldn't have, is the right force anyone to always agree with us."

"Now that's where you're wrong. The men who founded this country intended for it to be a christian country, with conservative values. Each and everyone of them was a devout christian. They hated liberals and atheists. Those are the people causing all the problems. Their behavior has brought the wrath of God upon us. So we have the right to tell them what to do."

Mack looked at Lisa. His eyes alone said everything to her he needed to say. Staying any longer with Liam was second only to hopeless. If they left now, they might be able to return some future time. If they stayed, it would likely end up destroying any chance of that. Liam was obviously a man very ignorant of the history of his country, even if he came across like his was sure of his knowledge. People with his conservative beliefs were rarely willing to listen to anything other than what they wanted to hear. The truth was irrelevant to them.

Mack and Lisa stood to leave. Liam gave them a look of surprise when they did. "I'm sorry, Liam," Mack explained. "I didn't realize how late it's getting. We're scheduled to meet another couple at our campgrounds in less than an hour, so we have to get going. Hopefully we can stop back in the near future and visit with you again."

"Well, yeah, I think I'd like that. It can get mighty lonesome, being an old man and living alone. Seems like the young folks are too busy to visit these days. Most of the rest of the people I once knew are dead now, or locked up in one of them nursing homes."

"We can understand that," Lisa said. "At the end, that's very much the way it was for your brother. He was totally alone."

Liam walked them to the door. He looked profoundly sad when they went out. "Please," he said, "come back when you can. It would be good to talk more about Jasper."

"We'll try hard to do that," Mack said. He almost wished they'd stayed longer as he watched Liam's shoulders slump just before he closed the door.

"I think we're right in leaving," Lisa told him. "What with his screwed up beliefs. At the same time, it's so damn sad to see how lonely that old man is. The way we deal with older people is still a piece of American society that needs a lot of fixing."

Mack nodded in agreement. It was a subject that filled his thoughts until they got to the campground. Roy and Wanda were naturally glad to see them. Especially since there were campers in a forty foot, class A RV at the other side of the campground. The men in the RV were young, loud, and had already been drinking rather heavily. There were ten of them.

Wanda, who was wearing a bikini until shortly after they arrived, looked a lot less than happy. Lisa's mood quickly matched Wanda's after she heard the crude comments about her body as soon as she got out of the Jeep.

"I think it'd be wise," Roy told Mack right away, "to pack it up and find another place to park these rigs. It's my guess, given how much those fools over there have had to drink, that the four of us can handle them if we need too. I think though, it'll be better if we don't have too."

"I agree," Mack said. "What do you two think about it?" he asked Wanda and Lisa. "Should we avoid the problem those guys are likely to be?"

"As far as I'm concerned," Wanda said, "they aren't worth the effort it'll take to kick their sorry asses. So yes, let's just get the hell out of here."

Lisa said, "As much as I hate the idea of letting those jerk-off boys, who are desperately trying to be men, push us out of here, I agree with Wanda. They just aren't worth the effort today."

Mack moved the Jeep behind his RV to hook it up for towing. Lisa helped him line everything up. Wanda and Roy loaded up the few things they'd taken out of the RVs. When they were ready to go, the ten men decided to join them.

"What, you people leaving?" asked the man among them who appeared to be their leader. "We were just thinking that it was getting to be party time." He moved up close to Roy. "And we were thinking that these two ladies he would be more than happy to join us."

"Not likely," Roy told him. "So you can go back to your campsite. we're leaving now."

"I don't think so. Whether you like it or not, those two fine looking women are going to party with us for a while. That's all we want. A little party time. And whatever else they're likely to want to give us."

Before Roy could answer him, Lisa did. "It's like this faggot face. We will not be partying, or doing any other damn thing with you. So back your simple minded self the hell out of our way, and you won't end up hurt."

The man laughed. "I guess that's the end of our being nice. You two broads are now going to have the chance to find out what real men are like." He glared at Lisa. "And I'll be the first one to teach you what's what."

That was a threat that Lisa wasn't about to tolerate. Without any warning, she took the man down. When he tried to get up, she slammed her doubled up fist against the back of his head, knocking him out. At the same time, Mack landed a solid right hand to the gut of the man in front of him. As he doubled over Mack grabbed his hair, pulled his head down and slammed his knee into his face. As he wilted to the ground, Mack spun around with his right elbow held high. It connected with the side of the next man's head, just hard enough to knock him out. Without needing any kind of recovery, Mack swung his fist straight into the windpipe of the man trying to hit him hard enough to hurt him.

As the man fell to the ground, struggling to breath, Mack looked around. Lisa and Wanda were each standing over two men. None of them were moving. Roy decided then to finish the man he'd been toying with for a while. A hard left under his chin did the job nicely.

"What now?" Roy asked.

Mack shrugged, then looked at the ten men on the ground. He shook his head a couple to times, then told the others what he had in mind.

They proceeded to load all the men in their RV. They gather up all their cell phones and threw them as far out into the lake as they could. Mack then drove their tow vehicle into the lake until it stalled. Roy backed the RV into the lake until its back wheels couldn't do any more than spin in the mud at the bottom of the lake. He then threw the keys for it into the water.

They'd already picked out the next campgrounds, so that's where they went. It was a lot more crowded there, but it was free of creeps who's only goal was to rape a couple of women, just because they thought they could. As soon as they were settled in, they started to talk about where they should go next. That's when Wanda surprised all of them.

"I'd like to go to Canada," she told them. "I think we're overdue checking on Larry."

Roy was even more surprised by her request than Lisa and Mack were. Roy and Wanda met Larry during an investigation which partially took place in Canada. During and after the investigation, she had first liked him a lot. He visited them, and he and Sue fell in love. But he deserted her in the end, and Wanda was a lot less than fond of him now, because of that.

Roy had to ask. "Why the hell do you want to go to Canada and see him?"

"Because I want to know why he did what he did to Sue. It hurt her a lot, and the way things worked out, it normally would even have had a negative effect on us. If we didn't love each other the way we do, you know damn well that it would have."

"I know. A lot could have happened that didn't. But enough did, so I still wonder why you want to go there to see him. There's got to be more to it than just wanting to ask him about Sue."

Wanda shrugged, looked at the floor, then at Roy. "I want to know if he's coming back to see Sue again. If he's not, why not. There didn't seem to be much in the way of available women up there in Canada while we were there. Why would anyone want to live the kind of a lonely life he lives?"

"I can understand his way of life," Roy said. "But living it alone has got to leave a lot to be desired."

"It think that it's got its good points and bad points," Mack said. "As far as living totally alone, I don't think I'd like it for any longer than a week or two. And that would only be if I was doing something Lisa couldn't be a part of. For a short time though, I think any of us could find something special about spending time alone in some wilderness area."

"You kind of do that, Mack," Lisa said, "when you take those solo walks in the refuge."

"I guess I do. That's probably why I kind of understand why Larry did what he did. I don't agree with it, but as lousy as he treated Sue, I can understand him. At least somewhat. I'm also curious about him and the way he lives. So I'm with Wanda. I think we should go to Canada and find Larry. We can pick up Jasper's trail later."

Lisa offered her opinion. "I agree with Mack and Wanda. We should go to Canada and check out Larry. I'm curious about his way of living too. I realize that we live a lot more of a self-sufficient life than most people, but I often would like to do even more. I think he's probably got a lot to teach us in that department."

"Lisa's right about that," Mack agreed. "The one thing I'm wondering about though, is Sue. I think we should tell her what we're planing on doing. She might even want to come along."

"That's true," Wanda said. "I'll give her a call and see what she thinks." Wanda called her right away, and explained what they were going to do. She listened for a few minutes, then said, "You can still ride with us. I'm not at all worried about that. We both know why it happened. All that's okay now." She paused again, and as she did, Mack looked over at Roy. He was staring at his left foot, which was nervously moving a small pile of dirt around. His face had slightly more color to it than normal. Finally, Wanda spoke again. "I understand. But just so you know, it was a long way from the end of the world then, and wouldn't be all that terrible if it happened again. I'll give you call after we get settled in up there, to let you know how it's going."

As soon as Wanda hung up the phone, she looked over at Roy. She smiled at the expression on his face. She then walked over to him, put her arms around his neck, and kissed him in a way that left no doubt that he'd been kissed. "I told you then, and like I said to Sue, I'm telling you now. It's okay, Roy. Everything is just fine."

Mack and Lisa both suspected what Wanda's words were about, but knew that the best thing they could do was to ignore them. Her words did one thing for them. The words told them that they were not alone when I came to sharing intimately with someone else. They also knew that it was Wanda's idea for Roy to comfort Sue after Larry left her.

Roy continued to look somewhat uncomfortable the rest of the day. He didn't relax until the day was gone and they decided to go to bed. He looked much relieved when he closed the door to his and Wanda's RV.

As soon as he did, Lisa moved Mack's lap. She hugged him tight, then kissed him deeply. "At least," she said, her eyes filled with the love she had for him, "we aren't alone. What has happened to us, can happen to anyone. But tonight, I'm glad that whatever happens, only happens with you and I. That's when it's always the best. Just you and I, Mack."

He agreed. He held her as he stood up, then carried her to their RV. He set her down as they went inside, but as soon as the door was closed, he picked her up again. She had her blouse opened just before he laid her down on the kingsize bed.

CHAPTER 6

They took their time the next day, breaking camp and getting ready for the trip into Canada. The last night in Minnesota was spent in an RV park near the Canadian border.

Before they ever started out on their journey, Sue had made sure they had every kind of ID so that anyone, anywhere, would be satisfied with the paperwork. The crossing into Canada the next morning went without a hitch. The trip to the town near Larry's home was also without problems, but it was late when they got there. Rather than go directly to his home, they decided to wait until morning.

They found a small RV park just outside of town and decided to spend the night there. The local police chief arrived less than an hour after they were parked. Wanda and Roy recognized him from their previous visit to Canada.

He was smiling when he got out of his car. "So you're back again," he said to Roy as he stuck out his hand to shake Roy's. "Plan on staying long this time?"

"The truth is, we don't really have any plans, other than what will probably be a short visit with Larry Jameson."

"Is there a special reason for the visit?"

"Not really. The four of us are on a long overdue vacation, so on a whim we decided to visit Larry. He became a good friend when he visited us a while back." Roy took the time then to introduce Mack and Lisa to the police chief.

"Well, that sounds reasonable. As far as I'm concerned, you folks are welcome here for however long you feel like staying. But I have to warn you, some of the men around here who took a licking from you back then, are still more than a little unhappy about it. So it might be wise to stay out of the bars and all of the eating places. You'll be asking for trouble if you don't."

"No problem," Roy told him. "We've got plenty to eat in the RVs, and we can leave any drinking for another place and time."

"Sounds good," the chief said. "I hope for your sake, your stay in Canada this time is a lot more pleasant than your last one was." He left then.

"I think," Mack said, "from listening to the cop, that the idea of a short visit is a good one."

Wanda had other thoughts about all of it. "I don't agree with you, Mack," she complained. "We've had too many times in too many places, that we were forced into doing something we shouldn't be forced into doing. We are, damnit, on vacation. We aren't cops. We aren't looking for trouble. And I damn well don't feel like cooking tonight. I want to find a bar in town tonight and have a hamburger. A couple of beers will taste good too."

Roy heaved an extremely heavy sigh. He wasn't sure whether to frown or laugh when he looked a Wanda. "I think, Wanda, you've forgotten how close we came to having our asses kicked the last time we were here. And what those boys would have done to you if we wouldn't have gotten the help we did, would have been worse than a beating. Given the kind of town this is, that could happen to both you and Lisa."

"I don't think anything's going to happen, so long as we stick up for ourselves."

Mack was about to agree with Roy, when Lisa stepped in. "I'm the one here who's been raped. It is a kind of hell that no one should ever have to go through. Even so, I'd rather risk it than let some punk-ass macho males tell us what we can and what we cannot do. No matter what, I think Wanda and I deserve to eat hamburgers tonight."

Mack wanted to give the subject further discussion when two pickups drove in the park and up close to the parked RVs. Four guys got out of each of the trucks.

Mack waited until they got close enough to hear him, then told Roy, "Only eight this time. Shouldn't be much of a problem."

The smallest of the men, who stood near six feet tall, walked directly up to Roy. He stuck his nose in Roy's face. "It's like this, old man," he tried to snarl, but his voice squeaked a couple of times, "you've got an hour to pack it up and get the hell out of here. Your kind just ain't wanted in this town."

Rather than retreat from the man, Roy moved in on him. "You can either move your pointy little nose out of my face, asshole, or I can move it for you."

The man tried to push his nose even closer to Roy's face. It was exactly what Roy expected him to do. Moving so fast the man never knew what hit him, Roy reached up, grabbed his nose, and tweaked it hard enough to break it. He then push the man hard enough to knock him down.

Wanda and Lisa then did something that always threw pseudo tough guys off balance. Standing next to Roy, they lifted their hands in front of them. With the backs of their hands facing the men who were not having a serious nose bleed, they waved their fingers as an invitation. It said to the men as clearly as anything ever could, "You want a fight? Then come right on. Let's have us a brawl."

The men stood still, with none of them having the slightest idea what to do next. Mack decided then to make a suggestion. He moved in tight against the man closest to Lisa.

"You're crowding my wife," he said as he slammed the palm of his hand against the man. The blow was strong enough to stagger the man back a few feet. "I don't like punk-ass jerks like you to do that."

Roy followed Mack's move. The only difference was, Roy's man went down when he was pushed. Another man pulled a knife and lunged at Mack. Before he got halfway to him, Lisa took him out before he even realized that she'd moved.

Wanda quickly moved up to her closest man. She was in the mood now to do her own kind of intimidation. She also wanted to lay a serious insult on him. She slapped him across the face, putting every bit of strength she had in the swing. The sound of it was unmistakable. Her man was visible shaken by it.

"Time for you assholes to pick it up and get the hell out of here. And if we run across you again, we will get you next time."

None of the would be tough guys knew what to do, but their fearless leader was still bleeding from his tweaked nose. He walked over the pickup he rode in on, then waved his troops over to him. A couple of minutes later, they were on their way out of the RV park.

Late in the afternoon, Wanda declared it time to go out to eat. The first time they'd been in Canada, Roy and Wanda were threatened by a group of men much like the ones they'd just seen. That was the bar where Wanda wanted to go to eat. So they did.

It wasn't at all crowded. Mack parked their Jeep in front of the place. Inside, they sat in a place where they could watch the Jeep. It didn't take long for a couple of men to park next to it. They got out of their pickup and checked out the jeep. They were looking for a way to lift the hood.

"Those two are mine," Lisa said. She left the table where they were sitting. "If I get into trouble, you can come and rescue me. Otherwise, let me handle it. No one's likely to arrest a helpless little girl like me for defending myself against those two big men."

Mack gave his okay, but stood near the door to watch her when she went out. He wanted to be able to move as quickly as possible if she needed him.

Lisa didn't fool around with the men. "I think," she told them, "it would be a good idea for you to get your fucking hands off my Jeep."

The man fiddling with the hood on it, looked at her and laughed. "It's like this, girly, I'll do whatever the hell I choose to do with it. You want someone to do something about what I do, you best hustle up a half dozen American males to do it. Sure as shit, neither one of those wimps with you can do a damn thing about it. They ain't nothing but chickenshit, sending a child like you out here. So go back inside and get the rest of your group out here. You are finished here."

"And I'm telling you," Lisa said, a wide grin spreading across her face, "you've got one minute to get the hell away from the jeep and the hell out of here. You don't, then I'll have to take you out. I won't be nice doing it."

The man laughed hard. So hard he nearly doubled over. It was a big mistake on his part. Lisa knew better than to fool around with the man, so before he knew anything would or could happen, she hit him hard in the neck. That left a partially crushed windpipe. Her next blow was to his solar plexus, adding to his breathing difficulties. His look as she approached him now was priceless. It was shear terror. She didn't even hit him again. She just pushed him hard enough to sit him down hard on his boney ass.

The second man was totally confused. How could a beautiful young woman, as small as Lisa, kick ass the way she just did. She moved close to him. "Load him up and get the hell out of here. You don't, and you will find it painful."

The man did as he was told. The two would-be Jeep vandals were quickly gone. Lisa went back inside.

"I wonder," Roy asked, "how many more of this town's tough guys that little incident is going to attract?"

"I expect it'll be a bunch," Wanda answered. "But there will be a whole hell of a lot of them in a world of hurt before they get to us."

"If they get to us," Mack said. "If there is too many of them for us to beat, and they don't give us a choice, there might be a way to back them off." Mack explained his idea.

They were finished with their cheeseburgers and ready to leave when the macho men, along with some of their women, entered the bar's parking lot. They stood outside, waving their hands and screaming for Mack, Lisa, Roy, and Wanda to come out.

"How many do you think?" Roy asked.

"Around thirty, I'd guess," Mack answered.

"Think your plan will work, Mack?" Lisa asked.

"Not really," he answered. "There's about twice as many as I expected there'd be. This is one time I wish we would have brought our guns with us. They sure aren't worth anything back in the RVs."

"You're right there," Wanda agreed. "But I have another idea. Let's go out there and offer to fight each and every one of those bastards. But only two at a time."

"How's that going to work?"

"Simple. We stand back to back. Me behind Mack. Lisa behind Roy. They come at us. Eight of them against us four. We do it until all of them are laid out, or we are."

"Do you really think they'll go for it?"

"I don't know, but if they do It'll give us the chance to take out eight of them before they catch on."

"There's no reason not to give it a try, so let's got out there and get this over with."

Mack held Lisa's hand as they went outside. He glanced at her just before they stopped in front of the mob they were facing. The look she carried told him that some of the men there would be in very serious condition before this night ended. Win, lose, or draw, much of the mob would be regretting this before it was over.

Wanda then spoke up. "All right, tough guys," she told them, her voice a snarl. "You out number us near eight to one. I'm going to offer you a chance to prove you aren't the cowards I think you are. There isn't any doubt about what you want to do to us. So my offer is this. We'll take you on, two on one. That's eight of you against the four of us. We continue with the two on one until you beat us or you decide you've had enough."

About half of the mob laughed. A few of them just smiled. The smart ones frowned.

One of the men in the front of the group answered, "I don't think so. We want your women in decent shape, for the fun we're going to have with them shortly."

That was enough for Lisa. He never knew what hit him. Lisa stepped back as he wilted to the ground. "He's an example to what's going to happen to any of you scum-bag assholes who tries to put your hands on me."

"The same goes for me," Wanda added.

A large woman, wearing pants so short they barely covered her between her legs, and a man's shirt mostly unbuttoned, went after Lisa. She was sure Lisa would cringe in fear. It surprised her when Lisa manage to grab the ponytail she wore, snap her head around, then lay her out with a strong right hand under her chin. She too, wilted to the ground.

Just then two squad cars drove into the parking lot. About a third of the mob quietly left. The police chief was in one of the cars. He approached Roy. "I thought I warned you about eating here. You knew there'd be trouble if you did."

Roy shrugged. "All we wanted to do is have a hamburger for supper. These jackasses got here after we were done with our meal. We weren't looking for trouble. They were."

"Still, you shouldn't have come here. When you did, it meant you were looking for trouble."

"No. All that any of this means is that you've got a town full of a lot of semi-retarded jerks who are always looking for trouble. We, being who we are, are more than damn sick and tired of putting up with people like this bunch of cowards who are here."

"I don't think you need to get so insulting. These folks are plenty brave when they're on their own. Normally, they could take any of you on, one on one."

"No, they wouldn't. We offered to take them on two on one. Two of them against one of us. They declined. It was actually eight of them against us four. They were too chickenshit to take us up on our offer."

"You really have a cocky attitude. I don't think I can allow that kind of fighting here. But I am willing to compromise with you. We put up our best fighter, you put up yours. Our guy wins, you leave our town and don't return. Your guy wins, and you stay for as long as you want. No one pulls this mob shit again."

"Sounds good," Wanda said. "Bring him on."

The man who emerged from the crowd was very big. He stood around six foot six, was heavily muscled like a weight lifter, and moved as if his body was knotted together. As soon as they saw him, all four of them knew what the secret to beating him was. Speed. The instant she saw him, Wanda seriously wanted to take him on. She knew it would take some time and a lot of effort to beat him, but she had no doubts about whether or not she could do it. She knew she could.

"I want him," she told Roy. "I think I earned the privilege when I came up with the idea about fighting all of them."

"I don't know, Wanda," Roy argued. "He's awful big."

Wanda softened her voice enough so Roy was the only one who could hear her. "I know he's big. Probably extremely strong too. But look at the way he's built. He's not two problems, being muscle bound the way he is. He's not going to be very flexible. He is going to be slow. I don't have either problem. So let me kick his ass. I need the exorcise."

Roy couldn't help himself. He laughed. "I don't like it," he said, "but go ahead, do to him what you can." Even though he gave her his permission he knew he would step in, if needed, before she was seriously hurt.

The chief of police couldn't believe it when he was told Wanda would be the one fighting the crowd's champion. "I don't think I can let this continue," he complained. "If he so much as hits her, he'll probably kill her. One of you guys will have to do the fighting, or the deal is off."

Lisa answered him. "I think you are afraid of your guy losing to a female. Your saying Wanda can't fight him is really just saying you are chickenshit. Actually, I think the whole bunch of you are. Just because I stopped a couple of you boys from wrecking our Jeep, you have to come after us with more than thirty of you. All any of you are is gutless pissants. So, chickenshits, let's have at it. I'll enjoy putting a whole mess of you in the hospital." She waved her hand at them, as if she was ready to take on the whole mob.

The big guy, who was supposed to do their fighting for them, finally spoke up. "Don't know about the rest of you here, but I ain't fighting no woman. Tonight, I ain't fighting nobody. I'm going home." He started his Harley and drove away.

Roy glared at the people still there. "Now there goes a wise man," he told them. "He's going home. That beats the hell out of going to the hospital with multiple injuries. Any of the rest of you smart enough to do that? If not, let's have at it now. I've had enough of looking at a bunch of total assholes like you people."

About half of the remaining mob decided that trying to run the Americans out of town wasn't worth risking serious injury. They left.

"Would you look at that, Mack," Roy said to him. "There isn't enough of them any longer to make it a fair fight. The four of us need to be careful now, to be sure we don't break too many bones. We need to be especially careful to keep the breaks to legs and arms. Be tough on a small town like this one, if we put too many of them into permanent wheel chairs."

Roy moved in on the biggest man still there. He slapped him hard under the chin with the side of his hand. It jolted the man's head back. "What do you think," Roy asked, doing it again, "you ready to take me on yet. Shit! You don't stand a chance with either of these two women. One on one, what they'll be doing to you will be brutal. Lisa here, when she gets pissed, has been known to neuter more than one asshole like you." Roy did one more, final, slap under his chin.

The man did nothing to retaliate against what Roy did to him. No one else in the mob did either. Roy smiled, then moved his hands to his hips. Giving the mob three big smiles, Wanda, Lisa, and Mack also moved their hands to their hips. It left the impression that they'd be more than happy to take on the people still there.

"Well," Roy said, "we're waiting. So come and get us." He shook his head as he stared them down. "That is, if you all are stupid enough to still believe you can."

Three more people left then. Wanda and Lisa moved close to Roy. "Since all of you apparently aren't ready to take on all of us," Lisa told them, "I will fight any two of you. "I'm about the smallest one here, but I'm willing to have a go at any two of you. No matter how big."

The men in the crowd looked around at each other. There were no takers. Lisa lifted the middle finger on her right hand. Holding it high enough so everyone in the crowd would be sure to see it, she moved her hand back and forth at the crowd.

Some deep but muffled grumblings floated out of the mob. They were filled with anger, but didn't sound dangerous. It was far more of a frustrated anger.

Wanda spoke up this time. She moved in front of Lisa and Roy, all the time glaring at the mob. Her voice was loud, and left no doubt that she was pissed. "I don't know what the fuck is wrong with you people up here in Canada, other than you all seem to be a bunch of chickenshit assholes. We didn't do one goddamn thing, nor do you have one goddamn reason, for attacking us the way you have. So one of you shit for brains jerks is going to explain to me what your problem is, you are all going to leave now, or whether you want to fight or not, we are going to kick your asses. As in each and everyone of them who doesn't leave. You've got exactly two minutes to decide."

Since there were only about ten of them still there, they slowly turned away. Some got on their Harleys and the rest got in their pickups. They left as a group. The police followed them away without another word.

"Well," Mack said, watching them leave, "so much for our fun trip to Canada."

"It should get better tomorrow," Wanda answered, "when we get to Larry's."

Mack forced a smile. "I'm not going to hold my breath."

CHAPTER 7

They half expected to be raided by people from the mob during the night. If not, at least a visit from local law enforcement in the morning. Neither event occurred. Considering that they were in Canada, it felt to them like a rather pleasant morning.

They managed to get out of bed, use the showers, get dressed, and even eat breakfast without anyone threatening them about anything. Again, given the fact they were in Canada, it was a rare treat.

When they finished eating, they washed their dishes, then policed their campsite, leaving it cleaner than it was when they got there. Roy led the way to Larry's farm.

They almost didn't recognize it when they got there. It was completely rebuilt after it was burned out by a mob much like the one they'd faced the previous night. It was rebuilt from the ground up by a multi billionaire.

Shanty Lucas got involved with Mack, Refuge Rescuers, and Larry during a murder investigation. She liked Larry, so she paid for the rebuilding of his farm after it was destroyed. He was thankful for what she did, but felt uncomfortable with it. He was a recluse who lived a very simple life, and all of the many improvements done to his farm seemed to him to compromise his way of life.

He was also less than happy when the two RVs drove in. When he saw who it was, he wasn't sure whether he should be happy to see them or run away. When he left Minnesota he promised Sue that he would contact her as soon as he knew things were going okay. He never did. Because he didn't, he expected that Roy, Wanda, Lisa, and Mack would be angry with him.

They weren't smiling when they saw him, but didn't look particularly angry either. The hand shakes with Mack and Roy were friendly enough. Then he got a hug from Lisa. The one he received from Wanda was somewhat more than just friendly.

When she stepped back from him, the look on his face was one of surprise and confusion. Wanda couldn't help but smile. "That was from Sue. She doesn't know she did it, but it's what I think she'd do if she could."

"I doubt she'd do that if she saw me. A knife in my ribs would be more like it. I wouldn't blame her for doing it either."

"Nor would I. There are a lot of better ways to leave a person, than what you did to her." She sighed, knowing she was pushing it by bringing up this conversation so soon. But it was started now, so she decided not to let it slip by her. "So why the hell did you do it to her?"

"I don't think I can ever explain it to you, Wanda, in any meaningful way. All I can say is that Sue and I live in two very worlds. Neither one of us had any interest in living in that other world. So when I got back home, it seemed like making the split between us permanent was the most logical thing to do. More goodbyes weren't going to help either one of us. So I didn't call her."

"You did more than just not call her. You dodged her in every way it's possible to do it. You hurt her when you did that, Larry. You hurt her a lot."

"I imagine I did. I'm damn sorry for it, but it's too damn late to do anything about it. So unless you plan on kicking my ass for it, you've made your point. There's no need for you to lecture me any more to make me feel really lousy about it. I don't think I can feel any worse than what I do now. It didn't take me too long to realize how big a mistake I made. I've regretted it everyday since."

"If you really feel that way, then you should damn well call her and tell her that. Even if you two can't work it out between you, you'll both feel better for trying."

Roy, Lisa, and Mack all told him the same thing. He still hesitated, so Wanda being Wanda, she immediately called Sue. When she answered, Wanda simply said, "Someone wants to talk to you." She handed the phone to Larry and said, "Now talk. No excuses. Talk."

As soon as he said hello, he turned away from them and walked a few steps away. "Please, Sue," he said, "don't cry." The rest of his conversation was too muffled for them to understand what was said.

He had tears in his eyes when he handed the phone back to her. "She'll be on the plane tomorrow. I'll be picking her up at the airport. Now come on. We'll find a place to park your RVs."

Larry went to the airport alone to pick up Sue around mid-morning the next day. The chief of police arrived shortly after he left. The man didn't look happy. He marched up to them, his face filled with frustration. He frowned at them for a moment before he talked.

"Where were the four of you last night?" He demanded to know. His voice sounding like he was sure their answer would be a lie.

Roy returned his frown. "Right here."

"Can you prove it?"

"Why the hell should we have too? Don't you have any real police work to do. Or is harassing Americans all you know how to do?"

"It's like this. I asked you a question and I expect an answer. And you better know, I'm not in the mood for any of your bullshit."

"I'm not in the mood for yours either. So until you can ask me a question in a civilized manner, and tell me why you're asking the question, you won't be getting any answer."

"That's where you're wrong. I will be getting answers, or you will be in jail, and I'll be tearing apart you RVs, looking for evidence."

"Not today. Today you are going to leave. You can come back here later, after Larry returns from the airport. If he's in the mood, he might talk to you. In the meantime, go somewhere else to throw your weight around."

The chief knew then that Roy wasn't about let anyone push him. And because of the situation that brought the chief there, he couldn't call for any backup. There wasn't any backup. Everyone normally available was involved in the same thing. A young girl, age eleven, was missing. She had disappeared from the campsite she was in with her father, sometime during the night.

It was now a matter of searching the surrounding forest for her. The girl's father though, was demanding more. She was taken, he was sure, and he wanted everyone even slightly suspicious to be checked out. He particularly mentioned Roy, Wanda, Mack, and Lisa. He didn't know them at all, but he remembered them being camped close by.

Since the chief already considered them trouble makers, he was now there to be sure they hadn't taken the girl. As impatient as he was with them, the chief was still sure the girl had wondered off and gotten lost. So he reluctantly told them what the problem was.

After he finished explaining the problem, Roy said, "Why the hell didn't you tell us that to start with? We've all spent enough time outdoors to be able to help with the search without getting ourselves lost or in any other trouble. I don't doubt that you have a lot of people out searching for her, but it sure can't hurt to have a few more. And we damn sure would like to help."

"I doubt anyone wants your help. You people aren't exactly popular around here."

"An eleven year old girl is missing. From what you've told us, the odds are that she's alone, lost in these woods. And you're worried about popularity contests? What kind of total nonsense is that? I think finding that kid is far more important than whether anyone around here likes us or hates us."

"You mean you actually want to help find her. Why?"

"Why wouldn't I? Kids are kids, and they should be taken care of. As soon as we put together our gear, we'll join the search."

They followed the chief to the campground, talked to the man coordinating the rescue efforts, then entered the forest. There were five trails leaving the campground. They each took one of them. Lisa took the trail everyone thought was the least likely one the missing girl would have taken, if she in fact did wander off as they suspected.

In the beginning, the trail didn't go very deep into the trees. Lisa soon questioned her decision to take the trail, and was about to turn around. She then spotted a mark in the mud in a low spot in the trail. She couldn't tell who or what made the mark, but it was enough to keep her walking.

The trail quickly narrowed and the walking became difficult. As the trail moved deeper into the forrest and on lower ground, she ran into ever more frequent stretches of mud. That alone might have been enough for her to turn around, if she hadn't so frequently seen new marks in the mud. She still couldn't tell what made the marks, but from the way they looked it was obvious that whatever it was, was often sliding in the mud. She didn't think that animals large enough to leave the marks would have near so much trouble with their footing.

An eleven year old girl, out alone on this narrow, muddy trail in the dark of night, likely would have. Lisa thought then, that she had to continue on the trail, no matter how difficult it was. She knew, from looking back at her own tracks, that if an adult would have been there ahead of her, the marks in the mud would be a lot more significant.

Lisa walked for another thirty minutes or so, until the trail split. The larger trail turned off to the left, and seemed to continue turning in that direction. Lisa was fairly certain then, that it was a circle trail, and that it would end up back at the campgrounds.

She followed the trail to the right, which quickly proved to be an animal trail. Not one normally used be humans. She continued following it until it grew so narrow, with so many low tree branches blocking the way, that she decided to turn around. Realizing that's what she'd have to do was a huge letdown for her.

She found a dry spot near an ancient maple tree, and sat down with her back against the tree to rest a moment before heading back. She closed her eyes and let her body relax as she listened to the sounds of the forest.

They were sounds she knew well, and she found them soothing. Enough so, that her frustration from having to go back and start her search over eased up some.

Just as she was actually feeling pretty decent, something interfered with the comforting sounds surrounding her. It was close to the sound of a puppy spending its first night away from its mama. A few minutes went by before she heard the new sound again. Because she was listening closely for it, it was more distinct this time. And this time she knew it wasn't a puppy. It almost sounded human, so she tried walking in the direction she thought the sound came from.

She didn't get far before she was crawling. The cries were coming steady now, but Lisa was forced to continually change directions to get through the thick brush. The end of it came suddenly, as she burst through the vegetation and into a clearing. She immediately stood up, then looked around. Across the meadow, the little girl lay curled up into as tight a ball as she could make herself into.

When she walked up to the girl and bent down to touch her shoulder, the girl jumped up and backed away. She was obviously terrified. "Did you come to take me back?" she asked. "I don't want to go back."

This was not the response Lisa had expected. She assumed when she started the search that the girl had just foolishly walked off on her own and gotten lost.

"Are you Emma ?" Lisa asked her.

"Who told you my name? Did my daddy? I don't want to go back to him. I don't want him to do it to me again."

"There are a lot of people looking for you Emma. Everyone is afraid you're lost out here. They all want you to be able to go home."

"I'm not lost. I want to live here now. I don't want to live with my daddy anymore. He always makes me do those things. It hurts when he does it to me."

There was no doubt in Lisa's mind now, that this girls father had been raping her. Having been a victim of kidnapping and rape herself when she was still a kid, meant that she understood what this girl had gone through. So the last thing she wanted to do was bring her to her father. At the same time, she knew she couldn't leave her here. If she did, there was little to no chance that she would survive.

"I think though, Emma , we have to go back. It's impossible for us to survive here. We don't have any food, very little water, and no survival gear. I will try to protect you from your father, and if I can't do that, I'll help you escape to a better place than this."

"But this is the only kind of place where he won't find me. He always finds me in the other places I go. Nobody ever helps me either. They just say he is my daddy and I belong with him. So I want to stay here. It's okay if I die. Then he can't do it to me anymore."

Lisa's heart was breaking for the girl. She knew how she felt, and couldn't blame her for not wanting to go back to her father. But she couldn't, for any reason, let her stay out in this forest and die. So she needed to convince Emma that she would be able to protect her.

Convincing her took over two hours of serious talking and pleading to convince Emma to return to the campgrounds. Rain started shortly after they started back, making the trail that much muddier, and the walking constantly more difficult. It slowed them so much, that evening shadows were drifting over the campground when they reached it.

Lisa immediately brought Emma to the large tent setup as the head quarters of the search. The man in charge was shocked when he saw Lisa bring Emma in. They were both splattered heavily with mud, and generally looked to be in rough condition. They were also exhausted.

The man ignored Lisa and kneeled down in front of Emma . "Are you alright?" he asked her.

"I want to stay with Lisa," she answered. "Don't tell daddy I'm here. I don't want him to take me with him."

The man looked up at Lisa. "What the hell have you been telling her. Why did you put ideas like this in her head?"

"I didn't tell her anything like that. She doesn't want to go to her father because he's been consistently raping her. She disappeared because she was running away from him. She needs to be protected from him."

The man got up on his feet. "I don't know what you're up to," he snarled at Lisa, "but you're not going to get away with it here." He took Emma's hand. "We'll go find your dad now. Things will be okay, once you're away from this bitch here."

Emma pulled herself free of the man. She moved behind Lisa. "I don't want my daddy to do it to me again. I want to stay with Lisa."

The man then made a huge mistake. He tried to hit Lisa to get her out of the way. He didn't know what hit him. He quickly found himself on the ground. She stood over him with her foot on his throat. He tried to pull away, but she pushed down with her foot just hard enough to tell him she could stop his breathing if she wanted to.

"It's like this, asshole," she told him. "Emma's been raped countless times by her father. She doesn't want him to do it anymore. So she ran away. I can understand why. But I couldn't leave her out there in those woods to die. No more than I can let you turn her over to her father. So if you don't want me to hurt you, or maybe even kill you, you'd better cooperate."

She gave his throat another not so gentle push, then moved her foot so he could get up. "I'm going to have you arrested for assault," he whined, rubbing his neck.

"I don't doubt that. You're a typical chickenshit male who just can't take it. Just think about what your buddies are going to have to say about you when you charge me for assaulting you. You're close to a foot taller than me and outweigh me by near a hundred pounds. But just so I don't have to kick your sorry ass again, let's get some people in here, so we can find someone with at least some kind of sense of responsibility, and maybe even a brain, to take care of Emma. She damn sure isn't going back to her rapist daddy."

Dark was closing in now, so searchers were returning to the campground. Emma's father, Willie Flynn, was among them. He rushed to Emma the moment he saw her. Before he could touch her, she moved behind Lisa.

"She doesn't want you anywhere near her," Lisa told him. "So be smart and back the hell off."

The father glared at Lisa. "What did you do to my little girl? You must have brain washed her when you took her from me."

"No, you pervert. I didn't do anything to her other than find her deep in the woods, where she was hiding from you. I told her when I talked her into coming back, that I would help her stay away from you. You aren't going to touch her again."

The father looked around at the people there. "Can't you see what she's doing. She has my daughters head filled with horrible things that aren't true."

Mack walked out of the trees then. He quickly moved to Lisa's side. "Are you the one who found her?" he asked.

"I am. But we've got a big problem, Mack. She didn't wander away and get lost. She ran away, because her father's been repeatedly raping her. He claims that I've filled her head up with those ideas. And I don't know how many of these people here are smart enough to realize the truth of what's going on. Given the way we've been treated since we got up here in this pathetic little town, I doubt many are."

Mack looked around at the people there. "Ask the girl. Ask Emma. As difficult as it is for you to listen, try to do it anyway. But if you decided to turn this little girl over to a goddamn rapist, there'll probably be some trouble."

The chief came out of the woods then, and took the time to get the stories from the father, Lisa, and Emma. He watched her closely, especially her eyes, as she talked. When he stood, he pulled out his handcuffs and slapped them on Willie's wrists.

"I'll have to let you people figure out what to do with Emma . I'll be taking this man to jail. I'll be a while, filling out the paperwork. There's a lot of crimes to charge him with."

One of the returning searchers called out, "You can't do that. Willie is her father. He knows what's best for his daughter."

Lisa didn't wait for the chief to answer. "No, he damn well does not know, nor does he care, what's best for his daughter. He's a sick pervert who's been raping his own daughter. And if you think that's what is best for her, then you are as sick as he is."

The man charged out of the crowd, ready to attack Lisa. "You goddamn bitch," he swore, "you can't talk to me that way."

Mack moved to stop him. Lisa touched his arm and said, "Let him come, Mack. I've about had enough of the kind of treatment we've been getting from this self righteousness bunch of ignorant pecker woods here."

Mack quickly realized, from the look on her face, that this time Lisa was right, and would be justified in whatever she did to him. Besides, he was damn sick of it too. He stepped aside.

The man came at her, swinging a hard, open right hand at her. She easily stepped out of his way, grabbed the little finger of his open right hand as it flew by her face, and with a quick twist, broke it. It made an audible snap. He grabbed his broken finger with his left hand. She buried her right hand deep in his gut. When he doubled over, she slammed him in the back of his head with both hands, which were folded together.

When he landed on the ground, she looked down on him. "Be damn glad, asshole, that I don't kick your fucking teeth out." She looked at the rest of the people. "Anyone else want to attack me for protecting Emma from her rapist father. "I'm ready to face anyone of you who is. If more than one of you comes after me. there'll be four of us to greet you." She paused and waved at Roy and Wanda, who just entered the tent. They quickly moved up next to Lisa and Mack.

Roy looked at the crowd, then told them, "I don't know what the dispute is about this time, and frankly, I don't care. But if you people are harassing my friends here, you'd best back off. And I mean now."

He saw Emma then, still behind Lisa. He turned to her, and she told him in as few words as she could, what was going on. That was all Roy needed to hear.

"This is what we're going to do now," he said, loud enough for everyone to hear every word. "Those of you who are concerned about Emma can stay and help us figure out what's the next best step for her. Those of you who are so stupid you want to turn her over to her rapist father, had best leave. None of us who care about Emma, and know the difference between right and wrong, have any more patience for you."

There was a lot of mumbling about parent's rights among the people leaving. Once they were gone, the discussion about Emma's short term future started. Most people thought that the best thing for her would be to turn her over to the juvenile authorities. Lisa absolutely disagreed with that idea. So did Emma.

The discussion went on for the next couple of hours, without a firm resolution to the problem. One thing was clear though. No one wanted to take responsibility for Emma's care. Lisa volunteered to take care of Emma until a more permanent solution could be found. At first, there were several strong objections to the idea. It didn't take long before it was obvious that the reason they didn't want Lisa to do it, was because she was an American. The people of this town simply didn't like people from the United States.

In the end, the discussion wore everyone down, and they acknowledged that Emma staying with Lisa was the best temporary solution. Especially, since she and Mack would be camping in their RVs on property owned by a Canadian native. Even if most of the people who finally went along with the idea, didn't much like Larry either.

When the meeting finally broke up, and they were ready to go back to Larry's, a squad car drove up. He went directly to Mack. "I've got some bad news," he said, his voice a bit shaky. "Willie Flynn somehow got the drop on the chief. He shot him. The chief's in the hospital. It doesn't look good. We can't say for sure, but most of us on the force think he'll probably be looking for you guys. So you'd best be on the alert."

Given their past experience, Mack and Lisa took him very seriously. Mack watched his mirrors closely, to be sure they weren't being followed as they followed Roy and Wanda back to Larry's. Larry and Sue were waiting for them when they got there. Together now, they looked as if they'd never been apart.

They were shocked, however, when they saw Emma, especially since she and Lisa were still covered with mud. Larry immediately told them to shower in the main house. It was bigger, and definitely could produce more hot water.

Lisa went inside her RV and got a complete change of clothes. Emma did the same out of her suitcase, that they'd salvaged from Willie's RV. Lisa let Emma shower first, then took one herself.

Larry prepared supper for all of them, while Emma got acquainted with Wanda and Sue, and talked more with Lisa. She and Sue seemed to find some kind of hidden bond between them as they talked. Rather than make Lisa feel left out or jealous, it gave her a sense of relief. She was already very fond of Emma, but not ready to take on the full-time responsibility for her. She also knew that it was highly unlikely that she'd be allowed to. But Sue, because of her relationship with Larry, who was a Canadien citizen, had a chance at taking custody of Emma.

It was also decided, before the evening was over, that Emma would sleep that night in the spare bedroom in the house. It would be the most comfortable spot, and with Emma's new found attachment to Sue, she was more than happy with the unexpected arrangement.

As much as Mack and Lisa were concerned about Emma, it was a bit of a relief for them to still be sleeping alone in their RV. Their lifestyle was not at all designed for a child as an overnight guest.

It didn't really matter though. Lisa was exhausted by the time they went to bed, She fell asleep within minutes of lying down and slept soundly through the night.

CHAPTER 8

Lisa showered and washed her hair again in the morning. Mack was outside, enjoying a cup of coffee when she finished. She sat down next to him and turned to kiss him good morning. She didn't finish it.

A loud gunshot rang out and Lisa fell sideways into Mack's lap. The blood rushing out of the wound in her arm almost instantly covering his pants with her blood.

In less than two minutes, Roy and Wanda ran out of their RV to see what happened. One look at them and Wanda said, "Take care of them Roy."

She went back into her RV and returned moments later. "I'll be back when I'm done hunting," she said. She was carrying her most powerful rifle, topped with the strongest scope she had. "What direction did the shot come from?" she asked Mack.

He pointed and she headed in that direction. Another shot rang out, and she picked up on the direction it came from right away. She didn't bother to finesse her way through the woods. Wanting to end the shooting before anyone else was wounded or killed, she moved as fast as possible toward the sound of the continuing gunshots.

She found Willie Flynn, up high in a large maple tree within minutes. Two branches below him was another man. They were both wearing camouflage suits. Willie even had some small branches stuck to his hat. Even so, both men were easy targets for Wanda's sharp eyes.

She lifted her rifle to her shoulder. Picked up Willie with her scope, hesitated for about one second, then fired. She did the same with the second man before Willie hit the ground. His leg caught in a tangle of branches. He stopped there, hanging upside-down.

Satisfied that they were no longer a danger, she turned away and walked back, hoping that when she got there she wouldn't find anyone dead. She didn't. Everyone took cover after the first shot, and Mack was already racing to the local hospital with Lisa.

"How bad was she?" Wanda asked Roy.

"I can't be sure. It was an arm wound and if it's typical, it's probably serious. It'll depend on how deep it was. Mack took off with her as soon as we got the bleeding slowed down. We weren't sure yet, when they left, how serious it was."

"Should we go to the hospital now? I'm really scared for her."

"Mack said to wait for his call." Roy studied her face for a moment, trying to read her feelings. He couldn't, so he asked, "Are you ready to tell me what went on out among those trees."

"Sure," she agreed. "There were two of them up in the trees. One's on the ground. The other got hung up when he fell, so he's hanging there."

"Are you sure it was a good idea to just leave them there? They could try the same thing with us again."

"It's not like you to be asking silly questions, Roy. So why are you now?"

"Does that mean you killed them?"

"Of course I killed them. They were shooting at you. I wasn't about to let them keep it up. So when I shot them, I picked a spot that would make them very dead. I don't miss, Roy. I didn't miss this time. As far as the bodies go, if they get hauled out of there, it damn sure won't be me who does it. And as far as I'm concerned, they can lay there and rot."

"You sound awful angry, Wanda."

"I am angry. Those bastards shot Lisa. If they wouldn't have still been shooting at you and the others, I would have picked them apart. I would have liked to make them suffer. But I knew it couldn't wait. So I just killed them."

"I don't believe I can fault you for what you did. Because you were right. If they would have continued firing, sooner or later they would have gotten at least one more of us. So, do you think we should notify the authorities?"

"Definitely not. There'll be plenty of time for that after we hear from Mack."

"Okay," Roy agreed. "We'll wait."

Larry, Sue, and Emma came out from under cover then. "Sorry I wasn't more help," Larry said, "but I figured it would be best to stay where I could protect these two." He pointed at Emma and Sue.

"It's okay," Roy told him. "I wasn't any help either. It was all Wanda."

"I'm not surprised," Larry told him. "I've seen her shoot. I doubt there's anyone better." He turned to Wanda. "So, Wanda, did you send them running?"

"Not hardly. One of them is on the ground. The other's still hanging from a tree."

"How bad are they wounded?"

"Bad enough to be genuinely dead."

"You killed them? Jesus, that could be real trouble. We're going to have to do something before the cops get here."

"Why? I shot them in total self defense."

"You've seen the way the people around here react to you. You don't honestly believe they'll let this go past them, do you?"

"I haven't thought about it either way. I can't change what happened though, so I guess I'll have to face them when they get here."

"No, Wanda, you won't. All that happened here was an attack on Lisa and the rest of you. Roy, you and I need to get busy. We need to make sure that those two men do run off and disappear."

Larry and Roy walked into the woods. They returned about five minutes before the law arrived. Two squad cars with two patrolmen in each one. They were visibly upset.

The one in charge marched directly up to Larry. "I have to tell you," he howled, "we aren't happy with you people. Our chief is in the hospital, gravely wounded. All because that woman came between a father and his daughter. Now that father is desperately trying to escape after being forced to shoot the chief to regain his freedom. We want to know if you've been involved with him since he escaped?"

"We sure have," Wanda answered. "He and that friend of his got up in the trees and shot Lisa. She's the one who found Emma. They continued to shoot at the rest of us. I went in after them. I shot at them a few times and they ran off. I sure as hell hope you guys hang on to them after you catch them this time."

"Lisa was shot? Where the hell is she? We want to talk to her. Gunshot wounds are required to be reported to us."

"She's at the hospital. Taking her there seemed to us to be more important than following your rules. Not to mention that following your rules probably would have killed her."

"Nothing is more important than following the rules. Not even getting shot."

That comment was enough to embarrass even his fellow officers. "She probably wasn't in any condition to report to us," one of them told his leader. "Where was she shot?" he asked Wanda.

"In the arm. We don't know how serious. Mack, her husband, rushed her to the hospital. If the wound killed her, he would have called by now. So she's likely still alive."

"I guess we'd better get to the hospital then," the leader said. "So we can question her."

"Are you actually that goddamn stupid?" Roy asked. "What in hell do you think you can learn by questioning her. She had just sat down next to Mack when she was shot. Mack and I immediately got her into his truck and he rushed her to the hospital. She can't possibly tell you anything."

"I want to question her anyway. She had no business interfering with Willie and Emma. What ever went on with with them was between a father and his daughter. Lisa had no right to cause the trouble she did."

Emma was still there. Standing between Sue and Larry, holding Sue's hand. Even at eleven years old, it was obvious to her how ridiculous the cop sounded. She reacted to what he said.

"I know," she said to him, "that I'm supposed to be nice when I talk to policemen. But you are way too kind of dumb to be nice too. My daddy is always doing mean stuff to me. He takes off my clothes and pushes that thing he has into me. It hurts a lot. What he does is nasty too. Boys aren't supposed to do that to girls until they grow up and get married. Daddy's aren't supposed to ever do that stuff to their kids. That means what you say is wrong. You should go away now, and quit trying to be mean to me and Lisa."

"I think she nailed it," Roy added. "You've run off at the mouth enough. I, and I'm sure everyone else here, have heard enough from you. So if you intend on continuing to side with a rapist, you've said all you're going to say. The man's a pedaphile. Now get the hell out of here and catch him before he shoots or rapes someone else."

One of the patrolmen with the leader took his elbow and led him away. The four of them got in their patrol cars and left.

Emma took Wanda's hand and gave it a light squeeze. "I've been listening to what you guys have been talking about. Did you shoot my daddy?"

Wanda was surprised at the question, and wasn't sure how to answer it. But after thinking about it for a while, she decided to give the kid an honest answer. "Yes, Emma, I shot your daddy. He won't ever do to you again, what he was doing."

Emma's face filled with a broad smile. "Good," she said, "then I can stay with Sue and Larry. They can adopt me."

Since this was news to Sue and Larry, they quickly looked at each other, surprise written on their faces. Gradually, Larry's face was filled with a smile. Sue's quickly followed. Still holding Emma's hand, she kissed Larry. It lasted a while.

Wanda's cell phone rang. It was Mack. Lisa's wound was superficial. The bullet just lightly scraped her arm. It hit hard enough to shock her, and she bled a lot the way gunshot wounds often do, but she was leaving the hospital before day's end.

Roy and Wanda had the RVs packed and ready to go by the the time Mack and Lisa got back. Sue had enough of her equipment with her to be able to solve most problems that might need solving before she returned home with Larry and Emma.

They left in the RVs in the morning. When they got home, they let Lisa rest and heal up some before setting out for the next piece of their somewhat strange vacation.

CHAPTER 9

It was close to three AM when Lisa woke up. This was their fourth night sleeping in their own bed since they returned from Canada. Mack was still sleeping, with his back to her. He'd slept that way since she was shot. He was afraid he might somehow hurt her if he did more than sleep next to her.

She did appreciate his consideration, but enough time had gone by since the shooting to make her want another kind of consideration. She snuggled up close to him, and wrapped her arm around him. She let her hand drift up and down his chest, then his stomach, then lower. When she was low enough, he woke up.

Mack turned to face her. He groaned softly, then said, "It's too soon for this, isn't it?"

She laughed softly. "Not hardly. Not soon enough is more like it."

"But I'm afraid I might hurt you. You got shot. You can't be healed up enough already."

"Sometimes, Mack, you worry about the wrong things the wrong way." She pushed him over onto his back. She moved over him, and using her hand to give him direction, she showed him how much he wasn't going to hurt her.

They moved slow to start, but as he realized that what they were doing wasn't going to hurt her, their movements grew stronger. It had been, for them, a long time, so it was over rather quickly. Lisa stayed where she was anyway. They didn't need to hold each other very long before they were ready to start over. This time it took them far longer.

"Now," Lisa told Mack, "I am ready for us to continue our vacation. Sue and Larry will be getting here in a few days, Dale's going to be able to get away for at least a week, and Kathy has made sure she hasn't been scheduled for any kind of concerts or appearances for the next three weeks. So unless you want to cancel it, I think we should go again. Real soon."

"I agree. From what I just experienced, I can tell that your wound isn't bothering you a whole lot anymore. Where do you want to go this time?"

"I think that since Kathy and Dale will be our traveling companions this time, we should pick up on Jasper's trail again."

"Where do you want to start?"

"Well, we've seen his brother, and where that visit was interesting, I think we should do something different from looking up any of his relatives this time. There was that part in the book about his buddy he served in Korea with. They fought together in more than one battle. Let's go to Iowa and try to find him. If we can, it will be interesting to see what he has to tell us."

"That it could. I'll call Sue in the morning, and have her start searching for him. The book said he lived in Waterloo, Iowa. But you never know. He could have moved. I sure am glad she brought her laptop with her when she went to Canada."

"That is good," she said. "Now, before we go to sleep, it would be nice if we could…"

So it was a while before they slept again. Then, as so often happened, they were last to join the group for breakfast in the morning.

Roy greeted them with a smile and a comment. "I see that Lisa must be pretty much healed up. It's been a while since you two were this late for breakfast."

Mack had an answer for him. "She's more that healed, Roy. Somewhere in the night, she turned into some kind of dynamo. Just about did me in."

That brought on a good laugh for everyone, and was enough to stop Roy's teasing. At least for a while. It also gave Mack the chance to tell them that he and Lisa would be leaving soon to start the next leg of their vacation.

Dale and Kathy, who were now somewhat regulars for breakfast, were happy to hear the news. They knew that they were the next couple scheduled to go with Mack and Lisa, but had been afraid if there was too much more of a wait before they went, something would interfere with their ability to go.

For the rest of the morning after breakfast, Mack was on the phone with Sue, going over what she discovered about Jasper's friend from when he was in the service. Lisa spent her time organizing the RVs, so they'd be ready when they left again.

It was around four that afternoon when she got an unexpected call from Beth, her father's second wife. The news wasn't good. Her father, Bob Anderson, was a dairy farmer. He and Beth milked a hundred cows twice a day, along with doing everything else busy dairy farmers do. Lisa was shocked when Beth told her they would were going to quit farming.

Bob had developed a serious heart problem. The same one that eventually killed Bob's father, James. Bob's was even worse than James's, so he had no choice but to quit. The only saving grace in the whole thing was the fact that the auction they had scheduled to liquidate the farm cows and equipment wouldn't be for another three weeks. That would give Mack and Lisa enough time to go to Iowa and check out Jasper's friend. That is, if they could actually find him.

They planned on leaving early the first day, but it was afternoon before they could. They arrived at the planned RV park a couple of hours before dark. So they started their evening relaxing with a glass of wine for Kathy and Lisa and beers for Mack and Dale.

Both Lisa and Kathy changed into more comfortable clothes when they got there. Lisa wore a light skirt with an even lighter blouse. Kathy wore a light cotton dress that buttoned down the entire front. It wasn't at all difficult for Mack and Dale to see that neither one of them wore a bra.

Kathy sat down next to Mack on the bench that was part of the campsite. The way her hands landed on various parts of his body when she talked, made it obvious what she had on her mind.

Lisa wasn't bothered by her flirting. She intended to do her share of it with Dale. But she had something on her mind that she needed to tell all of them.

She smiled when she said it. "It's pretty obvious, especially from watching Kathy and Mack, what's probably going to happen on this trip. At least once anyway. But not tonight. If it happens it will be during the day. I can spend a few hours alone with Dale. I'll probably love it if I do.

But I won't sleep with him. And I won't let Mack sleep with you, Kathy. I can't do that. I can't let go of him long enough to do that. Never again. As much as I love all of you, as much as I can share with you, I can't not sleep with Mack. I hope you understand. In the meantime, there's no rule about touching right now."

No one said anything to Lisa right away, one way or the other, about her sleeping rule. They all just followed it for the entire trip. But Mack did ask about it when they settled in for the night.

"I'm not at all upset or anything," he told her. "I am curious though, the reason for your little talk earlier."

"That's another somewhat of an are you sure you want to know question. Are you sure you want to know, Mack?"

"I am. We both know what will probably happen between all of us while we are on this part of our vacation. I'm fine with it. The thing I don't understand is, if you're perfectly willing to do that, what is it that brought on the no sleeping together rule?"

She gave hm a heavy sigh, letting her shoulders slump forward as she sat on the edge of the bed. "It's because of us, Mack. It's the way we live. For us, we can't wait until we get old to start to live as if our time on this planet is limited. We always need to live that way. What happened to me in Canada has happened too many times. We both know that the next one could kill either one of us. If it's you, I don't want to spend the rest of my life wondering why I didn't spend more time with you. That includes sleeping time, or anytime I'm sharing you, even if I am with Dale. Most of all, when I fall asleep, I don't want to wake up next to anyone other than you."

"Why then, are you willing to share with Kathy and Dale, if you are so concerned about time away from me?"

"To start with, because it adds too, rather than taking away from what you and I have. What I share with Dale is always something that goes beyond pure pleasure. It's sharing who I am with another human in a way that can't be duplicated. Even so, and this is something I think is really special, it's never what you and I have. What we have almost seems to come from some other world. Another reason, which I think is every bit as important. It always makes you a little jealous. The same way I get when you're with Kathy."

"Do you really think getting jealous is a good thing. Jealousy has done a lot of harm to a lot of marriages."

"It only does when there's too much of it. In our case, it mostly just helps keep our interest in each other strong. I'm sure that you're like me. When you feel it, it makes you wonder if I'll still be there for you later. And when you once again know that I am, it's like our love is brand new again. We need to keep that feeling, Mack. Again, because of who we are, we can't ever let things got to the point that we want to be apart for even a minute. Of all the things he said, that's what Jasper was most right about. For us, our time might well be too short to ever let that happen."

Mack took her in his arms. He kissed her, then said, "I don't know how you got so smart, but I'm sure glad you are. You just took something that the world would judge us harshly for, and made it for us some kind of gift. And you are right. Every time you return to me, I fall in love again."

Lisa had tears in her eyes when she fell asleep that night. They rolled down her cheeks and over her smile.

CHAPTER 10

They found Jasper's friend, Edgar McKenna, living in an assisted living complex on the outskirts of Waterloo. He used a walker to move around, and appeared less than happy to see four strangers standing outside his door when he opened it. The odds are that he would have slammed it shut if it weren't for the beautiful smiles on the faces of Lisa and Wanda.

"If you're selling something," he told them, "I can't afford it even if I want it. And it's not collection time for your insurance payment until tomorrow. Except you don't look like you're here to collect the insurance. You're too old and you don't look like those people. So what is it that you want? My back hurts too much for me to stand here much longer."

Lisa answered him. "Are you Edgar McKenna?" she asked him. "Because if you are, we'd like to talk you about Jasper Klug."

"How do you know him. Last I heard, he kind of disappeared. His family pretty much deserted him, from what I understand."

"They did. He was homeless when he died."

"He's dead?" Edgar swiped a big hand over his face, trying to wipe the tears away that were now covering it. "Damn! That sure as hell ain't fair. I was hoping I could somehow see him one more time. Talk to him anyway. So you know how he went? What happened?"

"As far as we know," Mack explained, "he died of natural causes. We found him out in the country, just off the road and under a weeping willow tree. We had him buried next to his wife."

"Did his family bother to come to his funeral?"

"Only us. But Kathy here sang for it. It was a small ceremony, but I think it was a nice one."

At the mention of Kathy's name, Edgar finally looked at her. "You look kind of familiar," he told her. "Is there some way I could know you?"

"I guess you could kind of know me. I'm a singer, so you might have seen my picture somewhere."

Edgar tipped his head to one side, still starring at Kathy. "Who are you people anyway?"

Mack then introduced the four of them to Edgar. His eyes got wide when Mack gave him Kathy's full name.

"My god," he said. "You're famous. I've seen you on Youtube. I love your music. I can't believe this. Kathy Magee in my home. I'm nobody. What are you doing here?"

Kathy answered his question. "We are all here to talk to you about Jasper. And you are not a nobody. You matter as much as any of us."

He suddenly took a deep breath, then shook his head. "Where the hell are my manners," he said. "Please come into my apartment, such as it is."

Lisa rested a hand on his arm as they went inside. "I think you have a nice place here," she told him. "I don't think anyone else could do anything to improve it. It makes a person feel at home."

Lisa was right about it. His small apartment was crowded, but neat and clean. What crowded it the most was the number of books he owned. They seemed to be tucked in corners, resting on table tops, and filling three small book cases. They were a mixture of good fiction, history, and science, with the science heavy on the environment and evolution.

After a quick look around, with a short stop at each of the bookcases, Mack told Edgar how they met Jasper, the evening spent with him, and how he found him after he left them.

"And," Mack finished with, "I think the only goal he had left in life, was too in no way ever be a burden to anyone.

"That sounds like him," Edgar answered. "During the war, he always looked out for his men before himself. He was a master sergeant. The best of all I ever saw. And I saw some damn good ones."

"Did you serve in combat with him?"

"Oh yes. The things is, in some ways it's hard to say I served with him. For the most part, it was him leading and us following. But he didn't just lead us. He always seemed to be serving us while he was doing it."

"Was he a tough leader?"

"No, tough isn't the right word. He was firm in what he said and what he expected. When he gave an order, it was followed. The men did it out of respect for him, far more than because they were intimidated by him. He could get on you if you screwed up. He always did it though, so when it was done, a person came out of it knowing you wouldn't make that mistake again. It made you feel better about yourself, rather than worse. I wasn't worth a damn when I joined his outfit. I felt pretty good about myself in just a few weeks, thanks to him. And it was thanks to him that I could feel anything. He saved my life more than once."

"Do you mean that literally or figuratively?"

"Literally. Be my guess, no one told you that he won a silver star and a medal of honor. The man had a kind of courage no ordinary person could even imagine. He got the medal of honor for holding the enemy back, while his men literally crawled away. There must have been more than a hundred of them. He was wounded twice. He spent more than a month in the hospital recovering."

Lisa turned to Kathy. "That must be where those scars came from. From the size of them, he must have been hurt pretty bad."

"I think so too," Kathy answered, "I wish now we wouldn't have been so polite to him. It would have been special to hear him tell us how he got them."

Edgar asked them then, "How would you know about his scars. They weren't where anyone would normally see them."

Lisa answered. "We gave him a bath. He was in bad shape, so we helped him into the shower."

Kathy told him the rest. "We got him into the shower, then washed him. We couldn't miss the scars. He needed the washing, so he didn't seem to mind it at all."

"That doesn't sound like him. He always wanted to do for himself by himself."

"I think he would liked to have this time too. At least to start. But when the both of us joined him in the showered, he appeared to think it was okay."

"You mean you got undressed and got in the shower with him?"

Lisa laughed. "Most of the way, yes. We thought he was just an old man and wouldn't notice. We were wrong. He did. He remained a gentleman the whole time anyway."

"His reaction didn't bother you then?"

"Not really. He seemed like someone special from the time we first found him. That feeling just grew as we spent more time with him. Now, we all wish we would have had a lot more time with him. That's why we're here. We want to, as much as possible, get to know him better. And we have. There was very little in his book about his war experience. So you've already helped us get to know him better."

"Well, that's reassuring. At my age, it's hard to do much other than get in the way or make work for someone. Hearing that I actually did something to help someone feels good. Even a strange group like you four."

"Do you really think we're strange?" Kathy asked. "I don't think we're that much different than anyone else."

"Well, Kathy, you are. I don't know what these other three do for a living, but just having you as part of your group makes you strange. You're a world famous singer. One of the very best. Just the fact that you want to know something I might be able to tell you makes this whole visit strange."

Mack spoke up then. He decided to tell Edgar what they all did for a living, as much to see the look on his face when he did it as anything.

"Dale here," he said, "is the sheriff of Clayborne County, Minnesota. Lisa and I used to be deputy sheriffs for him. We now own a detective agency. We are private detectives."

"This is getting weirder all the time. You people are in no way ordinary. Before I forget to ask though, you said something about his book. Did he keep some kind of journal or something?"

"It's more like an autobiography," Mack explained, "that he wrote like a novel. If you have a reader or tablet, I can download a copy of it for you."

"No, I don't have anything like that. I'm surprised that Jasper could put something like that together. As far as I know, he wasn't very technical savvy."

"He probably wasn't. We got it the way he wrote it. On paper from yellow legal pads. Hand printed. The people at the detective agency put it together into the ebook format."

Before Edgar could say anything more, there was a loud hammering on the door. "That's probably the insurance guys. I think it would be best if you all wait here. I'll deal with them."

There were four men on the other side of the door when Edgar opened it. Three were white and one was black. The black one spoke up. "We seen what you gots yerself some company. We come here ta see who it is. You knows we don't like someone snoopin' around territory what's ours."

He pushed Edgar out of the way, nearly knocking him down as he did. A big grin filled his face as soon as he saw Kathy and Lisa.

"Well now lookee what we done got here. Some sure fire sweet ass white pussy, just all a hot and waiting for the likes of us. Man oh man, is we gonna have us some real good fun now." He waved his hand at his three companions. "Be best iffen you'd be gettin' rid of theses two white boys. We be not wantin' them in the way for us to be doing these two fine young womans."

He moved in on Lisa first. It was the biggest mistake he ever made in his entire live. She instantly took command of the situation. Fingers on the two hands trying to grab her breasts were broken to start with. His nose was second. She broke his left knee next, and when he went down, she kicked his manhood twice, using every bit of strength in her leg she could put into it. When she looked up, two other of the men were down and quite still. Dale was holding the hair of the man who thought he could put his hands on Kathy, and turning his face into putty.

Kathy was the one who dialed 911. The Waterloo police were quick to arrive. At first they didn't know what to make of the fact that they'd so easily taken out four well known gang members. It made sense to them when Dale explained who they were.

The cops had all the needed paper work on a large iPad, and Dale signed it. The four men were escorted to the hospital to get patched up, and from there they would go to jail. The cops left no doubt that they'd be there for a fair amount of time.

After the police finished up, Mack asked Edgar about the insurance thing.

"It's a gang. There's probably at least a couple of dozen of them. A few are black, but most are white. They come around once a month to collect the money they say we owe them for protecting us. We're forced to pay in cash."

"What about the cops? Can't they put a stop to it?"

"They try to help. But they can't be everywhere, and the few who have been caught collecting money have had lawyers good enough to get them light sentences. The people who've fought back have paid for it. Just like I'll pay for what happened here today. They'll be around soon, to get even. And there won't be a damn thing I can do about it."

This was not at all what they came to Iowa for. All they wanted was the chance to learn more about Jasper. Which they had already done. And they were sure they would learn more. If, that is, those hoodlums hadn't interfered.

It didn't take a lot of discussion for them to decide that the only thing they could do was settle the problem with the gang. They also decided that if they couldn't handle it themselves, they would call in reinforcements from home.

Their first step in dealing with it was to watch for the so-called insurance collectors. They traveled around all the senior developments in pairs. Their favorites were the people in the assisted living apartments. It was rare for them to be able to do anything to defend themselves from the gang members. Especially since they always worked in pairs.

As mean and nasty as all the gang members were, none of them had the abilities of Lisa, Mack, or Dale. Even Kathy, thanks to the intensive training she'd been getting, especially from Lisa, could do a respectable job of defending herself.

They split up, with Mack and Lisa covering part of the area, and Dale and Kathy the other. Before the first day of hunting, Mack and Lisa had disabled eight gang members. Dale and Kathy took six out. They didn't bother the police with what they were doing, nor did they put many of the gang into the hospital, but everyone of them who dealt with either Mack and Lisa or Dale and Kathy, had a good understanding of the meaning of the word pain.

On the second day they hunted, there was always three members together to do the collecting. Kathy and Dale then rejoined up with Mack and Lisa. This time, Lisa got very upset with two of the collectors, so they did go to the hospital.

From then on, the collecting was being done in groups of six. That gave all the gang members a whole new confidence. Something Mack, Dale, and Lisa proceeded to destroy.

Lisa did the most damage. The further they got into hunting the relatively feeble minded gang members who were terrorizing innocent seniors, the angrier she got. For her, what was being done to these people was even worse that what was done to Jasper. And she considered what was done to him by his own family to not only be small and petty, but downright evil.

That meant that life for the gang members, who thought they could do nearly anything the wanted to do, was getting downright dangerous. Mack finally was forced to tell her to back off some. He didn't want her arrested for murder, even if they all did consider her attitude justified.

By the end of their third day in Iowa, the gang was down to just under ten members in fit enough shape to continue to try to collect their so called insurance. That's when their collecting days came to an end. Three different people living in a seniors mobil home park were inspired by what was being done. They decided to do something about the gang themselves.

They took out guns from closets, that hadn't so much as been touched for years, then cleaned, oiled, and loaded them. The first senior to use his rifle on a collector only wounded him. But it was a gut shot and he was permanently out of it. The second man, who was still in excellent shape and who had served in Vietnam, shot three of them. He used a shotgun. Two were killed and the other spent a couple of months in the hospital. The third man wounded two of them before they ran off. After that there weren't enough gang members to do anything to anybody.

None of the seniors were ever even taken into custody, let alone arrested. And Mack, Lisa, Kathy, and Dale were able to spend more time with Edgar McKenna, talking about the life of Jasper Klug.

They bought a tablet at a discount store and downloaded Jasper's book. Lisa taught him how to use it, and he read it right away.

"The book is interesting," Edgar commented when he finished. "But like everything else he did, Jasper was kind to all of us when he wrote it. He did a pretty thorough job of covering the good things and the good times, but he sure did gloss over or skip the hard, sometimes mean times. He also skipped some things about himself. He must have thought he'd be showing off or something, if he told it all about who he was and what he did."

"Are those times something you can talk about to us?" Mack asked him. "Or would you rather not?"

"I'd rather not tell you the truth about somethings." Edgar took a couple of deep breaths. "I will though. You've all done way too much for me, to allow me to let you go home wondering. The hardest part of his life was his wife. She was the best thing for him, the last eighteen years or so, but before that, she hurt him. She hurt him a lot. After the war, there was a short time those of us who knew him the best, we were afraid he might end it all. Instead, in the end, he forgave those of us who hurt him so bad.

"She cheated on him the whole time he was away, serving his country. It was more than one man who spent a night with her. He found out about it when he came home. She promised then, that it would never happen again. He forgave her, and for him it seemed for a long time that everything was okay between them.

"It wasn't. She was seeing one man. The one man she should have stayed the furthest away from. Me. When he finally caught us, I was sure it was over. Their marriage and for sure our friendship. I damn sure didn't deserve his friendship. Still wouldn't if he was alive. He gave it anyway. That's the kind of man he was. About as decent as they come." He shook his head, almost as if the memories were causing him physical pain.

"When they got back together, he told her to see me one more time. To say goodbye. He said he didn't care how she did it, as long it was the last time we were together. We made love that one last time. She cried then. Not because we were splitting. It was because of what we'd just done, and what we'd been doing. She said we never should have done any of it. After that, she was the best wife to him anyone could have ever been. For the rest of her life, she pretty much avoided me. She was right in doing it. It eased Jasper's worry considerably.

"They had those last good years. I'm glad they did, even if I wasn't much of a part of them. I left Minnesota the day after my last time with her. I've lived in Waterloo ever since. Jasper forgave me too. Even so, our close friendship was over. Our times together were always pleasant enough, even if there was always something missing. Loving her was the hardest thing I ever did. I betrayed the best friend I ever had, and I never really had the only woman I truly loved. It all would have been a lot worse though, if Jasper wouldn't have been such a good man."

Edgar's head dropped, and he stared at the floor. His face was hidden, his tears weren't.

"I remember when she died. He must have loved her something god awful. I've never seen a man so tore up as he was. I think part of him gave up then. It maybe had something to do with him ending up homeless. I don't think life meant near so much to him once she was gone. He wasn't much more than an empty shell. I've always wished I could have done something for him that mattered. He should never have had to spend the end of his life alone the way he did. I will always wonder how the world could be so blind that it couldn't see what a good man he was."

The four of them stood quietly for a while, feeling Edgar's grief. When they started the disjointed journey to learn more about Jasper Klug, they expected to learn about a good, but simple man. An ordinary, but good person who lived a rather ordinary life. So far from what they'd learned about him, he was anything but ordinary.

They made their goodbyes to Edgar a little later, promising to stay in touch. It was something they all honestly wanted to do. It was a quiet ride back to the RV park in the jeep. Mack and Dale each drank a beer when they got there. Lisa and Kathy drank a glass of wine. It seemed as though none of them knew what to say.

Finally, when the silence between them grew too loud, Kathy left the chair she was in. She walked over to Mack. Without a word, she took his hand and pulled him to his feet. She led him to the RV he shared with Lisa, and they went inside.

Dale and Lisa watched them. Lisa was pulling him to his feet before Mack shut the door on his RV.

CHAPTER 11

They ate a pleasant supper together. It started as quiet as they were when they left Edgar. It was Mack who managed to bring some life into their quiet. "I guess what happened this afternoon is not going to be all that damn easy to deal with. It shouldn't be like this though. We all know what we did and why we did it. We are all still here, and it doesn't appear to me that any harm has come to any of us. As far as the jealousy we all feel right now, Lisa told me about it. It keeps all of us that much more interested in our partner. As long as we don't get too carried away with it, it's good for us."

"Aren't you afraid sometimes, Mack," Dale asked, "that this kind of thing could split us up? It could happen to all of us."

"It could. Odds are though, it's never going to. In this life, we are meant to be with who we are with. The rest is only something extra special that we share. Kathy and I love each other, but we don't have any plans to make anything we do together permanent. Not in this lifetime. So be jealous, Dale. At the same time, be reassured that no harm is going to come to you because of the way we feel."

"Mack's right," Kathy said. "Not that long ago, I never would have dreamed I could be part of what the four of us have now. I'm glad though, that things have changed into what they are now. I loved you, Dale, before any of this happened. I love you even more now."

They were quiet for a while, then Lisa spoke up. "I agree with what you guys were talking about, even if it was a little embarrassing to listen to. It settled the questions I think we all had after we were in the RVs. It think it's time to move on though. We've still got time left, so there do we go now? Someplace just for fun, or more Jasper?"

"I think another Jasper stop," Mack suggested, "before we decide on the something fun. Sue sent me a text message this afternoon, about his daughter. She lives out in the country. Her and her husband own about a hundred acres, and their place is between here and home."

Dale further lightened things up between them when he said, "Mack's right. Let's look up Jasper's daughter. We all had plenty of fun this afternoon. We can have more later fun later. Even if it is a different kind."

They all got a bit of a chuckle from his comment. Real laughter though, was unlikely. They all took the afternoon too serious to laugh at it. That didn't stop them, however, from appreciating the fact that Dale was able to treat it lightly. He was normally the one most likely to get uptight about it.

Kathy and Lisa got up then, to get the RVs ready to go in the morning. Mack and Dale volunteered to help, but their wives shooed them away. They were told that too many hands doing the job would only make a mess of things. Either way, it didn't matter much. They had the RVs ready to go in much less than an hour.

In the morning, they opted for a fast food breakfast. They decided to eat their takeout breakfast sandwiches inside the place, to save making a mess in either of the RVs. Mack and Dale already felt that they were leaving too much of the domestic work to their wives. Kathy and Lisa didn't agree about that. They went along with eating inside anyway.

They were just finishing their meal, which had turned out to be better than expected, when five men came in. They were wearing various kinds of fishing hats and vests, a were all obviously very much under the influence of alcohol.

The men started out loud, and steadily got worse. They quickly got verbally abusive to the limited staff working there. Only two of them were male. One was the fry cook, and the other one they took to be the manager. The rest were females, and none of them appeared to be any older than around eighteen.

Mack was the first of his group to get up and leave his seat, when one of the fishermen got mildly violent. When he unwrapped the sandwich he'd just been served, he threw it at one of the young ladies at the cash registers.

"That ain't what I ordered," he yelled. "You gave me sausage. I wanted bacon. Now make me the right fucking sandwich."

This, of course, discouraged Mack from leaving the place. The three people with him were every bit as unlikely to want to leave. Given their considerable experience in law enforcement, three of them knew how much trouble the men could be. Kathy had enough experience with creeps in crowds at her concerts, to know how it was too.

Dale was the one to approach the acting manager, to ask if he wanted help dealing with the drunks.

"It would be nice," he answered Dale. "The thing is, there's five of them and only two of you. That doesn't look to me that you could be much help."

"I know what it looks like, but we can help if you want it. You could also call the police. Either way, those guys are only going to get worse."

"The cops won't be much help. We've had to call them too many times. Some of those times, we should have been able to handle the problem ourselves. They're more than a little tired of us."

"I guess the choice is yours then. You can tell me you want our help if they get worse, or we can leave you at their mercy."

"Well, okay. But if I do ask for your help, what the hell can just two of you do to stop them from making trouble, if that's what they start to do."

"Whatever it takes. And there's four of us." He pointed out Lisa. "The truth about her is the fact that she could take on any two of them without any kind of a problem. With her, the biggest problem is hoping they don't piss her off too bad. She can get awful rough when someone does that."

The manager shrugged, gave Dale a half a smile, and said. "Okay, if they get worse, I'll be glad to have your help."

It didn't take long for the drunks to throw more food. When the second sandwich was in the air, Lisa was the first one out of her seat. In seconds she was behind the man who threw it. She didn't fool around. She knock his silly hat off, then slapped him up side the head with her open hand. All of her strength went into it.

His head snapped to one side when she hit him. He quickly got to his feet and turned to her, his hands balled into fists. He grinned as soon as he was able to focus on her.

"You did that?"

"You don't see anyone else standing here," she asked, "do you, asshole?"

"Sure don't," he said, reaching for her. "Now my teaching you some manners is going to be pure fun."

"The only fun you're going to have," she told him, dodging his hands, "is cleaning up the mess you made."

"Oh yeah? And who do you think can make me do that?"

"I can, you drunken piece of shit."

He laughed, then lunged at her. She was already tired of him, so she just used the palm of her hand to break his nose. She then grabbed his hair, pulled his head up and back, then landed her best right hand into his soft, protruding gut. He curled into a ball after he landed on the floor.

Lisa looked at the rest of the drunks. "It's time to pay your bill," she told them. "You can leave an extra hundred for the mess you made. You can take your food with you when you go. Or not. I don't care. Now pay up and get the hell out of here." She gave the drunk on the floor a not to gentle kick in the ribs. "And be sure to take your garbage with you."

The four men who could still function exchanged looks. One of them then got up and took some money out of his pocket and left it on the table. "Be a good idea if the rest of you leave some too," he told the others. "We've been out of line since we got here."

They each left some money, Then two of them half dragged, half carried their drunken friend out of the place. They then left the parking lot in the large SUV they came in.

The four of them waited an hour to be sure the drunks didn't return, then went on their way. They had planned on stopping to see Jasper's daughter that day, but because of the delay at breakfast, they decided to find a reasonably close RV park and visit the daughter in the morning.

It was a family type park, and filled with friendly people. Shortly after the got their RVs setup, the couple from the next campsite stopped to introduce themselves. They were also told they were welcome to join everyone in the singalong they had every night.

"It doesn't matter if any of you know how to sing," the man told then. "It's all just for fun."

They thanked the man for telling them about the singalong and he left. Three of the smiled as they turned to Kathy. Dale was the one to tell her. "None of us will mind skipping that tonight. I can't imagine you will want to sing with a bunch of strangers."

Kathy got a mischievous grin on her face. "You know what, Dale? Let's not tell them who I am. I don't get to sing just for the pure hell of it very often anymore. I think it might be fun."

"It's unlikely you'll get through it without someone recognizing you."

"Probably not. I think it'll be kind of fun anyway."

They ate a simple supper that night. Hot dogs and macaroni and cheese that came out of a box. Not very nutritious, but filling enough. The singalong started shortly after they finished eating.

Kathy asked that they sit near the back of the group of people singing, and didn't put near as much into her voice as she could have. She was having fun doing it, and liked the fact that no one had noticed her. They were about half way through it when she made her mistake.

They sang one of her earliest hit songs. It was one of her personal favorites, of all of her recordings. It was also a song that she gave it her all whenever she'd sing it in one of her concerts. This time, as soon as she started singing, she forgot where she was. It didn't take long before her powerful voice rose out of the crowd. Soon, everyone there had turned behind them, to see who was singing.

It was a young mother, holding onto her baby that first recognized her, "Oh my god," she cried out. "That's Kathy Magee. Kathy Magee is singing with us. How can that be?"

Kathy didn't hesitate. She stood and finished singing the song. She put as much of herself into it as she'd ever put into a song. When she finished, she waited for the applause to die down, then told the group. "I appreciate the fact that you like my music, and I'll sing a couple more for you. But then I'd really like it if we all sing together. You are a great bunch of people, and it's a real treat for me to be able to share music with all of you."

She sang two songs for them, and got a round of applause, as strong as the group could make it, for each one of them. They then finished out the evening singing together. And no one bothered Kathy for an autograph until it was over.

It proved to be an altogether nice way to spend an evening, and helped ease the gloom they all felt from learning how Jasper was all too often treated.

CHAPTER 12

While they were eating breakfast in the morning, most of the people stopped to tell Kathy how much they appreciated having her a part of the singalong. They all were hoping she'd be there another night, and all of them who stopped to thank her were disappointed to learn she'd be leaving right after breakfast.

There were no glitches in the GPS system in Mack and Lisa's RV, so they got to Jasper's daughters within thirty minutes of leaving the RV park. The concrete driveway from the dirt road they were on to the daughters house was a long one. The house was huge. It was two stories, and had five bedrooms and four full bathrooms. It was built on a small knoll, so the finished basement was a walkout. Behind and down the hill from the house was a horse barn.

Inside the barn were stalls for a dozen horses. Out in the pasture eight, well trained horses were contentedly grazing on the deep green grass covering every inch of the ground. Six head of young stock completed the picture. Chickens also used the pasture during the day. They spent their nights in a coop not far from the barn. Because of the numerous predators, it was too dangerous for them to be out at night. All the fences were wood. They not only defined the pasture and corrals, they surrounded the entire farm.

Mack knew enough about the cost of all kinds of fencing materials, so he knew the money it cost to build all of them on this land was more than he and Lisa had spent on their house. Looking at the place, he couldn't help but wonder why the people who lived here didn't give Jasper the help he deserved when he needed it. If they could afford to live here, they could have supported him for many many years without hurting their budget.

Because they were on their way home, they drove into the place in the RVs. The woman who came out of the house to greet them, even before the RVs came to a complete stop, had a large hand gun in her right hand. She didn't appear to be in anyway friendly.

"Whatever it is that you're selling," she snarled the instant Mack got out of the RV, "we don't want any. If you're not selling, we don't contribute to charities either. And no, you may definitely not camp on the back forty. So it would be best if you'd just drive the hell out of here now."

Mack held up his hands, trying to show her that he meant no harm. "All we want is a few minutes of your time to talk. If you are Gladys Jeffers, that is?"

"Whether I am or not is irrelevant. I surely don't see any reason I would want to talk to you."

"From your answer, I can't help but assume you are Gladys. All we want to do is ask you about your father."

"Why? He's just a difficult old man who never listens to reason. That's all anyone needs to know about him."

"You don't know," Mack asked, "do you?"

"Know what? I doubt any scar faced fake cowboy could possibly know anything I don't."

"Maybe not. You should know then, that Jasper's dead. The man who was your father is dead."

Gladys's body suddenly seemed to fold into itself as she absorbed what Mack said. Her shaking head dropped and she softly said, "No." No other sound came out of her and her eyes stayed dry. Only her shoulders shook slightly. When she did manage to look up at Mack, she asked, "When, where, how?" Her look now was of one who was lost, and whose world was now devoid of meaning. "Why? Did he die alone?"

Mack told her how they met Jasper and the evening they spent with him. He explained how he found him. When he reached the part about the willow tree, she finally cried. Lisa and Kathy tried to comfort her then. She pushed them away.

When she recovered enough to talk, she immediately asked, "Who the hell are you people, that you come around here wanting to ask me questions about my father. Nothing about him is your business."

"I'm Mack Thomas," he told her, "and this is my wife Lisa. My friend here is Dale Magee. He is the sheriff of Clayborne County. It's about a hundred miles north of here. This other lady is his wife, Kathy Magee."

"Really now? You come here and introduce yourselves, and one of you has the same name as a famous singer. A person, I'm sure, is so far above any of you that it would be impossible to describe how far."

Mack couldn't do much other than smile at her answer. He looked at Kathy to see if she wanted to tell Gladys who she was. She shook her head no. Mack could see that she wanted the woman to be shocked when she realized who Kathy was.

"You are right about us ma'am. We aren't anybody special. Well, maybe Kathy is some. We didn't come here to take anything, or get anything, from you. We just became quite fond of Jasper in the very short time we knew him. As I told you, he gave us his book that told his story. We've all read it. It told us a lot about him. About his life. We have since learned though, that he left a lot out. Too much really. He was apparently a humble man, and he left out a lot of who he really was. All we want is to learn as much about him as we can. That way, maybe we can some day finish his book for him. Mostly, we're trying to learn more about him because of the deep impression he made on us."

"As far as that book goes," Gladys claimed, "it belongs to me, and to the rest of his family. Not to a group of nobodies like you. So I'd appreciate it if you'd turn it over to me."

"I can't do that right now. We don't have it with us. If you have a reader or a tablet, we can download it for you so you can read it."

"How can you do that? Jasper didn't know anything about modern technology."

"We turned it into an ebook." Mack explained how it was original written and about all the people who wanted to read it. He finished with, "As far as the original goes, your family will get that at a more appropriate time."

"I still don't think you have any right to it."

"He did. I'm the one he gave it too. And I still have the letter he sent me with the key for the safe deposit box it was in."

"Well, if that's the case, I don't think I'll be inclined to talk to you until I get the book from you."

"Does that mean you don't want to read it now? If not, we will be on our way. We can't wait for you to decide. We will have to be back home in a few days." Mack exaggerated that. Kathy and Dale still had slightly over a week that they could spend on their uncommon vacation. "Kathy has a concert coming up. They always take some preparation ahead of time."

Gladys cocked her head to one side when Mack mentioned Kathy having a concert. For the first time since they got there, she actually looked at Kathy. She then blushed. "You aren't really her, are you? You do look like her. A lot like her. You can't be though. I've been a fan of Kathy Magee's since the first time I ever heard her sing on the radio. If you were her, why would you care any about my father? He wasn't anyone important."

Kathy answered her. "Not to you maybe. To me, to all four of us, he was important. He still is important. I guess I got to know him, and who he was, better in one evening than you did in a lifetime. I know him well enough now, to want to know him better."

"You sound so sincere. Yet you come here pretending to be a famous singer, just to impress me. It doesn't. I think you are all probably just a bunch of swindlers or something. I think you should all leave now."

"I'm so sorry you feel the way you do, Gladys. I wish there was some way we could convince you that we really only do want to learn about Jasper. We don't want to take anything away from you. We only want to share with you."

"Well, smarty pants. Why don't you try singing. That'll prove to both of us who you aren't."

"Okay, but I'm used to singing with music." she turned to Dale. "Will you get my guitar for me, Hon?" Dale got the guitar from the RV. "This is one of my most recent recordings. They've been playing the video a lot on YouTube and the other music channels." Kathy sang the love song. Because it was such a strong reminder of the love her parents had for each other, it brought tears to her eyes. They were flowing freely when she finished.

Gladys finally realized that she was mistaken about them. She shook her head a couple of times, waved her hand for them to follow her, and said, "Come on into the house. I'll tell you what I can about my father."

They were barely settled in the family room of the big house, when a late model BMW came screaming up the driveway. It came to a screeching halt in front of the house. A tall young man leaped out, and slamming the car door behind him, he rushed into the house.

"What the hell do you think you're doing, Mother?" he bellowed at Gladys. "Who the hell are these people? You know father said no company if he's not here."

Although she was obviously afraid of him, she told him, "They were friends of your grandfather. They came here to talk to me about him."

"Too damn bad. The talking's done. It's time for all of you to get the hell out of here, before I throw you out."

What was beginning to be a frequent happening, Lisa was the first to respond to him. She stood up and moved within inches of him. "It's like this, Ollie," Lisa said, "Gladys invited us in. We'll leave when she says so. Not before." She knew his name was Oliver, from reading Jasper's book. She called him Ollie to intentionally piss him off. She simply wasn't at all in the mood for bully boys like him.

He put his hand high on her chest and tried to push her away. The last thing he expected was how fast she could move, and the things she could do when she did. She twisted his right hand until his wrist was ready to break. She then put her hand on his chest and pushed him. He nearly fell as he stumbled back.

"If you put either of your hands on me again, you will find yourself very full of regrets for being such a total asshole."

Gladys watched the episode with a surprised look. The smirk on her face said she wasn't at all upset with what Lisa did.

Oliver, however was. "You goddamn whore," he screamed at Lisa, "you are damn well going to pay for that."

Mack stood up at that point. He stepped between Lisa and Oliver. "You just called my wife a whore. She doesn't like you doing that at all. I'm going to be nice anyway, and let you walk out of here and leave. If you don't, I'm going to get out of her way. If I have to do that, I won't stop her until you are hospital bound."

"Fuck you, Cowboy. Ain't none of you going to do anything but get to hell out of my mother's house. I'm black belt karate, and I can kick all your asses. That slut wife of yours will be easiest of all."

The word slut did it for Lisa. Before he could signal either of his karate legs to kick her, he was laid out on the floor. His nose was bleeding and he was curled into a tight ball.

"I'm sorry, Mack. But you know how much I hate it when a piece of shit like him uses words like that on me."

He turned to Gladys. "Can we still talk, or do you want us to leave?"

"We can talk. Do we need to call an ambulance for Oliver?"

"Not really. His nose is probably broken, but he should be able to drive himself when he recovers."

"Okay." She was quiet for a while as she moved her eyes back and forth from Mack to Lisa, then back to him again. "And no, I'm not upset about what Lisa did to him. Just surprised. He actually does have a black belt in karate."

"She was a deputy sheriff for a while. She's been attacked way too many times, so she learned how to defend herself. There aren't many men she couldn't handle if she had to."

"Unfortunately, there is one man I know she couldn't beat. My husband. He's a big, very strong man. He fought heavy weight in Gold Gloves in his younger days. He knows karate and a couple of other styles of fighting. He still works out regularly, so he's in great shape. He'll be home in a couple of hours."

"If you're at all worried about us meeting him," Mack said. "We could always try to get together sometime in the future." As soon as he finished talking, Mack realized that it was too late to leave.

The husband arrived home early. He charged into the house, his face a deep red and his expression said he was ready to kill. "What the hell?" he bellowed like a bull in heat when he saw his son trying to get up from the floor. Axton Jeffers was not a happy man. "What the hell's going on, Gladys?" he demanded. "Who the hell are these people?"

"They came here to talk to me about, Dad," she answered. Her voice trembled slightly, yet it was obvious she was gaining confidence about them being there.

"He's thankfully gone the hell out of here, so there's nothing for you to talk about him." He looked up. "All you people get the hell out of here," he growled. "And I mean now, before I'm forced to throw you out."

Gladys stood, facing him. "Not this time Axton. I'm sorry, but my father's dead and these kind people came here to tell me what happened to him. They want to know more about him, so I told them I would talk to them. So I am going to talk to them."

"You will not. You will only do what I tell you to do. And you have to know, my patience is wearing thin. Someone's going to get hurt if I need to literally throw them all out of here. I won't be gentle."

"For your wife's sake," Mack said, "we'll be leaving. But if I ever hear, sometime in the future, that you in any way hurt her because we were here, I will be back."

Axton laughed. "You can come back all you want. I can kick your ass from here to hell and back without thinking about it much. Primitive cowboys don't scare me in any way, shape, or form."

Lisa tugged on Mack's arm. "If I promise I for sure won't kill this childish boy in a man's body, will you let me kick his ass? He's an even bigger jerk off than his jellyfish son."

"You'd best watch your mouth, Bitch," Axton told her. "Before I take you over my knee and paddle your cute little bare ass."

"Not even two of you could ever do that. Maybe three of you could, but I'm thinking more like four of you. Even then, before it was over, you'd be wishing you hadn't done it."

Gladys realized then, that Lisa wasn't kidding, and that she probably could beat her husband if it came to a fight. "I'm sorry, Lisa," she said. "I guess you guys should go now. It will be better for everyone if you don't put Axton in the hospital. Rich as he is, he still needs to go to work every day."

Axton grabbed her, then slapped her face. "You don't ever talk about me that way." He slapped her again.

Lisa grabbed his arm when he raised it to hit her with his fist. Before he could realize what was happening she jammed it up behind it until they all heard it snap. He screamed from the pain. With a look of total disgust, she pushed him away.

"Sorry again, Mack," Lisa said, "but he was hitting her."

"No need to be sorry. All of us were ready to do the same or worse to him."

Oliver was finally on his feet then. Without talking, Mack and Dale helped him and Axton to his car. "Be best if you both go to the nearest hospital and get patched up. When that's done, it'll be good if you remember before you harm Gladys, that we don't live far away. If we have to come back, it will be much worse for you."

After they left, they went inside to say goodbye to Gladys. "I don't feel much like talking right now. I do want to talk to you about my father, so I hope we'll get the chance to sometime in the future. I think you can see now why I didn't take care of him. Those two wouldn't let me. It's too late to help dad. It isn't for me. I think I'll be talking to a divorce lawyer before the sun sets tomorrow."

"I think you've got a good idea there," Lisa said. "And if you need any help, let us know. We own a private detective agency." She gave Gladys all the information connected to it.

They were a disappointed bunch as they started out on their ride, heading for home. The only saving grace from the visit with Gladys was the fact they'd learned that Jasper wasn't all that wrong when he chose not to live with his daughter.

CHAPTER 13

When they arrived home, they decided to postpone any future vacation time until after Lisa's father, Bob Anderson, and his wife, Beth, had their auction. It took a tremendous amount of effort to get a hundred milking cow dairy operation ready for one.

Along with the cows being milked, there was nearly a hundred head of other cattle to be sold. Along with the heifers waiting to calve the first time, there were a lot of them of various ages, scheduled to be bred as soon as they hit the right age.

Bob was planning to quit farming entirely, so all of his machinery would also be put up for auction. The farm itself was already sold. Bob and Beth had already found a house, which was less than half the size of their farm house. That meant a lot of household goods would be sold too. All in all, it would be an all day auction.

Mack and Lisa decided that since they were still technically on vacation, they would assist in getting ready for it. It was a good idea to do it. Lisa found a few things that had a lot of memories connected to them, and Bob insisted that she keep them. She agreed to keep the things that had little monetary value, but insisted to bid on the other things, the same as anyone else.

All the prep work moved along smoothly, with one not so small glitch. Beth gradually developed a habit of working as close to Mack as she could. She tried to make it look like a coincidence, but given her history with Mack, it was impossible for her to pull it off. She was also such an open and honest person, that she was lousy at faking anything.

Lisa did her best to ignore what Beth was doing. It still finally came to a head when it became too much for Lisa to watch any longer. She talked to Mack about it.

"I know, Lisa," he said when she complained. "I've more than noticed. I just don't know what to do about it exactly. I did tell her that she was getting too forward toward me. She just smiled and said, "I know. My world is coming apart, and you are the only anchor I can see anywhere. I'll still try to back off some."

"She hasn't though," Lisa complained. "It seems to me that her only activity everyday is flirting with you, Mack."

"I'll try to get her to back off further, Lisa. I know I could have done more when it comes to that, but I've been trying not to hurt her. She is feeling pretty bad right now. With your dad's health being as bad as it is, and now them having to give up the farm, it's pretty tough on both of them."

"Well, do what you can." Lisa paused to gather her thoughts. "I guess I'll just have to look the other way for a while. Until this damn auction is over anyway."

Mack took a moment to think. He wondered if he should tell Lisa right then, everything about Beth, or if he should wait until after the auction. He finally decided that the truth now would be the best thing.

"There's more than just her flirting," Mack explained. "She wants, if it's possible, to have your permission to spend time with me occasionally."

"What kind of time? Time like walking in the refuge? Or time like the two of you in bed?"

"A lot of the latter, I'm afraid."

Lisa gritted her teeth, trying not to scream or groan or beat on Mack. "And what did you tell her?"

"No. I told her a flat out, loud no. I told her that the no wasn't just for me. It was for you and your dad too."

"What did she say to that?"

"That the no was only for you and me. Not for Bob. He's sicker than we realized, Lisa. The only way he'll ever get back to anywhere near normal is with a transplant. Everyone knows how long the list is, for those waiting for a heart."

"Damnit, Mack. What the hell else is going to happen, that you and I have to deal with?"

Mack sighed heavily. Shaking his head, he said, "There is one more thing."

"Oh my god! What?"

"She asked me if we had any openings in the agency. She wants to work for us."

"And you told her what?"

"That it would have to be a wait and see proposition."

"Well, Mack, it might be a long wait. Right now, I think our lives are plenty far away from normal the way it is. If you end up doing anything with Beth, I'm not going to like it at all. Kathy would absolutely hate it. So we'd best try to figure out how to deal with this. If we don't, it can only lead to trouble. We just don't need that."

"You're right. I'll do the best that I can to deal with it. I just want you to know. You are the most important thing in my life. No one could ever replace you. So please don't worry too much. I have no desire to do anything to mess it up between us."

Lisa did a good job of ignoring Beth's moves on Mack for the rest of the time they were making the auction preparations. It was enough of a strain, however, that she was greatly relieved when auction day finally rolled around.

They lucked out with the weather. The day started with a bright blue sky. The early morning temperature was in the high sixties, and never got above seventy-five degrees all day. Bob was well enough known for the auction to draw a large crowd of auction buyers.

The auctioneer started with the smaller, miscellaneous items first. People were in a buying mood that day, so many of the household goods sold for close to their original retail price.

The machinery went next, and again, the prices were as good as Bob and Beth and the auctioneer could have anticipated. It was a good crowd, but what drew them to the machinery was Bob's reputation. He was well know for the fact that he always did his best to properly maintain his equipment.

Because the price of milk was now in a downward trend, they expected that none of the cattle would bring any better than moderate prices. And that would only include the best in Bob's herd.

Fortunately, they were wrong. About fifty miles south of Bob's farm, there was a dairy farm owned by a large, agricultural corporation. Money was never a problem for them, and they were currently concentrating on expansion, rather than maximum profits.

They were also aware of the quality of Bob's herd, and were interested in owning as many of his cows as they could. They had considered offering to purchase his herd, but decided that they should be able to buy them cheaper at the auction.

They were badly mistaken. Since there weren't very many dairy farmers left in Minnesota, they all knew about each other. Even if they might not know each other personally. So there were several other dairy farmers there, eager to buy Bob's cows.

From the first cow, the bidding was vigorous. It continued to be until the last cow was sold. The corporation that thought they'd buy the cows cheaper were proved to be wrong. They ended up owning somewhat less than half of Bob's herd, and it cost them slightly more than the whole herd would have, had they offered to buy all of it before the auction.

When the receipts were counted up at the end of the day, the auctioneer was more than pleased to tell Bob that the auction brought in close to double what was originally expected. It was the first time in his life of a farmer that Bob was paid close to what all his hard work was actually worth.

It didn't mean much at the time. As he stood near the gate, watching his cattle being loaded on trucks, he felt as though a large part of his life was slipping away from him. Standing with him, Beth, Lisa, his other daughter, Julie, and his son Ricky, were all feeling a sense of loss. They all had tears in their eyes. Beth was suffering the worst. She was crying hard. Of all of them, she had spent the least amount of time on the farm. It didn't matter. She changed her entire life when she married Bob. She loved him, but the farm was one of the other reasons she married him. She loved the hard work and the consistent routine of it. She was sure that nothing could ever replace the way of life she had while working on it. The good thing was the success of the auction. She at least had some choices now.

It was much the same for Bob. The best part of it all as far as he was concerned, was that it meant that he and Beth had enough money so she could take the time to choose the job she wanted, rather than be forced to take something just for the money. Mack and Lisa, on the other hand, weren't quite as excited about that. They knew what job she wanted, and they knew that if they gave it to her, it could lead to trouble.

The solution came to them as a gift. A gift that turned out as beneficial to the giver as it was to Mack and Lisa. Dale offered Beth a job working for him, inside the sheriff's office. To convince her to take the job, he promised to also train her to become a deputy. The fact that one of his people in the office gave notice the day before the auction is what allowed him to hire her.

He stuck his neck out a long way, and probably wouldn't have done it on his own. Kathy was the one who convinced him to do it. When she learned about Beth's constant flirting with Mack, it didn't take her long to figure out a way to put a stop to it. Or at least slow it down. So she suggested to Dale that he hire her.

Beth accepted the job for two reasons. One, it sounded interesting. Two, it meant that she would be working in the same field, law enforcement, as Mack. It would, she hoped, occasionally allow her to have contact with him. She knew it wouldn't be as often as she wanted, but hoped it would be more often than she might otherwise have.

Mack and Lisa were greatly relieved from the news about Beth's new job. It was also time, they knew, to leave on their next part of their vacation. Roy and Wanda were more than willing to have Emma for a while, so Sue and Larry were going to be the next couple in the second RV.

Before they left, they talked about where to go and what to do this time. Lisa and Sue wanted to make the first stop at Jasper's son's. Mack wasn't quite as adamant about it, but went along with the idea. Larry thought the whole idea of trying to learn about a dead old man they hardly knew was a bit crazy. He went along with it anyway. As far as he was concerned, the entire clan he was now part of was a bit crazy anyway.

CHAPTER 14

Beth was more than anxious to start her new job. Her life was full all the years she was married to Bob. Between doing all the things any housewife did, and the twice a day three hours in the barn milking the cows, she was always busy. And until recently, she also was a mother to Bob's daughter Julie and his son Ricky.

Now her biggest responsibility was taking care of Bob. It wasn't close to enough to keep her busy. Even with his bad heart, he still managed to do nearly everything for himself.

She loved the hard work on the farm, and missed being busy all the time, so she now constantly found herself bored. Bob tried to alleviate some of it, but because he was becoming constantly more limited in the activities he could take part in, his help with her problem was negligible.

She knew that Mack and Lisa would be leaving for more vacation soon, so she debated whether to call him or not. She hoped to convince him to take her on one of his walks in the refuge. After debating the idea with herself for a couple of days, she decided to call Lisa for permission to ask Mack if he'd take her.

She was sure Lisa would say no. She had every reason too, and little to no reason to say yes. Beth knew that's what she'd do, if the situation were reversed. If Mack was her husband, there's no way she'd want him to spend a day in the refuge with another woman.

That meant that Lisa's answer was a surprise. "It's fine with me for you go for a walk in the refuge with Mack," she told Beth. "As long as it's okay with Mack. And…you follow the rules."

"I will Lisa. What are the rules?"

Lisa laughed. "They are real simple. Kissing and holding hands only. No touching, and absolutely nothing that goes beyond touching. If you follow them, you will probably get more than one chance to walk the refuge with him. You don't, and walks will be forbidden. Can you handle that?"

"I'll do my best." She couldn't help but smile. "It sounds like such an easy thing to do, when we talk about. It isn't so easy out there, holding his hand. Or kneeling down next to him, to look at some interesting thing or another. You know how his voice changes while he explains something. The way it softens, and he talks to you like you're the only other person in the whole world. And his eyes. The way they penetrate you down to your very soul. That's the hardest part. Resisting those eyes." She paused a moment, just long enough for a deep sigh. She met Lisa's gaze. "I love your father dearly, Lisa. I always will. He is such a good, decent man. Mack, however, fills parts of me I only know exists when I'm alone with him."

Lisa wasn't at all surprised by Beth's words. It didn't matter that she was married to Mack, and slept in the same bed with him every night. She got much the same feelings from him as Beth did, every one of those nights. That fact was what concerned her about him. As aware as he was of the world around him, he didn't realize what he so frequently did to a woman. It just never seemed to occur to him.

In spite of all that, she trusted him enough to know he'd never cheat of her. Not in the traditional sense of the word anyway. If he somehow did make a mistake and something happened between them, she knew he'd never try to hide it. And given all the things they'd experienced together, she knew their bond would remain strong, regardless.

Beth got her wish then, and two days before Mack and Lisa planned to leave with Sue and Larry for the next part of their vacation, Mack and Beth started their refuge walk.

She didn't wait to take advantage of the fact holding hands was permitted. She had her hand in his before they took their first step. By the fourth step she stopped him and planted the most passionate kiss on him she could. He responded, but when they broke it he pulled away.

"That went beyond something nice, Beth. It was fantastic. The trouble is, we've both made promises. I think we should keep them."

"It was only a kiss, Mack. Lisa said kisses were okay."

"And they are. Problem is, what you just gave me went far beyond a simple kiss. Any more of that, and I could too easily lose control. You are way   too beautiful, too wonderful a woman for me as a mere mortal man be able to control the situation when you do that to me. And this time, we really need to keep this under control."

"I know, Mack. I also know that I want to be as close to you as I can be today. I don't expect that we'll go beyond holding hands and sharing a few kisses. It would be nice though, if we could let some real, honest passion be part of it. Life being what it is right now, I could use some passion in it."

He answered her with a second kiss, then took her hand to start her down the trail with him. He was determined to make it a good day for her while at the same time, keeping it a day Lisa would approve of.

Although they did break the touching rule some, Mack managed to keep it to touching only. Beth seemed okay with it, and actually did pay attention to him when they stopped to study something he found interesting.

They were watching a couple of lizards playing some kind of game only members of their world in the refuge could understand, when Beth took Mack's hand and moved it up to her face. She put it against her cheek as her eyes filled with tears.

"I'm sorry, Mack," she said. "I was wrong when I chose Bob over you. I wish I'd been braver then. I do love Bob. He's such a good man. Part of what I did though, was because it was safer. You are a different kind of man. With Bob, everything was safe and steady. With you, it's always an unknown thing. For me now, I wish life could be something that would allow us, you and I, to share those things we have in us to share. Why are we expected to only give what we are to one person? I don't want to hurt Lisa or Bob, yet I don't understand why it will hurt them if we, even for a brief moment, were who we should be with each other."

"It's pretty much because of religion. It's also the male macho bullshit that dictates that a man owns his wife. It's the idea at the same time, that marriage must show ownership. That was one of the great things about knowing Linda. She didn't believe any of that, and she lived her life accordingly. And because of it, her and Dave had one of the best marriages I've ever seen. And from what she told me, their sex lives were still going very strong up until the day she was murdered."

"So you don't think there would be anything wrong with you and I making love?"

"No, I don't."

"Then why don't we?"

"Because of the promises we made. As much as that, it would hurt other people. It's true that I don't think it would be wrong for you and I to make love again. But right now, it would hurt Lisa. I think the time will come when it will be okay, but not right now. Right now, she needs to know that I will respect her wishes. You know what she's been through. You were a big part of getting her past it. So you have to understand why I can't do with you what we both wish we could do."

"I do, Mack. And I respect both you and Lisa enough to not push this any further. I'm just afraid this might be our last chance."

"I wish you wouldn't feel that way. I'll always care about you."

"I know that, Mack. I know that you will always be there for me. That you will always try to protect me, the same way you do with everyone you care about. But you can't always be there. That somehow scares me right now."

"Lisa often feels just the opposite. Before we started making our little trips to learn about the man who made such a big impression on our lives, we had a big fight one night." Mack went on to tell her about finding Jasper, and why they were spending so much time trying to learn more about him.

"So when you go again, you will be going to visit his son?"

"We will. After we do that, we'll probably find a decent place to camp. Somewhere we can kick back and relax. Maybe do some fishing. And in the case of Lisa and I, spend some significant time in bed."

Beth laughed at his comment about time in bed. "I can't tell you how much I wish it was me you were talking about." She took a couple of deep breaths. "You see, Mack, it's been a while. Roy's sicker then he wants his kids to know. One of the things that have adversely affected has been that."

"I'm sorry. I didn't know."

"I know. Bob would like to keep it that way for now."

"Of course. I won't say anything to anyone until you say it's okay to talk to Lisa about it."

They left the lizards then, and walked the trail again. This time Mack took her hand, giving it a light squeeze. She returned it, and leaned her head against his shoulder. He very much liked the feeling of having her so close, but knew that no matter what, he wasn't going to go against Lisa's wishes. He didn't object though, when she thoroughly kissed him several times along the way.

The rest of the afternoon was a pleasant day for them. Two people enjoying the time, the place, and most of all, each other. It was just as they reached the end of the trail that Mack got a call from Lisa.

"Sorry to bother you," she said. "But we all have decided to go out tonight. So when you two finish your walk, take Beth home, have her put on a pretty dress, and meet us at the Mystic Curve. We'll be eating dinner there, and then doing some dancing."

"Who all is coming?"

"All of us. Even Emma. Don't be too late. We'll be leaving in about an hour."

"I assume Bob's up to a night out?"

"He's more than ready to go. He said he might even try a slow dance or two with Beth. He promised a dance with me too. It's been a long time since I danced with my dad."

"Okay, Lisa. We'll be there. We're almost to the end of the trail."

"Good. Dad's here now, so it's up to you to make sure Beth wears a pretty dress tonight. I think he'd like it a lot if she does."

"Will do. We'll see you there. And I love you, Lisa."

"I love you too, Mack."

Mack went in with Beth when he got her home. She left him in the living room while she went to shower and change clothes. When she was drying herself off, she realized that she wasn't told of any rules about what someone could see, so she decided to tease Mack. More than just a little bit. She wrapped a towel around herself, got her dress from the bedroom, and brought it into the living room.

"I'm going to do something I suppose I'm not supposed to do," she said.

He didn't know what to say. He wasn't sure what she was up too. Seeing the look on his face was all she needed to convince her to finish what she started. She dropped the towel, and proceeded to do a reverse strip tease. She dressed slowly, and enjoyed watching him squirm as she did.

When she finished, she said, "I wanted you to see, one more time, what you could have had today, if you would have wanted it bad enough."

"I already knew that, Beth. But I thoroughly enjoyed being reminded. We'd better get going now. Otherwise they'll all be wondering why we're so late."

"We aren't late. We have plenty of time to get there."

"I know. It's just that if you start to take off what you just put on, we will in fact, be very late."

Her eyes lit up when he said that, and she reached behind her for the zipper on the back of her dress. He quickly stopped her. "Maybe sometime soon," he said, "but not tonight."

She sighed heavily, nodded her head, and took his arm as they went out the door.

CHAPTER 15

Lisa gave her own wardrobe considerable thought before she dressed for dinner and dancing. She was determined to look the best she could. She wanted Mack to more than notice her. She hoped to make him anxious. At the end of the night, her aim was to have a hungry husband. It wasn't difficult to pick out clothes she knew he'd like. He always told her when she looked extra nice. This night, however, she wanted to get past nice. She wanted to be beautiful and sexy. She wanted to have the kind of effect on him that made him want her. Enough so that he couldn't wait to get her home.

She finally settled on a blue dress that she'd only worn once. It proved to be a mistake when she did, because she wore it for Dale that night, not Mack. Kathy had just asked Dale for a divorce the previous night. Lisa spent most of the day with him, trying to comfort him. She then thought a kind of date with him would be a good idea. That way she could let him know that he was still desirable. She also called Mack and told him to bring Sue and meet her and Dale for the evening.

It was a big mistake on her part. Mack was decidedly unhappy with the arrangement. She should have let Sue be his date, and she should have been Mack's. She bought the blue dress that day to wear on her date with Dale. As great as it looked on her, it still wasn't one that Mack cared much for.

She did some quick alterations on it though, making it just enough more revealing to be noticeable. Everything else she wore was special for him too. When she looked at herself in the mirror, she knew she looked really good. And if she carefully moved just the right way, it could be revealing. That would be something she'd have to make sure she only allowed Mack to see. The last thing she knew she would need to careful of, was time spent with and flirting with Dale.

Hoping the looks of the dress would outweigh the negative aspects of it, she and Bob left for the Mystic Curve. They were close to the first of their group to arrive. Lisa's sister Julie, and Refuge Rescuers relatively new receptionist, Donna, were among those already there. With their help. Lisa rearranged tables so everyone could sit together. They were just finishing the arranging when two guys from a group of eight approached them.

"We're gonna need to take two of your chairs," one of them told Lisa. He cocked his head to one side, as if to say, don't argue with me, bitch.

"I'm sorry," Lisa said, keeping her voice as pleasant as possible, "but we'll be using all of these chairs. You'll just have to find your chairs somewhere else."

"I don't think so. I think you can hunt up more chairs if you need them." They each grabbed a chair, intending to carry them away.

Lisa didn't say another word. She just did a number on his hand until he dropped the chair he thought he was going to haul away. She put additional pressure on his hand until he groaned, then let it go.

"If you would have asked, like any decent person, I would have let you take the chairs. You didn't. Find some somewhere else or find another bar."

He and his friend reluctantly walked away. As she watched them go, Lisa silently hoped that the rest of the evening would go better than this encounter did. Before she could brood on the subject, Mack and Beth arrived. They were all smiles until Mack noticed what Lisa was wearing. He obviously wasn't happy with the dress.

She kissed him, then led him aside to explain why she wore it. Before she got the chance to do it, he said, "So, do you and Dale have plans for later?"

"No, Mack. God no. I wore this dress because I wanted to look extra special nice for you. What I'm wearing under it is most especially for you."

"Really," he said, still sounding somewhat unhappy. "And what would that be?"

She couldn't help herself. She smiled. She moved her mouth close to his ear. "Not a thing, Mack. Just for you tonight, the only thing I have on is this dress and my shoes." Slowly and carefully, she moved so he could see how revealing the dress could be. "I made some adjustments to the dress, just so I could do that for you. Tonight I'm here for you. Only you. If you want, I won't dance with anyone else tonight. With the possible exception of my dad. If he's up to it, I'd like to have a couple of dances with him."

"I'm sorry, Lisa, for over reacting like that. It's just seeing the dress that brought back memories of that night, when you chose Dale over me. They aren't the best."

"You know that I never intended it to seem that way. I was just desperately trying to comfort a friend who was hurting real bad."

"I know. And I understand how that night was so different for you than it was for me. Let's forget it now. It's over and done with. We have so many friends with us here tonight that we should try to enjoy. So let's do that. And you can dance with whoever you want to dance with. I'll get even with you for it when we get home tonight."

"Is that a promise?"

"It most certainly is."

"Good," she said. "Very good." She then moved her special way, and gave him a glimpse of what was waiting for him later.

They all sat down then. Lisa was on one side of him, and he fully expected either Kathy or Beth to be on the other side. Instead it was Donna. For the first time that evening, Mack actually looked at her. She normally was a very pretty woman, but tonight she was beautiful. The dress she was wearing was molded to her body. It wasn't exactly overtly sexual. It was very sexy though. The first thought that came to Mack as soon as he noticed her, was that Refuge Rescuers would be looking for a new receptionist in the near future. She wasn't going to have any trouble finding a husband, if she decided she wanted one.

The only thing that might stop that from happening, would be because she was leery of most men right now. She started out with Refuge Rescuers as a client. She came to them for help to escape an abusive husband. While they were solving her problems, they ended up as good friends. She was now working for them, and living in the cottage that Mack lived in before he had the house built that he and Lisa now lived in.

As the meal progressed, Mack also noticed that Donna frequently touched him somewhere while they talked. Lisa took note of that fact too, and made a mental note to do her best to keep Mack as far away from her as possible during the dancing later. She already felt a lot of competition from Kathy, and some from Beth. She figured that was more than enough.

Donna had other ideas. She knew she would never interest Mack enough to any more than help her if she really needed help, and if she was lucky, maybe dance with her a couple of times this night. She wanted as much attention from him as she could get anyway.

The band started not too long after they finished eating. They immediately apologized for not having a lead singer, explaining that she was home in bed with a mild case of covid. They did their best with the vocals, but by the third song it was obvious that it was going to be a long night for the band and the audience.

Kathy and Mack danced to that third song. When it ended, she said, "I normally wouldn't consider doing this. The thing is though, we have so many good friends here, and I know they'd all like to be able to enjoy a night of decent music and dancing." She kissed Mack on the cheek. "Tell Dale I said I'll dance with him next time."

She went up on the stage, took the microphone from the guy who was trying to do the singing, and said something to the band. Then, without introducing herself to the people in the bar, she started to sing. As soon as they heard her voice, shock waves flew through them.

Nearly everyone there shook their heads in disbelief as they realized who was up on stage singing. Kathy was midway through her second song before the dancing started again.

Lisa was kept busy dancing. As good as she looked, there wasn't a man there who didn't hope to get a chance to dance with her. So she and Mack had not connected for one. He was kept busy too. His first two dances after Kathy started singing were with Donna. Wanda was next. He then danced with Sue. They were going to do it again, when Kathy called him up on the stage.

She kissed him when he got there. "This is my friend, Mack," she said. "This next song is for him." She put her arm around him, pulled him close, then sang a love song that they had decided a while back, was special for them. While she sang, she let the fact that her feelings for him went beyond friendship. Mack was blushing when he left the stage. Kathy was smiling.

Mack and Kathy were being watched closely while she sang to him. The same man watched the look on Lisa's face. The twinge of jealousy she felt showed. He decided that she was now fair game. Not to mention the fact that he was sure there was so much man to him that she couldn't possibly resist him.

He was the leader of the group of eight who wanted the chairs earlier. He was sure that wouldn't matter to Lisa anyway. She had to be pissed at her husband, after what he did on the stage. She should then be ready to welcome the attention of a man as handsome as he was.

He moved in on her as soon as the man she was dancing with left her to sit down. He asked her to dance, and since he was the first to ask, she said yes.

The eight men were quiet all through dinner and hadn't started any trouble, so she was sure it would be okay.

It was a good night so far, and it seemed as though everyone, including her, was having a good time. So she didn't notice as quickly as she should have, that he was trying to maneuver her into a back corner, somewhat out of sight from most of the other dancers. Once she did notice, it was too late. They were already there.

They were dancing to a slow song. Everything seemed okay until it was over and Kathy started singing another one. He pulled Lisa close. She didn't appreciate the gesture, so she pushed him back a little.

"You don't need to do that," he claimed. "That husband of yours is too dense to know what we're doing. He's not even going to figure it out when we spend some time out in my van. Time you're going to love. You'll be getting more out there than what you ever dreamed of before." He moved his hand over her breast and squeezed.

She instantly stopped moving and pushed him. She turned her back on him to walk away. She didn't want any trouble. She just wanted to get away from him.

He grabbed her arm and tried to swing her around. A big mistake on his part. She wasn't up for grabs. She put him where he belonged, which was on the floor, and walked away.

"You fucking bitch," he screamed at her. "You're going to pay for that."

His friends all rushed over to help him, certain that whatever was done to him, was done unfairly. Larry and Sue were dancing not far from where it happened. Lisa stopped walking when she got next to them. Larry, being the kind of man he was, stepped between Lisa and the rushing men.

Seeing the disturbance, Mack, Roy, Dale, Ben, and Wanda joined them. The bunch of eight regrouped, and thought they were ready to beat the hell out of Lisa's group. Mack stepped out of his group to greet them.

"If you bunch of morons want a fight," he told them. "It's more than fine with me. Let's take it outside. The folks who own this place didn't do anything to deserve having it busted up because you brainless wonders think you need to start a fight. If you insist on having it in here, along with paying for your own hospital bills, you will be paying for all the repairs that need to be done, along with all lost revenue caused by the fight you are about to start. Along with that, we will be inflicting extra damage to your bodies, simply because you just had to start a fight you can't possibly come even slightly close to winning. All of us, but particularly my wife who you planned on trying to rape, hate men like you. So the truth is, it is going to give us a great deal of pleasure when we beat each and everyone of you within and inch of your life. Your only other choice, is to walk the hell out of here now. While there's still enough left of you to walk."

Mack's speech was long enough to make everyone with him smile. Especially the way it left the gang of eight unsettled. The smiles then further unsettled them. They stood there grumbling for a while, then as a group turned around and left the Mystic Curve Bar. Everyone still there breathed a sigh of relief and Kathy started another song. Soon everything was back to normal, with everyone dancing and having a generally good time. With the exception of two of them.

Wanda stayed with Roy for a while, until the ache in her gut and the images in her head became too much. She took Roy's hand and said, "We have to find Mack."

Roy took one look at her and said, "They're back. The dreams are back." He was referring to dreams her and Mack sometimes had when something very wrong was about to happen. "Do you know who it is this time?"

"No. One of us though, I think. A body on some kind of tile floor. People around. Too much blood. It's bad, Roy."

Before they could hunt for him, Mack appeared. Lisa wasn't more than two minutes behind him. He met Wanda's eyes and she fell into his arms. He held on to her until her hard shaking stopped.

"This was going to be a good night," Lisa said. "What are we going to do now?"

"I think it would probably be a good idea to call it a night. It'll be closing time in less than an hour anyway."

Kathy decided to sing one more love song before they left the bar. She took Dale up on the stage and sang a love song to him. As she'd done with Mack, she left no doubt that her feelings for him were extremely deep.

As they made ready to leave, Mack suggested to everyone that they drive straight home. Donna made a face then, and apologized for the fact she needed to stop for gas. Bob and Beth volunteered to follow her, and since there was a new truck stop only a few miles down the highway, everyone thought a stop there would be safe enough.

Only Mack and Wanda continued to have uneasy feelings.

CHAPTER 16

The gang of eight drove around in their custom van after they left the Mystic Curve. Until they found another country bar. It proved to be a waste of time for them. The customers inside were made up of middle age and older people. They didn't see any women in the crowd they wanted to take out to their van and rape, so they left the place.

They were driving passed the Mystic Curve for the third time, when they saw people leaving. They watched the cars and pickups, and were sure that the two that drove out onto the highway had women in them. Since all the women in the group who requested they leave the bar were more than just pretty, they paid close attention to where they were going. When they drove into the nearby truck stop, they were sure they had their chance. They made a quick U turn and went back to the truck stop. They parked, got out of the van, and opened a compartment in the back of it.

Powerful semi-automatic handguns, with large magazines, were passed around. Their prey didn't notice them. Bob Anderson was pumping gas into his pickup. Beth, who was suddenly thirsty, was walking to the store to buy something to drink. In the next bay, Donna was busy washing her windows as gas was pumped into her tank. Lisa's sister Julie was half asleep as she waited in the passenger seat of Donna's car.

The gang of eight split up. One of them moved up behind Bob and pushed a gun into his ribs. He was told to keep it quiet, and his concern for the women around him dictated that he do so. Two men quickly took control of Donna and Julie. The rest of them went inside the truck stop. They spread out, as they had done in several other places they'd robbed, and then yelled at everyone to lie down. They were doing their thing by holding up the place.

One older lady, carrying a cane, could no longer bend well enough to be able to lie down on a floor. One of the eight shot her a couple of times, killing her. She bled a lot before she died, so the floor around her was covered with blood. He just grinned when she stopped breathing.

Two of the men then went after Beth. They stood her up and told her, "You are about to pay real good for being who you are. We seen you with that loud mouth at the bar. When we get done with you, he ain't gonna be able to know who the hell you are. It's just too damn bad he ain't here to watch."

Mack wasn't there to watch, but he was thinking about what had happened to Wanda and him. It was like a repeat of all the other times they'd gone through the terrifying dream sequence. This time, the memory of his fiancé, Mandy, lying in a hospital bed with tubes and wires seeming to be attached to her everywhere. Her voice, struggling so he could hear her. The way she gasped for breath, and suddenly was gone. He always felt as though he let her down by not being there when she was beaten. That guilt was a good part of the reason he tended to be what Lisa and others considered to be over protective. His eyes started to tear until the image changed from Mandy to Beth.

She was inside a building, and he could see some kind of shelves behind her. Slowly, the image faded and she formed into something with tubes and wires attached nearly every part of her. Then that was gone and all he could think about was he had to do something. It was the shelves behind her and remembering that Donna was going to stop for gas that did it. Bob and Beth were going to stop with her. He slammed on his brakes, nearly giving Lisa a heart attack, and threw the pickup into a spin. The instant it was facing in the direction he'd just come from, he slammed the accelerator to the floor.

"What the hell are you doing?" Mack, Lisa yelled. "Are you nuts?"

"It's Beth," he answered between deep breaths. "And probably your dad and Julie and Donna. At the truck stop. I don't know who or why yet, but we don't have much time. Call Dale."

He would have told her to call Roy too, but knew they'd be at the truck stop before she got the chance. Once they got there, her hands would be full of the gun she would soon be using.

He stopped his pickup up against back bumper of the the van belonging to the gang. "I want them to know we are here," he told Lisa. "They'll want to stop us before they kill anyone else. At least, I hope that's what they'll do."

"What if they do get us? Then what? They'll do their killing anyway."

"They'll probably try. Hopefully, before we are killed, we'll be able to take out a few of them. Maybe your dad will be able to get hold of a weapon by then. If he can hold them off long enough, maybe the cops will be here." What he wanted was to convince Lisa to back away. He knew she wouldn't. For her, if it was dangerous, she needed to be in the middle of it. If Mack tried to keep her out of it, she'd only accuse him of being overly protective.

Dale and Kathy drove in then. He stopped near the back of the parking lot. It was a wise move. It gave Kathy some protection if there was a lot of shooting. Dale left Kathy and hustled over to Mack and Lisa. Before he could say anything, Roy and Wanda drove in. Roy stopped at the very back of the parking lot.

Wanda was quickly out of the truck with a rifle in her hands. It had a scope. She used it to search through the store windows. She then called Mack with her cell phone. He instantly fished his out of his back pocket and answered it.

"It's like this, Mack," she said, speaking rapidly. "I can see them all. It's that bunch that we threw out of the bar. One of them is holding a gun against Beth's head. What I'm going to do, is take out the windows in the store. Then I'm going to start shooting those guys. They are all standing. Everyone else is on the floor. Trouble is, my rifle is a bolt action, so I won't be able to shoot fast enough. I need for you to add even more distraction so we can take them out before they kill Beth. As soon as you distract the one with the gun to Beth's head, he'll go down first. If you guys move fast enough, we should take them all out. Can you do that?"

"We can," he said, "so let's do this."

Shooting as fast as she could, Wanda took out the windows. Without hesitation, Mack ran to the closest window and dove headfirst through it. He rolled once and came up shooting. He heard the rifle shots coming from Wanda, then gunfire coming from someone about two feet away. The shooting from Mack, Lisa, and Dale was having its affect on the gang of eight. Between them they managed to hit four of the gang. They weren't dead, but they weren't good for much either. Wanda, being Wanda, took out the other four. They were dead. All four were head shots. Beth was unharmed and still standing.

As soon as the shooting stopped, Lisa told everyone one that it was safe to get up off the floor. Everyone did. Everyone, that is, except the old lady with the cane. As they got up, Mack and Lisa and Dale looked around them. Everything next too and behind them was riddled with bullet holes. It all happened so fast they hadn't noticed the bullets the gang of eight were shooting at them. The fact that they weren't hit by any of the bullets was luck. And only luck.

Mack looked at Lisa and shook his head. His instinct was to scold her for risking her life the way she'd just done. Never mind that he and Dale had just done the same thing. Knowing what he wanted to say, she was about to tell him to stop being so over protective. Instead, they both laughed. They'd done the right thing, Even if neither one of the had survived all the shooting, in the end, they'd done the right thing. Risking their own lives, they'd saved a lot of others.

It was Mack who said it, "I think, Lisa, we can stop saying the same old shit to each other. We just aren't going to change my being over protective and you taking too many chances."

"No, Mack, we aren't ever likely to be able to do that. So there is a good chance our lives might be shorter than what we'd like. And that means that you and I truly need to live as if today is our last." With that, she let the new, long rip in her blue dress move just enough to show him some of what she wanted him to think about until they managed to get home.

He just smiled at her move. "I think," he said, "I like that blue dress a lot better now."

As soon as Bob let her go, Beth moved into Mack's arms. Not caring that her husband and Mack's wife were standing next to them, she kissed him with all the passion she could pull together. She then turned to Lisa, and hugged her like she wanted to crack her spine.

Watching them, Donna did the same thing. That's when Mack got a big surprise. When Julie kissed him, he knew he could never think of her as a little girl again. Her kiss was followed by a lot of pecks on the cheek and hand shakes from the other customers who were in the place when the action went down.

Dale called in the backup team who handled that kind of incident, and the questions started. Because of his close relationship with Mack and Lisa, and his direct involvement in the shooting, he also called in the state police. They got lucky, and two of the state police knew Mack and Lisa, and also knew a lot about Refuge Rescuers. The gang of eight was also already wanted for nearly a dozen other robberies, three of which involved killings. That saved a lot of unnecessary accusations, and questions. As a result, everyone was allowed to go home quicker than would normally be expected.

When Mack and Lisa got home, she immediately said, "I need a shower."

"So do I," he agreed. "But they'll come later. Right now, I'm going to take that blue dress off you and make love to you the way you are. You are just as much a warrior lady as you are that sweet young thing fresh out of the shower. Tonight, I want to find out more about the warrior lady. Making love to her is the best way I know how to do that."

She didn't argue when her dress landed on the floor. His clothes quickly followed, and they fell on the bed. She moved over him, and proceeded to prove him right. She truly was a warrior lady. It was pushing morning before she stopped proving it.

When she did, she said, "I'm tired now. Let's shower later."

They did. Around noon. Together.

CHAPTER 17

Mack and Lisa were freshly showered and sitting outside on the deck on the back of their house. They shared the love seat, and Lisa was snuggled close to Mack. His arm was around her and his hand rested on her breast, when Larry Jameson walked into the small yard. Mack moved his hand, but only as far as was necessary to save Lisa's modesty. A modesty that didn't actually concern her much.

Larry cleared his throat to be sure they knew he was coming. Mack and Lisa both smiled inwardly when he blushed slightly. He was living with Sue now, but hadn't been part of the Refuge Rescuers group long enough to be used to the easy way they tended to show affection.

"I don't mean to bother you," he said. "I just thought I'd come by and see if you guys had decided when we're going to leave. Given all you've been through lately, it wouldn't surprise either Sue or I if you canceled the rest of your vacation."

Lisa answered him. "Don't worry about that, Larry. It's just plain isn't going to happen. I don't care if it takes us all summer, or even into the fall, we are going to finish our vacation. The only thing that will stop it, if we don't accomplish all we want to accomplish, will be winter."

"In that case, when do you think we'll be going?"

"We haven't set a time," Mack answered. "It won't be too long though, before we go. We'll let you know the day before we leave. So why don't you go into the kitchen and get yourself a beer and sit with us a while. It's a beautiful day for doing nothing but enjoying what's here."

"Sounds good. I can't stay too long. We promised Emma we'd take her out for an ice cream later."

He got a beer, then sat down on a chair facing the love seat. It was obvious that he appreciated the invitation to join them. It was equally obvious that he was somewhat uncomfortable. There were normally several people around when he socialized with anyone other than Sue.

"We've been kind of wondering," Mack said, leading into a conversation Larry would be familiar with, and therefore more comfortable. "about how it's going with Emma? Is she taking it okay living with and around a bunch of strangers?"

Larry immediately perked up. "Are you kidding me? She loves it. After all she went through with that evil father of hers, living here is for her almost paradise. I don't think she could be much happier."

"How about for you and Sue? Being new parents to a child her age must lead to some difficulties?"

"Not really. I'm sure we'll have some problems somewhere down the line, but right now taking care of her couldn't be easier. I haven't been doing anything else but care for her since we got here, and Sue hasn't been near as busy as she says she normally is. Add to that, having all the great baby-sitters that you all guys are, means there's almost zero stress."

"Well, that is good to hear. Things keep on going good with her, maybe she'll get her biggest wish. What do you think are the chances she will?"

Larry looked at the floor, shaking his head. Without looking up, he said, "I wish I had the right answer for you right now, Mack," he said. "I guess I could lie and tell you everything was going to work out perfect for everyone. I just can't do that. It's going to take some time before I or Sue knows for sure what's going to happen next. Part of why we're going with you on the next part of your vacation is to kind of test our relationship on neutral ground. I'm a big part of our problem. I don't know if I can adjust to a permanent life here. I lived alone, out in the wilds, for a long time. As far as Emma is concerned, we don't have the slightest idea what the officials up home are going to decide to do. It's hard to know that. Canadien officials can be every bit as flakey as the ones you have here in the states."

He paused and looked up. He caught Mack's eye and they both could see the concern the other's. It told them both that with all their concerns, it would take time to find the answer to Emma's wish. Her wish to stay with Sue and Larry, and if possible, be adopted by them. And added to that wish, the hope and dream that they would get married and live where they were now. Like Sue, Emma didn't want to live as a recluse in the Canadien wilds.

"I imagine," Mack said, "that it would be easier to deal with the officials up there if you and Sue were there, rather than here."

"It would, but that's not going to happen. She's made it clear that she loves me and wants to spend the rest of her life with me. Just not in Canada and definitely not in the wilds. I tend to be a recluse. I can get along without seeing too much of people. She can't. And I can't blame her for that. It's natural to want people around. Especially good friends. Relatives, not always so much. So we're different that way. Otherwise, our wants and needs seem to be much the same. And for me, I found life pretty much empty since I left her and lived alone again."

"You won't let that one difference split you up, will you?" Their conversation was now drifting into a place that he and Lisa had just fought their way through. Letting one difference lead to a disagreement that came close to splitting them apart. "If you really care about each other, if you really do love each other, the worst thing you can possibly do is split up." He squeezed Lisa close to him, kissed her, and said to her, "Tell him. Tell him what we've been going through. Tell I'm what we've learned. And tell him about Jasper and what he said about you and I always being together. We can't let them split up again for one reason not that difficult to solve."

Lisa started telling him then. She only got as far as the fight she and Mack had about his being too overprotective, and her taking too many chances. She was about to tell him about finding Jasper in the refuge, when Sue and Emma joined them. It was time, Emma explained with all the seriousness an eleven year old girl could muster, for them to go out for ice cream. Mack and Lisa were invited to go with, but they begged off. They said that after the events of the day before, they were too tired to want to do anything more than stay at home and relax.

The problem was, they didn't get that chance. Sue, Larry, and Emma were no more than around the corner of their house and out of sight, when Dale and Kathy joined them. They were walking. It was only a few hundred yards across a still wild meadow from their house to Mack and Lisa's.

Lisa commented right away about Dale being there on work day. "I was put on administrated leave for a few days," he told them.

"What the hell for?" Lisa asked.

"It has to do with the shootings last night. Someone thought it best for me to have a few days off, until the investigation of it has been completed."

"Who the hell is the idiot who thought that one up?"

Dale gave them a sheepish smile, then answered the question with one word. "Me."

Mack did a double take on him, then laughed. "What you mean is, you wanted some time off and now you are taking it."

"Pretty much, yes. Kathy and I needed some time to do some catching up with each other. And the truth is, I didn't want to have anything to do with the required investigation. I don't want some fast talking defense attorney claim I did something wrong, just because I was involved in the whole fiasco from when it started at the Mystic Curve."

"That makes sense," Mack said. "So what brings you guys over here this afternoon?"

"Just us wanting to spend some quiet time with our best friends. I hope you don't mind the company."

"Of course not. You know you are welcome here any time. No matter what."

Kathy spoke up then. "Even if part of the reson is me being a lot jealous of you and Beth?"

"Not even then, Kathy. The thing is though, there's nothing for you to be jealous about when it comes to me and Beth. She just wanted to spend some time with me, walking in the refuge. She's learning how to appreciate it. You know how I like to encourage anyone when they take an interest in it. The more people who are, the better the chance it'll continue to exist."

"I understand that, Mack," Kathy told him. "It's the other kind of understanding she wants from you that bothers me."

Seeing how serious and jealous Kathy was, told Lisa she should explain why she knew that Mack hadn't done anything with Beth that Kathy wouldn't approve of.

"You don't have to worry about what Mack and Beth did yesterday, Kathy," Lisa explained. "I know without a doubt that he behaved himself."

"How could you possibly know that. You weren't there."

"No, I sure wasn't. The thing is though, I was with him, in the same bed as him, from the time we got home last night, until some time late this morning. He couldn't have possibly done what I loved him doing, so often or for so long, if he'd spent the day messing around with Beth."

Kathy let what she said settle into her brain before she answered Lisa. When she did, it was with a smile. "That's good. He doesn't need anything more than what he's already got. And I'm glad that everything is okay between you two. I thought there might be some kind of disagreement between you after what you did last night. It was incredibly wild, going in there the way you three did, with all those guns shooting at you."

"Those disagreements are now over, Kathy. When we got home, he called me his warrior lady. He wouldn't even let me take a shower right away. He said it was time he learned what it was like to make love to his warrior lady."

"He actually did that? How was it?"

"It was awesome. So now you have to be careful, Kathy. He might show up in your dressing room after one of your concerts. I think he's wondering now, what it's like to make love to a singer who's famous around the world. Especially one who is so incredibly beautiful."

Blushing from Lisa's compliment, Kathy turned to Mack. "Is that what you're thinking now?"

"Pretty much, yes."

"Do you actually plan on doing it?

"Only if Dale says it's okay."

Dale responded to Mack's comment. "It's only okay, if I get to make love to the warrior lady."

That was what they all needed, and their laughter lasted for a while. The rest of the afternoon was a relaxing quiet, that helped lift much of the stress they were feeling from the night before.

CHAPTER 18

The three men parked on the road. They paid little attention to the house, set back from the road. To them, it just wasn't impressive. It was the type of place that any ordinary family, from medium to somewhat low income, would live in.

They also moved through the trees and into the open meadow as if they owned it. They lived all their lives in a place far wilder than this small place relatively untouched be humans. They were also concentrating on getting passed another house, as equally unimpressive as the first one. Their goal was an even smaller house, which they were sure was originally a manufactured home.

A almost new class C motor home was parked next to it. Eleven year old Emma Flynn was sitting in a rocking chair on a recently added deck. She was their target. Their problem was Sue Sartor, who was busy loading personal items into the class C RV. An added problem was Larry Jameson. A man they planned to kill the first chance they had. They knew him all too well, given they came from the same area in Canada as he did. So they knew how dangerous he was to their plans.

As they moved forward, they grew ever more frustrated. There were too many houses nearby. Given his previous way of life, they'd expected him to be a lot more isolated. They even considered giving up their quest, but she was too enticing to give up their chance of grabbing her. Before he disappeared, Willie Flynn had promised all of them a chance at his daughter Emma. Each of the three men had been craving his chance to rape her ever since. For them, she was near the perfect age to enjoy sex with. Young girls were so much better than grown women who could fight back and throw insults at a man. Young girls never complained about a man's performance. For them, no complaints about performance was a sure ego booster. Cries because of fear and pain meant nothing.

As much as possible, they stayed in the trees at the edge of the meadow. If they possibly could, they wanted to grab Emma before they created too much disturbance. They also hoped to see Larry before he saw them, thereby improving their chances of killing him.

They were far less concerned about anyone in the other homes. They were all experienced hunters, and had no doubts that they could outshoot any of the ordinary people who might live there.

They hadn't done their research on Sue. As soon as they figured out where she lived, they decided to go after Emma. She was just too promising to pass up. That left them totally unprepared for what was going to happen to them. They knew nothing about Sue's neighbors.

Ben, Mack's father, was out among a field of tomatoes when he saw them. At the end of a row he was walking down, he could see the well armed men trying to creep along the meadows edge. He knew that they were up to some kind of no good, so he used his cell phone to call Mack. Mack immediately called Sheriff Dale Magee, who was home. He lived in the house by the road that the three men ignored earlier. Ben called Roy, then made a fast walk home to arm himself.

It was only a matter of minutes until the three men found themselves surrounded by men and women with guns pointed at them. They were instructed to drop their own weapons and they did. The biggest of the three men, standing in the middle of them, wet his pants.

"Do you mind telling us what you think you are doing here?" Mack asked them.

Before they could answer, Emma, who Sue had left with Theresa, Ben's wife, broke loose and ran up to them. She stopped next to Wanda, yanked on her arm, and asked, "Are you going to shoot them like you did daddy? They are his friends. They did stuff to hurt me too, just like daddy did. I don't care if you shoot them. They were mean to me."

True to form, that was all it took to set Lisa off. She walked up to the middle man with the wet pants. "Is that what this is about? You came here to get Emma?"

When the man didn't answer, but moved his bowels instead, Lisa slapped him across the face a half dozen times. His face was crimson and blood trickled from his mouth when she stopped. She waited a couple of minutes for him to answer.

When he didn't, she said to Mack, "Fire up the backhoe. Dig deep enough for all three of them. You know the spot. Back where we buried all the rest of them."

They had never buried anyone anywhere, but the three men did not know that. And now the air was filled with a putrid odor, as they all filled their pants. The mighty hunters, who were nothing more than totally useless creatures who preyed on children, were terrified. Lisa was very convincing when she told Mack to get the backhoe.

Losing her patience with the men, Lisa moved as close to them as she could. "Either you talk. You tell us exactly what you came here to do, or you die. Before you do, however, I will personally cut off your balls. I will then stuff them down your throats. That is how you will die. Slowly choking to death on your balls. If you don't bleed out first. We will end it, by each of us shitting in your grave before we fill it."

She stepped back from them and glared. The big one in the middle started to cry. "You can't do any of that. Murder is against the law. And God would never forgive you if you shit in our grave." He was now shaking uncontrollably.

This told Lisa a lot. The men were essentially cowards. She initially wanted to beat the living hell out of them. Now though, she realized that terrifying them as bad as they possibly could, would be even better punishment. After all, that was exactly what they'd do to Emma if they'd had their way.

"Mack," she said, "fire up the backhoe and start digging. I'm going to sharpen up the neuter knife."

By then, everyone there, other than the three men and Emma, knew what was going on. In order to be sure that Emma learned the right lesson from what they are doing, Sue and Larry took her home to explain to her what was really happening.

Mack started up the backhoe and played with the motor to make it sound like it was digging. Lisa started sharpening one of Ben's gardening knives in front of the men.

After a few minutes, the big man in the middle said, "I'll tell you everything if you'll promise not to cut my balls off.

"Start talking," Lisa ordered. "And don't try to lie you way out of this. You do, and I'll make it even worse. I'll use a knife I haven't sharpened."

Given the look in her eyes, he believed her, and told her the whole story. What he said was recorded as videos on several cell phones. When he finished, they tried to figure out what to do with the men.

Dale finally decided to lock them up in the county jail, and then turn them over to the Canadien authorities. Before he did, Lisa was given one last chance to talk to them.

"If you ever are free men again, and think you can come here and get some revenge, think twice about it. You lucked out this time. You come back, it won't matter who or how many of you there are. You will all end up dead. For the most part, the hard way."

The three men were locked up, but because of someone's mistake, didn't get a chance to shower until the next day. Their clothes were destroyed and they were issued regulation prison wear.

The Canadien officials who picked them up all lived a long way from the part of Canada the three rapists came from. They also came from a religious sect who considered women to be superior to men. They especially held young girls to be something to be protected and cared for. They could no longer except Emma as part of their religious family, but they could hate the men who, in their eyes, destroyed her. Somewhere on the ride north, there was a serious accident when the van they were being transported in hit a giant oak tree. The bodies of the three men were found in the burned out van.

The bodies of the driver and the guard were never found, partly because there was no official record of the three men being transported anywhere. The theory was that when the accident happened the unofficial driver and guard must have caught fire too, and run off into the woods as they tried to escape the pain. That was never proven though, since no one ever searched for their bodies.

CHAPTER 19

They went through a full day with no disasters before they decided to resume their vacation. They were somewhat worried about Sue and Larry leaving Emma with Roy and Wanda while they were going to be gone. But it proved to not be any kind of a problem. Emma was much happier with her life then she was with her father, so staying with other people she loved while Sue and Larry were gone was not a problem.

They also hadn't as yet made a decision as to what they were going to do with the bulk of their time. They knew though, that the first thing they were going to do was visit Jasper Klug's son. The only glitch too that was Larry's not being sure he could understand why they would bother. Jasper was dead. Why try to get to know him better by visiting his son. After they were settled in the first RV park they would visit on this trip, they talked about it.

"It's not really complicated," Mack explained. "Jasper made a strong impression on us those few hours we spent with him. He came across as a good, intelligent man. He not only didn't try to get anything from us, at first he tried to reject what we had to offer him. He said he didn't want to be burden to anyone, and I have no doubt that he meant it."

"If that's true, why did he stay with you as long as he did?" Larry asked.

"Essentially, because we didn't let him leave. He was in rough shape when we found him, so he couldn't fight us too hard. I don't think it took him long to realize that he wasn't putting us out much, if at all. So he finally gave up and let us help him."

"And after a while," Lisa added, "he even let Kathy and me bath him."

"And how did that go, you guys giving a bath to an old man you didn't even know."

Lisa chuckled. "We put him in the shower to do it. We sat him on a stool, which was okay, but I couldn't quite reach a lot of him. So I stripped down to my panties and bra, and got in the shower with him.

I was still having some problems, because he wasn't steady sitting there. Kathy did the same thing I did and came into the shower to help. We managed to do a thorough job of cleaning him up then."

"You actually stripped down like that in front of an old man you didn't even know?" Larry gave Mack a curious look. "I sure wouldn't want my wife doing something like that. Didn't it bother you, her doing that in front of a man you didn't know?"

"No," Mack answered, without any hesitation. "Not in the slightest. It made a lot more sense than getting all of her clothes soaking wet and dirty."

"I don't know. Stripping down that way for a stranger seems pretty radical to me."

Mack frowned at his words. "Your tone of voice just now made your comment sound like you think what she did was something sexual. I think you should know, that kind of petty male attitude doesn't go very far with me. Lisa and I don't live in the kind of world where I'm the only one who can make a decision. She was doing a kindness for an old man who obviously needed help, and if taking off some of her clothes was the best way to do that, I damn sure won't ever fault her for it. You might have live up there in a wild part of Canada, where nothing's changed in more than two hundred years, but where we live, the relationships between men and women has changed since then. A lot. So if you're laying judgements on her for what she did, I suggest you straighten your head out."

"I think, Mack," Sue told him, "you're being too hard on Larry. And I don't think he's trying to accuse Lisa of doing anything wrong."

Lisa interrupted them. "It's like this, you guys. This is the first night for this part of our vacation. I don't think this kind of argument is at all a good thing. So let's knock it off. If Larry doesn't approve of what I did with Jasper, let's leave it with him." She turned to Mack. "You and I can live with that, can't we?"

"Not really," Mack answered. "If we just let this go, it will hang over us the whole time we're together. It will be part of everything we do. Something as simple as us taking some kind of bath if we're somewhere without facilities. Everyone's going to be worried about bare skin. No matter what skin is bare. It'll interfere other ways too, but I won't go into that now. So I think, come morning, we should think about splitting up. Larry has no interest in learning about Jasper anyway. But it is our main interest."

Mack reached into his pocket and took out his billfold. He took out a credit card and handed it to Larry. This will cover any and all expenses you have while you and Sue do your thing, whatever it is. Sue will give one of you approval to use the card. She's an expert at anything like that. Tonight, when you two decide what you're going to do tomorrow, you won't have to worry about the money part."

When Mack looked up at Sue, she was chalk white and her hands were shaking slightly. Tears were rolling down her cheeks. "Why, Mack?" she asked. "Why are you being so hard?"

"I don't mean to be hard, Sue. But Lisa and I started trying to have some kind of vacation to get some rest, and to find some peace. Neither one of us want any conflict while we're doing this. If we can avoid it that is. We've only talked for a little while, and we already have a major disagreement. If we stay together now, we'll most likely have more. Doing that makes no sense for any of us. That's why I want all of us to think about whether or not to stay together in the morning."

"I think you're overreacting," Sue argued. "I don't think we should have to decide that. We should just stay together, the way we planed too."

Lisa surprised Mack then. "I agree with Sue. You're over reacting, Mack. I think we should stay together."

"Okay," Mack said, standing up. "But I still don't want a vacation full of conflicts. So tomorrow, Lisa, do you want to drop me off at the nearest bus station, so you can take the RV and I can get a ride home? Or do you want to ride with Sue and Larry for the rest of the trip? It looks like you've already decided about what you want to do, without thinking about it. In my opinion, which I realize isn't worth much, if we just continue on we'll have more conflicts. Like I said before, that's not the reason for this vacation. Since not giving this even some thought, some consideration, I no longer want to be part of it. You three can go on ahead without me."

Lisa looked at him, her face riddled with shock. "My god, Mack, what the hell's gotten in you. I thought you were looking forward to this trip. I thought you wanted to learn more about Jasper."

"I still do. But if I'm doing it alone, my pickup will be all I need."

"I don't want you to go alone. I want to be with you. And now you really are overreacting. I don't understand why."

"When you said that the first time, you broke your promise. We agreed that we weren't going to do this to each other anymore. I haven't tried to tell you what to do. I just don't think we should continue this trip under these circumstances. Sweeping differences like this under the rug is not the answer. They need to be talked about. We need to come to at least some kind of settlement. I have nothing against either Sue or Larry. I fully approve of their relationship, and Larry's more than welcome to stay here and share his life with Sue and Emma. He just isn't going to fit in our life the way we all would have liked. Our way of life is something he obviously doesn't approve of. I also don't want anything serious to come between you and me, Lisa. That's why I said you can continue this already disastrous vacation with them, if that's what you want to do. If it was only Sue in the second RV, or Sue and someone else, things would be fine. It's Larry and I who won't work. And you, Lisa, of all people should be able to see that. If we stay together on this trip, our differences are only going to get worse. But if my wanting for you and I to have some peaceful, actually quiet time together, then I guess I'm over reacting. In that case I'm wrong, and you'd best go with them. You can either ride with them, or take the RV. We'll be together again when we both get back home."

Larry spoke up then. "I'm sorry, Mack, to have upset you this way. I damn sure didn't intend to. But I don't really understand what it is that upset you so much."

"I don't expect you too. You and I are two very different men. The thing in my life I'm most proud of is my wife. No matter how bad she can aggravate me sometimes, I'm even proud of th0se things. I'm sure you know at least some about Lisa's history, but I don't think you have the slightest idea how it has affected her. For her to do what she did in that shower, only because she wanted to give a very much hurting old man a bath, took a tremendous act of courage. There was a time, not too long ago, that she never could have done anything even remotely like that. To you, she was doing something dirty. To me, what she did was something good and caring. I know, just from the way you talk, that you have a conservative bent to you. Now I suspect, you've got a lot of religion in you too. Both of those things keep you from knowing good from bad. All they do is give you an excuse to judge. And it doesn't matter that you know little or nothing of what you judge."

"What's wrong with religion? I don't belong to any church, but I do believe in God and the bible."

Mack was getting weary of the conversation, so his answer for Larry was short. "What's wrong with it," he said, "is the fact that it's mostly just so much bullshit. Read the gospels and follow what Jesus taught. Throw the rest in the trash where it belongs." He sighed heavily. "Well, Lisa, are you going to spend the night with me, or have I overreacted too much again?"

"Of course I'm staying with you, Mack. I'm staying with you tomorrow too. Where else would I stay? I've told you before, I'm staying with you for however long we are both alive. And I won't sleep anywhere but next to you. You and I probably don't have the kind of time to waste, sleeping any other way. But I think we should let Sue and Larry talk about all this tonight, and then we can all decide what to do in the morning."

Mack smiled. "Okay, sweet wife of mine. I don't ever want to sleep anywhere but next to you either. And you're right. It's best we sleep on this and make final decisions in the morning."

Once they were settled in their RV, Lisa asked Mack. "I know why you were upset with Larry, and I don't disagree with you. But when I agreed with Sue that you were over reacting, you instantly told me you were going on your own so I could go with them. Why""

"To tell you one more time that I wasn't going to expect you to do something you didn't want to do. When you agreed with Sue, you came across as if you wanted to continue with them. It was my way of telling you that you could do that if that's what you wanted to do. You still can, if that's what you want to do."

"That means, I guess, that there's no way you want to continue with them tomorrow."

"That's right. I don't. I know that I'm supposed to be tolerant of other peoples believes, opinions, and ideas. I try to do that. I intend on doing that with Larry as long as he and Sue are together. But to do it, we'll have to keep some space between us. I doubt that we will ever be what you could call friends. But if he'll at least admit that he's off base with the way he laid his judgements on you, I'm willing to try to continue traveling with them."

"What about Sue? Can she be your friend if she's living with him?"

"I don't see why not. After all she's done for us, she'll always be a friend. You feel the same way, don't you?"

"Of course I do. And I'm sorry if I sounded like I was taking sides when I said you were overreacting. I wasn't. I was just being me and reacting to you the way I always do, one way or the other."

Lisa moved over to the chair Mack was sitting in. She sat on his lap. "Now," she looked at him with most serious expression she could put on her face, "we have a serious problem to solve. Are you going to help me undress or do I have to do it myself?"

He let his fingers answer her questions as they began to do their work on her blouse. Her fingers did the same with his shirt. They shed the rest of their clothes on the way to the kingsize bed.

Later on, while they were lying in bed, holding on to each other, Lisa felt as though she and Mack needed to talk about what happened earlier. "I'll go along with whatever you decide Mack, because I think you are for the most part right. If we can't find a way to change things, it won't work with them. I have an idea, that if it works, will change everything. Especially Larry's ideas about what women should be, and how they should be treated. If we could show him how to be both respectful of women, and at the same time realize that we have the same rights as men do, we might be able to get past this conflict. And I think we should do our best to do it. Because if we don't, we might very well lose Sue. She can't, in any way, be replaced. I don't know about you, but I don't think Refuge Rescuers is going to be near as effective when she's gone."

"I agree with you on that, but I still don't see how you can possibly get Larry to see things differently. I think we'll just hope that things work out as far as Sue staying with us is concerned. We'll also do our best to help Larry adjust and find some kind of meaningful work."

"No matter what, we'll have to do that. But I have another idea. I know it's radical. Maybe even a little bit crazy. But I think it could make a big difference."

"Okay, Lisa. You've set the bait and got me hooked. What's your idea?"

"I think I should do exactly what he found so offensive. Not to the degree I did it with Jasper, but further than what Larry would ever expect a woman to go."

Mack a lot surprised by her suggestion. He sat up in the bed and stared at her before he could say anything. "You want to do what?" he finally asked, not totally sure he heard her right. "How far do you plan on going with it?"

Lisa, expecting his reaction, laughed softly. "I knew you would do that if I suggested it. I'm am serous though, when I say that you should think about it. What I have in mind is simple. You know how I like to lounge around in my soft white robe in the morning when we have days off? I think I should wear it tomorrow morning. If he reacts badly, we go home. If he excepts what I'm wearing, we try to continue with the vacation."

"That might work, Lisa. But I do have one question. Do you plan on wearing the robe the way you'd normally wear it around company? Or are you going to wear it the way you do when it's only the two of us?"

"I'm going to wear it exactly the way I do when it's just the two of us. If I wear it any other way, it won't mean anything."

"I don't know, Lisa. Even I can get jealous. I don't know that I'm up to sharing you like that. It will bother me some for you to be on display in front of him."

"I hear what you're saying. What I'm going to try to do is make him think he's seeing more than what he really is. I'm also hoping to make him want to see more than he is. He starts thinking that way, and it will be awful difficult for him to get very self-righteous."

"Are you sure doing what you just suggested will work on him that way? He seems to be uptight around women. Maybe he'll find your near perfect, incredibly beautiful body disgusting."

"That is entirely possible. And if it does, it will have accomplished exactly what we want it too. It will tell us that we will be best off finishing this trip on our own."

"Just so you know, I'm not particularly fond of your idea, but I'll go along with it. Mostly because I love you. Just bear in mind through this whole thing, that I'm way more than just jealous. There are times when I can share you. This isn't one of them. Not even in this small way."

"It won't be near as bad as you think, Mack. You will, after all, be busy watching Sue at the same time. And we both know how well you can handle that kind of thing. With luck, she might catch onto what I'm doing, and do some of the same with you."

Mack fell asleep with visions of Lisa, dressed the way she said she would be in the morning, floating around in his head.

They woke up in the small hours of morning. Lisa surprised Mack by moving over him without any foreplay. She was ready for him, and she pushed him inside. When she did, she was surprised at how ready he was for her. She then moved franticly, until she climaxed. Without hesitation when it was over, she slid off him and pulled him over her.

All she said was, "I love you, Mack."

When it was over, he asked, "What brought that on?. It was awesome, but what the hell got into you?"

"I don't know for sure, Mack. I think I was having some kind of dream that I can't remember. But mostly it was you who got into me. All I know is that I woke up wanting you real bad."

"Are you sure it was me you wanted?"

"Mack, you have to know. No matter what I do or why I do it, you are the only one I ever actually want. Anything else is just reasons, not a real want. But that's enough talk for now. I need you again."

Thoughts of her in her robe in the morning was all he needed to fulfill her need.

CHAPTER 20

Lisa woke up ahead of Mack. She left the bed and went directly to the shower. She took her time with it, and would have stayed in it even longer if she wasn't concerned that there be enough hot water for Mack's shower. She was at the vanity, applying just a light touch of makeup, when Mack got up.

Seeing what she was doing left him wondering why. So he asked, "You almost never wear that stuff, Lisa. Why this morning?"

She laughed. "You know damn well why. I want to push him enough so he shows his true colors. One way or the other. I'll wash it off before we leave here today. I don't really like having it on anymore than you like seeing it on me."

"Okay. I'll go along with it. But I won't go along with any kind of getting friendly with him. No lap sitting, hugging, or kissing. Nothing but shaking him up from looking at the parts of you that it's okay to uncover."

"Damnit, Mack, you sure don't sound like yourself today. Telling me what I can or can't do. That's a long way from, "it's your body, Lisa. I'm not going to tell you what to do with it. What's wrong, Mack? Do you want me to forget my idea?"

"No, it's a good idea. The problem is me. I trust you, but I also know how impulsive you can be. Sometimes when you are, you make mistakes. Making one with Larry this morning would be the worst thing you could possibly do to me. I don't think I could deal with it, Lisa. So you have to be double careful about what you do."

"It's not like you to be upset about something that hasn't happened and isn't going to happen. I think I better forget what I was going to do. The way you feel about something like this matters to me. It matters a lot."

"No. I don't want you to not give Larry a hard time. It would be bad for us if I made you do that. You just have to remember, it'll be even worse for us if you forget and push things too far. And it won't take much for it to go too far today. I don't ever have a problem when it's you and Dale. Right now, you and Larry could be the end of everything."

"I understand, Mack. I was feeling a lot like that the last time you and Beth spent the day in the refuge. If something had happened that day, it wouldn't have ended us, but it would have done a lot of damage."

"That's what I thought, and that's why I was so careful to ensure that nothing happened. Now let's go out and greet the day. And before I forget to tell you, you look outstandingly beautiful this morning."

Sue was still in the RV when they got outside. Larry was sitting close to the fire he lit shortly before Mack and Lisa joined him. He was studying the dancing flames, and didn't look up at them immediately. When he did, his eyes locked onto Lisa. He was somewhat shocked at the way she was dressed. He loved the way she looked, while at the same time was finding it impossible to believe she would dress the way she was. Especially after the argument he and Mack had the night before.

"Good morning," Lisa said to him, adding a broad smile to her greeting. She sat across the fire pit from him. As she did, she intentionally let the robe slide up her leg a couple of inches. Nothing else showed, but it was enough to make almost any man want to see more.

Mack only nodded his morning greeting to Larry when he sat down next to her. She reached out, taking his hand as he did. As Lisa knew it would, the movement of her arm moved the top of her robe, allowing a small amount of cleavage to show. She pretended not to notice.

Larry was now having a hard time, trying to control his eyes. More than anything, he now wanted to keep them on Lisa. Only his mindset about how much a woman should wear kept his eyes from locking tight on her.

Lisa knew by then, that she had him in a turmoil. As she and Mack sat quietly watching the fire, she frequently moved only her eyes to watch him. When she saw him start to move his head up to look at her again, she crossed her legs. It opened her up just enough so he could tell that she wasn't wearing any panties. Not enough though, for him to actually see anything.

He fought against it, but he blushed anyway. That's when Sue joined them. She was watching them out the window, and had picked up on what was going on. So, like Lisa, she was wearing a robe. It wasn't as short as Lisa's, but was made of a lighter material. It seemed to flow over her body. It wasn't overtly sexual, but it did tell the story, leaving no doubt she was all female.

"I thought you were going to get dressed," he said.

"I am dressed," she answered, a small smile crossing he lips. "This is more comfortable for breakfast, than regular clothes."

"It's not what you normally wear for breakfast."

"I'm normally a mom and at home. I also never know who might come over, wanting me to solve some kind of problem or another. Today, I'm on vacation. We're with friends who couldn't care less about what I'm wearing."

Larry looked around at the three people he was with. Lisa was grinning, Mack had a bit of a smirk on his face, and Sue was giving him a serious frown. He just shook his head, then turned to Mack. "Are you people setting me up? Are these two ladies dressed the way they are, just to see how I would react?"

"I don't know about Sue," Mack told him, "but Lisa definitely is. We wanted to know if she could dress this way in front of you, without you having a negative reaction. You were doing okay until Sue came out. Does what she wear really bother you that much?"

"To tell you the truth, no. I questioned her the way I did because of what happened yesterday, and because she pretty much doesn't dress this way. She generally saves it for evenings when we're alone. As far as what Lisa is wearing, I have rarely been allowed such a treat as seeing her the way she's dressed right now. As far as last night is concerned, I didn't really mean to come across so negative about what Lisa did with that old man. I was more confused that you could share something so beautiful as she is. Even something so simple as giving an old man a bath. So now I guess I should apologize for causing the conflict last night. I also have to admit, I'm not used to being around beautiful women. So yes, what they wear can make me uncomfortable. That makes me come off the wrong way. The fact is, I love the way these two ladies look. Wouldn't mind seeing more of them."

"Does that mean then," Lisa said, "you're not going to be judging me for every little mistake I make?"

"Of course I'm not. Who the hell am to judge anyone?"

"Are we good to go now?" Lisa then asked Mack.

"We are good to go. If Larry and Sue still want to."

"Of course we do," Sue said. "And since we've made our point clear to these guys, I think we can get dressed now. It'll be more comfortable cooking breakfast if we are dressed."

Lisa moved close to Sue and whispered something in her ear. Sue nodded yes. "Mack," Lisa then said to him, "I know I promised to behave today, but there's one little misbehave Sue and I want to do. But only if it's okay with you."

"Maybe you should tell me what it is before I say yes."

"I suppose I could. The trouble is, if I tell you ahead of time, it'll take most of the fun out of it. I can promise though, what we want to do won't hurt anyone in anyway."

Mack could tell from the fun in her voice that Lisa meant no harm, so he gave her a go ahead on her surprise. With twinkles in their eyes while watching Mack and Larry closely, they untied their robes. Slow, almost painfully slow, Lisa and Sue opened their robes wide, leaving nothing to anyone's imagination. Every bit as slow, they closed the robes. They then turned and went into their RVs.

"I don't know about you," Mack said to Larry, "but that's not quite what I was expecting."

"I wasn't expecting anything," Larry said. "I won't ever forget what I got. We are a couple of lucky men, Mack. Those two are about as beautiful as anyone could ever be."

"That they are. And I don't know about you, but I think we should have them dress that way again, before this trip is over."

"I think I could handle that."

They waited quietly then, until breakfast was ready. While they ate, their chatter was about leaving the RV park and the visit they were going to have with Jasper's son.

When they left the park, the animosity between them was at least temporarily gone, and they were looking forward to learning more about Jasper Klug.

CHAPTER 21

Sue found a phone number for Jasper junior, who was called Jay by everyone who knew him. Mack called and talked to Jay, so he knew they were coming when they got there. It was shortly before noon.

"We'll probably be interrupted," Jay told them, after they finished the standard introductions and were settled in comfortable lawn chairs. The wood deck they were on was fairly large. So was the split entry house it was attached to, and the back yard it was part of. "The middle school is only a couple of blocks down the street, so the kids come home for lunch. My wife only works part-time, in the morning, so she'll be home to give them their lunch. She'll be here this afternoon. She'll be able to help answer some of the questions you might have about my father."

Mack was somewhat surprised that a man Jay's obvious age would have children as young as his were, to be in middle school. But he wisely avoided that subject. "Before we ask you any questions, I'd like it if you would just tell us what you can about Jasper. Nothing has to be in any order or sequence. It's often easier to remember things if you just let your mind flow, rather than try too tightly control it."

"I'll try, but from what my sister Gladys has told me, you already know quite a lot about him. She said you have some kind of book that he wrote?"

"We do. We've converted it to an ebook, so if you have a tablet or reader, we can give you a copy. We can even download it onto your cell phone if you don't have any other way to do it."

"I'd much rather have the original. The book, or what ever it is, really does belong to our family. Not to you."

Mack sighed, knowing now that it was going to be difficult to learn much from Jay. If he was already worried about Jasper's book, and expected Mack to turn over the original version of it, their conversation wasn't likely to go very far.

"We don't have it with us," Mack explained. "It's too important to us to risk damaging it. And it doesn't belong to you. Jasper gave it to us. We will, however, copy it when we get back home, if seeing the original looks like is important to you. He wrote it on yellow legal pad paper, so it can be sometimes difficult to read. I suggest you take an ebook copy too."

"That'll be okay for now, I guess. The trouble I'm having, is understanding why you're so interested in him. My father was just an ordinary old man. He was a good man, I guess. Just nothing special about him."

"What you just said is one of the main reasons we are interested. You said there was nothing special about him. We only knew him for a few hours, and for the four of us who were there, he was a very special man. Old or not."

Jay was visibly upset from Mack's answer. "I suppose that now you are going to say that I did something wrong with him. We tried our best to give him a home here. He just didn't fit in. That was his fault, not ours."

"We aren't here to judge anyone for anything. Like I said, we would just like to learn as much as we can about your dad. The short autobiography he wrote about himself is incomplete. He was too modest. He left out too many of the special things he did. Lisa and I hope to add those things to what he wrote."

"He told me about that kind of stuff when I was growing up. I think he was just bragging. I never saw those medals he supposedly won. How can I know that he really did win them."

"He won them," Sue told Jay. "There's absolutely no doubt about it."

"You can say that, but I don't think you can actually know it."

Sue didn't hide her feelings about Jay. She didn't like him much. She took her laptop out of the bag she brought it in, turned it on, and after pushing a few buttons, she turned the screen for him to see.

"Is that proof enough?" she asked, after he read the stories about how Jasper won his medals, and looked at pictures of them.

"Yeah, well, so he won his medals. He maybe even did some of those other things I've been told about. That don't change anything about what it was like to try to have him live with us. That's the main reason you're here, isn't it? To tell me how it was all my fault he was homeless when he died?"

"That's not why we wanted to come here, no. All we want to do is learn as much about him as we can. We try to leave the judgements to someone else as much as we can."

"Maybe you do. Maybe not. The thing is, I'll bet there isn't anyway you people would have wanted him living in your home. Taking care of an old man is in no way a fun thing to do."

"Actually," Lisa said, "if he would have stayed the full night with us, instead of disappearing the way he did, in the morning we were going to invite him to stay with us. We have a guest bedroom. It could have been his for as long as he needed it."

"Why in hell are you lying to me that way. We all know that no one is ever going to want an old man living with them. Man or woman, old people always expect too much from a person. Taking care of old people is what them nursing homes are for."

Before Mack could answer him, Jay's wife, Bella, came home. She gave them a simple greeting. "So you're the people driving around, sticking your noses into other peoples business. People you don't even know." She was obviously ten to fifteen years younger than Jay. What was also obvious, was how much kinder the years had been on Jay than they were on her. Her looks were a good match for her apparent personality.

"I'm sorry you feel that way," Mack told her. "The only thing we want to learn about is Jasper. We aren't here to snoop into your personal business."

"What you're doing with Jasper is much the same thing. You got no business checking up on him either. Especially since there isn't anything about him worth even thinking about, let alone you poking into our life by claiming you want to learn about him."

The kids then came home from school. They literally barged into the house, and without any kind of greeting, demanded, "Where's lunch? You know, Bella, we don't have that long to eat."

Larry's the one who reacted to their behavior. "Are those two your's," he asked Bella, "or is the wind just blowing some shit around now?"

Her mouth dropped open and she glared at him. "How dare you speak of my children that way. You have no right."

"Maybe not. The problem is, what they need is for you to take them over your knee and act the way any good mother would. If you don't want to use your bare hands on them, I'm wearing a belt you are more than welcome to use for a teaching tool."

"She knows she can't do that," the girl said. "It's against the law to hit kids nowadays. We'll have her put in jail if she even tries."

Larry looked at Mack, his eyes telling him that dealing with these people was already a hopeless proposition. All four of them knew it was time to leave. It was Lisa though, who said what the were all thinking.

"It's no wonder Jasper didn't stay here. What a bunch of total losers you all are. I'll bet that you two brats only loved your grandpa while he still had money to spend on you."

"He wasn't our grandpa," the boy said. "Jay ain't our real dad. Bella told that bastard to leave a long time ago."

"Yeah," the girl said, "she liked Jay better than our dumb shit dad. We did too. But that Jasper. He was so old. I didn't like to sit next to him on the couch. Or in the back seat of the car. I don't like people that old. Kids shouldn't have to live with them. I'm glad he's gone."

"You're glad he's dead?"

"Well yeah. Now he won't come back and embarrass us when our friends come over"

"I'll tell you what, Bella," Larry said. "You do have a couple of prize winners here. It's no wonder Jasper died alone. I sure can't blame him for preferring homelessness over living with you people."

"That's not how it was," Jay protested. "We didn't make him homeless. He did that all on his own."

"Really now," Mack said. "And just how did he do that?"

"He wouldn't cooperate with us. He got upset when we told him he had to stay in his room when the kids had company. They didn't like it when he was around. Their friends didn't like it either."

"Did you lock him in his room?"

"Well, yeah. We had too. Otherwise, he would come out to use the bathroom. No one has to go as often as he did. He could have waited until the company was gone."

"You expected an old man to wait to use the bathroom? Are you an idiot?"

"No. And there's no reason he couldn't. He was just too lazy to try to hold it. It wasn't our fault he wet his pants right away. He did it the first time we told him to stay in his room."

"The first time you locked him in his room, you mean. How many times did that happen?"

"Only once," Bella said. "He left that night. He didn't even show us the courtesy of putting those dirty, wet clothes of his in the washing machine. He left them in a pile in the middle of the bedroom floor."

That was enough for all of them, but especially Larry. So he was the one who spoke up. "I know, Mack, how bad you want to learn more about Jasper. But I think you've learned about all you're going to from these people. If that's what you want to call them? In my opinion, human they are not. So if you don't mind, I'd like to get the hell out of here and breath some clean air again."

"Me too," Lisa agreed. "We know now why he found life better on the street than what he found here. We also know who to blame for his dying the way he did. Maybe they didn't kill him outright, but they goddamn sure contributed to it."

"I think too," Sue said, "that it's time to go. I've got everything that's been said here recorded, and most of it video taped. We'll be able to keep it accurate when you complete the book Jasper started."

"Wait a minute," Jay complained. "You were going to give me a copy of the ebook you made."

"That was when we were trying to show you some respect. That respect is gone now."

This visit didn't accomplish much as far as learning about Jasper, but it did bring about one big change. It brought Larry into their group, as far as taking an interest in the life of Jasper Klug. He read the book while they were camped that night.

CHAPTER 22

They hadn't made a decision about what to do next, so they decided spend the day camped in the RV park they found the previous day. All four of them were disappointed from their visit with Jasper's son, Jay, yet they were still optimistic enough to believe that the rest of the trip could be turned into a rewarding and fun time.

They were enjoying the breakfast Mack and Larry put together, when two county sheriff's cars drove into the park and stopped between their campsites. They were about four counties away from Clayborne county, so they didn't know any of the deputies.

The driver of the lead car was a somewhat skinny male, who was just tall enough to look Sue in the eye. The only one there who was just a little bit shorter than him was Lisa.

"We need to see some ID," he ordered without giving them any kind of greeting. "And we need to do it now."

His belligerent attitude irritated all four of them, but it did a bigger number on Mack and Lisa than it did to Sue and Larry. And as always, the kind of behavior the pushy deputy was displaying hit Lisa hardest of all. So she didn't hesitate to face down the cop.

Pushing in so close to him that he could feel her breath on his face, she said to him, "I don't know who the hell you think you are, Ace, but there's no way you can come into our campsite claiming you want our ID without a damn good reason. So far, you haven't given us one. Since you haven't, you'd best back the hell off and come up with one. Or else get the hell out of here, and don't come back without a warrant and the sheriff."

The deputy foolishly tried to grab Lisa. He thought he could spin her around and cuff her. She not so gently helped him to the ground. She put her foot on his neck.

"If you put your hands on me again," she snarled at him, "I will first beat the hell out of you and then I will personally arrest you for attempted rape. I will then follow through with whatever it takes to put your sorry ass in prison."

She moved her foot and let him get up. "Put cuffs on all four of these people," he told the other three deputies. "They can sit in a jail cell while we get to the bottom of this."

Sue held up her hand and told the deputies, "Before you get stupid enough to to listen to this dip twit deputy here, who thinks he's Rambo The Second, you'd best hear me out. You don't, you will be facing a lawsuit big enough to bankrupt not only you, but your entire county government. To start, what in the goddamn hell are you assholes doing here. What the hell is it that you want?"

Rambo wannabe answered her. "You people stole a book from Jay Klug. It was a valuable heirloom his father wrote. He wants it back. We are here to get it back, and while we are at it, arrest the bunch of you for the theft of it."

"The truth is," Mack snarled at him, "we do have the manuscript of a book Jasper wrote. It's in a safe place, where no one as stupid as you can get your hands on it. Jasper gave the book to us, and we have complete documentation to prove it."

"I don't care what you claim," Rambo man said, "I want to see your IDs. Now. And I mean right now."

All four of them were so pissed at Rambo by then, that any thought of being cooperative enough to show him their ID was gone. All he was going to get now was a look at the complete trail of documentation Sue had on her computer. After that, Mack had every intention of going back to Jay's and raising some hell with him. The man deserved a good scare.

Mack looked Rambo in the eye. "It's like this. We have no intention of showing you one damn piece of identification until after you look at what Sue has on her computer. At that point, we will talk about what's going to happen to Jay Klug, the damn fool who sent you here."

"That's it. Now you are going to have to turn your precious computer over to us."

"Not in a million years. Either you look at the evidence we have that explains what all of this is about, or the four of us are going to make citizen's arrests of the four of you. You're guilty of attempted false arrest and attempted rape of my wife. When our lawyers get involved, the list will surely grow. So what's it going to be?"

"Simple. You are under arrest. I'm the law here, not you."

Mack looked at the other three deputies. "What do you three want? To take the time and learn, without any doubt whatsoever, about is going on here? Or do you want to play the game Rambo here is trying to play? If you do follow him, I guaranty you will be hurt by it. And likely as not, it'll cost you your career in law enforcement."

"Before we decide," one of the three deputies said. "I want to know why you think you know so much about the law. Are you a lawyer or something?"

"I was a deputy for Clayborne County for several years. So was Lisa. That's why we know how far out of line Rambo is. Now choose. Do the four of us arrest the four of you, or do you want to listen to reason."

The deputy got affirmative nods from the other two deputies. Rambo was still red in the face and drooling onto his uniform. He tried to walk away when Sue turned the computer on. Lisa stopped him, and shaking her head no, let him know that he was required to watch the presentation.

It started with an interview with the postmaster, Charlene Leaf. She was wearing her uniform as she explained about the letter Mack got in the mail, and went through all they did. From talking to the people on the mail route to finding Jasper's body under the weeping willow tree. It ended with a picture of Jasper sitting there, obviously dead.

The letter was displayed next, then the cover of Jasper's manuscript. His funeral was followed, and only the people from Refuge Rescuers were there. Not one member of Jasper's family was there.

All the various receipts from the funeral costs were displayed. They all said what they were for, and showed that it was Mack who paid them. The documentation itself ended with a narration that Kathy did, explaining how they found Jasper, the time they spent with him, and why what happened to him mattered so much to all of them. It was followed with her singing Amazing Grace at his funeral. Three of the deputies gasped when they realized who was singing. A scan of those who were there showed a lot of tears for an old man most of them never even met. The video ended with the interviews of Jasper's children.

"Well, Rambo," Mack asked him, "what's next? Are you still hell bent on trying to arrest us?"

"Well, I guess not. But it don't make no sense to me at all why any of you should give a shit one way or the other. Jasper was okay, back when he was still a working man. Trouble is, in the end he was just an old man who couldn't do much but interfere with the lives of those who still mattered."

"Of course it doesn't make any sense to you. You're just another one of those people who don't know the difference between right and wrong. You are pretty much small scale nothing, but at the same time you're more like Donald Trump than like a decent deputy sheriff. You want nothing but power. You love being a bully, which is all that you are. A small, rather stupid, school yard bully."

"You'd best be careful what you call me. I can still bust your balls if that's what I decide to do."

"You could try, if you're stupid enough." Mack stopped to decide if he should bother to continue talking. It only took a few moments to decide to continue. "The fact is, Rambo, I kind of wish you would try. You have disgusted me enough, so that I'd enjoy kicking your ass."

"I hope you don't really believe you could get away with that. I've got backup. There's four of us and only two of you. You wouldn't stand a chance."

Mack chuckled. He'd heard the same comments from so many people that he'd long ago lost count of the times. He told Rambo, "I'll tell you what, tough guy. I'll give you a break. You can take your anger out on my wife." He waved at her to come over close to them. "Rambo here wants, real bad, to beat someone up. I told him he could go after you. Is that okay?"

Lisa smiled an answer so wide it almost looked as if it might split her face open. "Sure, Mack." She looked at Rambo. "This is going to be fun, don't you think? I do have to say I'm sorry though, Rambo. You probably won't be able the hear what I'm saying later. And by the time you regain consciousness, we won't be around here anymore."

Rambo suddenly remembered what happened when he tried to grab Lisa earlier. Then he turned his attention to her. It didn't take but an instant for him to realize that he was in trouble. She wasn't joking. He would end up unconscious and in the hospital if he took her on. It was time, he knew, for him and the other deputies to be on their way.

And their first stop would be to visit Jay Klug and his family. Lying to the police was never a wise thing to do.

"It's time we moved on," he said and got in his car.

The other three followed without comment. Mack, Lisa, Sue, And Larry had a few hours then, without any incidents.

It was near three o'clock that afternoon when the sound of an animal being tortured rang out through the entire RV park. Larry was the first to figure out where the screams were coming from. It was a very large, Class A RV. It had only been in and setup in the park for a couple of hours.

Before any of them could make a move to check out what was going on, a door to the Class A opened and a puppy flew out. It landed hard, and lay there unmoving. Without hesitation, Larry stormed over to check on the pup.

Mack followed him. Sue took out a camera and started recording what was going on. Lisa stayed in her chair, holding tight to each arm of it. She was struggling to calm herself. She knew that if she did anything immediately, her temper could get the best of her. She didn't want to go to jail for what she wanted to do to whoever it was that threw the pup out the door.

It was as bad for Larry. Even though he was doing his best to help the pup, he was still shaking with anger. He had seen too much cruelty to animals in his life to have any tolerance for it. Like Lisa, he knew he needed to be careful to control himself. It would be too easy to let himself go, and deal with the guilty one the way he would if he caught someone out in the woods torturing an animal, any animal, the way the puppy was just treated.

Mack was experiencing the same feelings as Lisa and Larry, but was doing a somewhat better job of controlling those feelings. So he was the one who knocked on the door of the big RV. Sue had a video camera on it.

A woman, somewhere in her mid-thirties, answered it. She wore a man's white t-shirt large enough to cover her almost as well as a very short dress. The problem with it was that it was very worn. That made it translucent enough to display her ample breasts almost as well as if she was nude.

She looked at Mack as if he were some sort of useless aberration, and asked, "And what the hell is it that you want, Cowboy?"

"I want the asshole who threw the pup out your door," Mack answered, not at all as impressed by her breasts as she expected him to be.

"Well, not that it's any of your business, but my boyfriend did. The goddamn dog shit on the carpet in the living room. That's why he got thrown out."

Lisa was now holding the pup, so Larry could join Mack by the door. "Tell your chickenshit, asshole of a boyfriend to get out here. I want to talk to him."

"No, I don't think you want to…"

Her answer was interrupted when her boyfriend appeared at the door. He was huge, weighing in at near three hundred pounds. Most of it muscle. "I don't know who you assholes are," he declared, "but I can tell you right now, you ain't welcome here. So leave, before I decide to make you leave. You stay, and you get hurt."

"I know you are big, tough man," Larry said. "Given how you overpowered that pup out here. But I doubt you can do anything that will bother me. So I'm staying until you first apologize for what you did to the pup, then graciously turn him over to us so we can take him to a vet."

The big boyfriend laughed. "Hell's bells, I can whip the both of you without making much of an effort to do it. So you best be moving on, before I put you in the hospital."

"You are more than welcome to come on down here and try. Because I fully intend to stay right here until you move that sorry ass of yours outside."

The big man came out then, moving down the stairs attached to his RV like he owned the world. He'd won both of the bar fights he'd been in since he stopped playing football, so he had no doubts about his ability to take on someone smaller than he was.

He was wrong. He managed to take one hard swing at Larry's head, which missed. Larry made the next six or seven moves. The football player made one more. When he landed on his face on the ground. He lay quite still then.

"I want you to know," Larry said to the woman, still standing near the door, "that there's no way I can allow you to keep the pup. You and your boyfriend are entirely too stupid and too cruel to ever own a dog, or any other animal as far as that goes."

"It's not my dog, it's his. I don't want it, so I don't care what you do with it. He will care. He'll be awful pissed if you take it. Most likely, he'll go to the law about it."

"I figured that." Larry turned to Sue. "Call the local animal control people. If we can't keep the pup, maybe they can take care of it."

Sue called and talked to someone. She was told that someone would be there shortly to pick up the pup. Ten minutes later a sheriff's car drove in. Rambo and the deputy riding with him got out of the car. Rambo swaggered over to the pup.

"I see that you people are at it again," he said. "Animal control called me. We're the one's they call for incidents like this. They don't have the staff to deal with it." He pointed to the other deputy. "Pick up the dog, and let's get the hell out of here. I'm not in the mood for dealing with this kind of crap."

"What about the guy on the ground?"

"I'm sure he'll come around." He pointed at Sue. "She'll have it all on video, which I have no doubt will show him to be the one who started the trouble."

"Well, okay, if you say so." The deputy carelessly took the pup from Lisa with one hand. I howled in pain.

Lisa instantly took the pup back. "You aren't taking this puppy anywhere," she told him. "Mack, we have to take this puppy to a vet. He's hurting. We can't let him get locked up in this condition."

"You're right. I'll get the jeep." He gave Rambo a hard enough look to tell him not to argue about what they were going to do. He said to Sue, "Find us a vet."

She found one who was willing to check out the pup, and had GPS coordinates on how to get there for Mack when he returned with the jeep. Lisa carefully got in with the pup in her arms, and Mack took off as soon as she got her seat belt on.

While they were gone, Larry and Sue explained what happened. The football player woke up as he finished. He was angry, but too groggy to do anything about it. He wasn't anxious to take on Larry again anyway.

"Do you want me to call you an ambulance to take you to the hospital?" Rambo asked him.

"No, I'm okay. Let's just forget the whole damn thing."

"You don't want to press charges against this guy then?"

"No. Like I said, let's just forget it."

"What about the dog? What do you want us to do with him?"

The football player groaned and got up from the ground. "Frankly, I don't care what you do with the mongrel. He shits in the house if we don't take him out every five minutes. There ain't no way I want to keep him. That's why I threw him out to start with."

"I think we'll keep him," Larry told Rambo. "We have a daughter at home who'd more than love to have a puppy of her own."

"You people are truly strange," Rambo told him. "After I left here earlier I went back to Jay's. He said the problem he has with the book is you guys snooping into their lives. Now you're sticking your noses into these folk's business. Why are you doing shit like that?"

"As far as Jasper is concerned, we just wanted to know more about him. I think it was so we could all better understand what happened to him. Why he had to die alone the way he did. With people he worked his whole life to take care of, flat not caring a damn. As far as the pup is concerned, none of us can put up with cruelty toward animals. From my own point of view, that pup has every bit as much worth as you do. Maybe even more. Finally, we get involved because we give a damn about what goes on in this world. We'd like to make it a little better, if we could."

When he stopped talking, Sue stopped taping him. She put her arms around him and kissed him. When they broke it, she said, "What you just said was what I needed to know. I love you. Let's get married and adopt Emma. Maybe we can't make the world all that much better, but we can try to make her's a whole lot better than it might otherwise be.."

"Yes. Just like you, I think we can. And now that I understand what Jasper's all about, and why he matters so much, I think living with you where you now live, is the right answer for us. We don't need anything more than we have right there. I only have one request."

"What's that?"

"For a week or two every year, I want you to let me go north and get lost in the wilds. Given the life I once lived, I'll need that."

"I'll gladly give you that Larry. And for the rest of the year, I'll be all yours."

"Good. I couldn't ask for more."

Mack and Lisa were surprised when they got back with the patched up puppy, to see Sue and Larry laughing and talking to Rambo. Especially since he didn't look at all like a Rambo any longer.

CHAPTER 23

They found a campground in a state forest with a half dozen spots large enough to accommodate RVs under thirty feet. Two spots near the lake the campgrounds was located next too were available. They considered themselves to be extremely lucky to have found a campground with spaces where they could park the RVs.

They were far happier to be camped there than they would have been in a commercial RV park, even if the accommodations were fewer. There were no showers with hot water, no flush toilets, and there were rules against foraging for wood to burn.

On the positive side, they had a great view of the lake. Their campsites were about thirty feet above the water, giving them the ability to see all the way across the rather large lake. Several hiking trails went through the campground, and a few more started there. The state forest surrounded them, and was large enough to provide habitat for a lot of wild critters.

Best of all, the campground wasn't crowded. A family with a couple of kids was camped in a tent camper at the far end, and in about the middle a group of four tents filled four campsites. There was a couple in each tent, and they appeared to be together. They were, thankfully, quiet, with only some soft, pleasant music playing from some kind of electronic device or another.

Lisa and Sue did the few things that needed doing inside the RVs while Mack and Larry started preparing the evening meal. Mack trimmed up the three steaks they'd brought from home, while Larry went to work on the vegetables. Both men were using charcoal grills. Mack was only cooking three steaks, because Larry didn't eat meat from any mammal or bird. He did eat fish, eggs and dairy products.

For this meal he roasted potatoes, broccoli, onions, green peppers, and tomatoes. He seasoned each vegetable with special seasonings he blended. Between them, the olive oil he basted them with, and the flavor from the grill, they all ate them with the same enthusiasm as they tackled the steaks.

Mack especially enjoyed the vegetables. He grew up eating the vegetables his father, Ben, grew, and learned to love them at a very young age. Watching everyone eat, especially Mack, Larry was both pleased and surprised by the way the vegetables disappeared into mouths and then stomachs as quickly as they did.

When the meal was done and there were no leftovers, he was sure he needed to ask, "Did I cook enough? The few times I've cooked like this for people in the past, there's always been a lot of left overs."

"There was more than enough," Lisa answered. "I always eat a lot, but tonight I outdid myself. The veggies were delicious."

"I agree with Lisa," Mack said. "If you would have cooked more, I would have eaten more. But I ate too much as it is. I think you did about perfect with what you cooked."

"I think," Sue said, "that I'm going to wish I'd brought some larger pants along. I don't think I've ever eaten that many vegetables. You did great, Larry."

Lisa and Sue insisted on doing the after dinner chores, while Mack and Larry relaxed in a couple of camp chairs overlooking the lake. They didn't get to relax long before they were disturbed by the four couples from the tents.

They ignored Mack and Larry as they walked over to a huge, old oak tree. They untied a rope from the trunk of the tree, and pulled it back, away from the lake. The other end of the rope was tied to a limb over the lake.

They waved the rope around some as they debated about who was going to swing out into the lake first. What young people usually did with that kind of setup, was swing out as far as they could, then let got of the rope and drop into the lake. The young lady who was going to be the first to try the rope was only going to swing out over the lake, then ride the rope back to land. She told them that she wasn't going to let go because she didn't know how to swim.

When she was ready, the guys she was with pulled her and the rope as far back as the rope allowed. They then gave her the hardest push they could and she started her swing. Everything went okay, until she reached the peak of the swing over the lake. The rope broke, and the extremely surprised girl went into a spin on her way down to the lake. As soon as she hit the water it was obvious that she was in trouble. Either she actually didn't know how to swim, or she was a very bad swimmer.

While everyone, Mack included, hesitated those first few seconds before acting, Larry left his chair at a run. Without the slightest hesitation, as he reached the edge of the thirty to forty foot cliff at the lake, he used his powerful legs to push himself off. His dive took him far enough out into the water to keep him from breaking his neck. Mack was running toward the lake, but stopped then. He knew he would be of more help if he could see what was happening before he tried to help.

Larry was a strong swimmer, so it didn't take him long to reach the girl. It was a good thing. She was totally panicked when he reached her, and had already swallowed a lot of water. In her panic, she fought him when he tried to help her stay above the water, so it took a bit of wrestling on his part to finally get control of her.

He kept his voice reasonably soft as he talked to her the whole time he worked to calm her. As soon as she realized he was there to help, she relaxed enough to let him bring her to shore. Once there, he picked her up and carried her up the path to the camp grounds. Lisa was already there waiting to wrap a blanket around her. The girl was trembling hard, so Lisa sat on the ground next to her, holding her as she softly told the girl everything was okay now.

Standing next to them, Larry was still breathing heavy. He had his hands on his hips, and his concern for the girl was written on his face. As the group the girl was part of moved around her, Larry asked, "Who the hell was it that decided she should swing on that rope? She doesn't know how to swim. She could have drowned."

One of the four young men ran up to Larry and slammed his hands into Larry's chest. "She was okay out there, you son of a bitch. She knows how to swim. She just said she didn't. Everyone knows how to swim. You didn't need to do what you did to her. You just went into the water so you could put your hands on her. I ought to knock you on your ass for what you did."

Larry was a reasonably patient man, but what he'd just listened to was more total nonsense than he was willing to put up with. "I don't know, nor do I care, what your problem is. But it'd be best if you'd back the hell off. Be a good idea if you grew up some too. Just for your limited ability to understand much, it is impossible to save someone from drowning without touching them. And, asshole, she was drowning."

"That's bullshit. She was doing fine. I saw you grab her tits. I saw you shove your hands down between her legs. Like I said before, you just went in the water so you could feel her up." He took a swing at Larry. He didn't have to move much to avoid the blow.

Too everyone's surprise, Sue stepped between them. She pushed the young man back. When he didn't move far enough to satisfy her, she did it again. "It's like this, you idiot. Your girl was drowning. It takes no brains at all to know that. I don't know what your real problem is. I also don't care one goddamn little bit what your problem is. But now I know this. If you don't immediately apologize to Larry here, and then get the hell out of our sight, I'm going to let him loose on you. If your friends here, try to help you in any way, you'll be taking all of us on. You do that, and you will spend the next few months wishing you hadn't." She looked at the group. "You all knew she was drowning, just as you all know what a damn fool this jackass is making out of himself. So why don't take him back to your campsite and calm him down?"

There was a lot of mumbling among the group, but when it was done, they took their less than aware friend by the arm and led him away. Larry turned his back on them as he shook his head in disbelief. Out in the water, wrestling with the girl to calm her down, he couldn't have felt anything no matter where he touched her. The water was too cold and his concentration while he worked to save her life eliminated the thoughts of anything other than pure survival.

It should have ended then, but the kid was determined to beat up Larry. He broke free, ran up to Larry, and slammed his fist into his the side of his head from behind. The punch lacked much power and didn't phase him. He turned and blocked a second punch with his forearm. Before the kid could throw another one, Larry decked him.

"You'll be best off," Larry told him, "if you stay on the ground."

Before the kid could say or do anything, the girl who fell in the lake got to her feet and looked down at him. "I knew you weren't the smartest boy I ever went out with, Gary," she told him. "But what you've been trying to do to the man who saved my life goes way beyond not being smart. You are the most stupid, and I mean really stupid, boy I ever went out with."

She gave Larry a hardy kiss on the lips, said, "Thank you for what you did," and joined her friends. The kid got to his feet, and head hanging, followed his group back to their campsite. A short time later, their tents started coming down.

It was easy for Larry to see as he watched the group pack up to leave, that Gary was no longer welcome among them. He sat alone on a rotting trunk of a fallen tree as they loaded up their gear. He was still alone when they left the campgrounds. His only saving grace was the fact that there was still a car left there for him to leave in. He sat there with his head hanging between his legs for a couple of hours before he finally did.

"Now there went a perfect example of how to screw up your own life," Sue said when he was gone.

"He sure was," Larry agreed. "Not only did he make a total fool of himself, he lost the girl."

"She was a pretty girl too," Mack said. "Makes a person wonder what makes some people tick. I also can't help but wonder, did he attack you, Larry, to try to show off for his girl? Or was he jealous?"

"I think it was both," Lisa suggested. Then she slapped Mack on the arm. "And of course you noticed that she was a pretty girl." But she was smiling when she did it.

The rest of their stay in that campground proved to be peaceful. All four of them finally got the chance to relax and refresh their minds and bodies for the next three days. It was the second evening they were there that while they were sitting around the campfire talking, that Larry mentioned that he didn't know what he was going to do to make a living if he stayed In Minnesota.

Being the one most concerned about their future, Sue responded to his comment. "You know how to do so many things, Larry," she said, "so there must be a lot of jobs you could do."

"Most of the things I'm ever likely to get hired to do, are things that would get a ways beyond just boring in a very short time. I've spent too much of my life earning a living by subsistence farming, and what the wilds provided me. I think I'm a reasonably patient man, but I just don't do boredom well."

Mack surprised all of them then, especially Larry. "I don't know if you have any interest in what we do or not. But Paul Danielson wants to retire. That means we'll be needing another detective. Would you be interested in going to work for us as a private detective?"

Larry jerked his head up and stared at Mack. The look on his face asked the question, "Are you nuts? Me, a detective?" His answer was, "I don't know the first thing about doing that kind of work. I'm really surprised you asked me that question."

"I'm aware that you don't have any experience in law enforcement. When I started as a deputy sheriff, I didn't have any training or experience. But that's what training is for, and Paul is willing to work with you for your first month to help train you. While he does, you will be getting experience. You will be amazed at how much he can teach you in a month. After that, you will work with each of us for anywhere from a couple of weeks to a month. Only then, will you go on your own. And even then it will only be on the simpler cases for a while. The question I asked you though, was are you interested in giving it a try. If you don't like it, you can always quit."

"Before I answer you, you'll have to tell me why you're making the offer. Did you do it so I'll stay here with Sue? I know you don't want me to ever take her away from you, and just as much, I know you're afraid that I'll walk out on her. Or did you do it just because you feel sorry for us and the situation we are in right now?"

"None of those reasons, actually. I made the offer out of pure selfishness. Replacing Paul is going to be impossible. Most of what Lisa and I, and all of our crew actually, learned what we know from our working with him. Finding someone who can be trusted is a near impossible task. The thing is, I know you now and I know I can trust you. You are a stand up guy. The fact that we won't always agree is, in reality, a good thing. That's why I made you the offer. I think you can learn and do the job, and I trust you."

"I'm still surprised you made me the offer," Larry said, still looking somewhat confused about it. "You've most of the time given me the feeling that you didn't much like me."

"When you left Sue the way you did, I hated you. I didn't like you much when we first got to Canada. By the time we left I decided I could tolerate you. When we started this part of our vacation, and you and I got into that argument, I once again didn't like you much. But now that I've gotten to know you some, I can better see who you really are. So I made the offer. And the main reason I want you to take it, is because I think you will be a definite asset to Refuge Rescuers."

Larry looked over to Sue to see what she thought about Mack's offer. Her face carried a broad smile. "I think you'll be good at it, Larry. And I have no doubts that most of the time you will love the work. We all seen to get the chance to help people. That's the best part of it, even if we do have to deal with some real downers occasionally. I think you should at least give it a try."

Still not sure what his answer should be, he turned to Lisa. She grinned at him. "You should definitely take the offer. As far as I'm concerned, I have no doubts about your ability to learn and do the job. As for me, it will give me the chance to make Sue jealous. She's so beautiful, and often makes me jealous. So I'm looking forward to working with you. I think a few weeks flirting with you will be an awesome experience."

Larry was stunned by her comments. How could she say something like that in front of her husband. Then the laughter broke out, and when he saw that all three of them were laughing, he knew that accepting the job offer was the right thing to do.

He shook hands with Mack, gave Sue a hug, but when he went to shake Lisa's hand, she kissed him. She winked at him as she moved away, then wrapped her arms around Mack and gave I'm a kiss with real passion in it.

"I think you did the right thing, offering Larry the job," she told him. "And I'm glad you still have your sense of humor. You know that even if I do flirt with Larry, neither one of us would ever take it beyond that." She kissed him again.

The next day, Lisa decided they should all try their luck fishing. They all had licenses just in case that's what they decided to do. Their tackle was lightweight and anything but fancy. So they fished mainly for panfish, using worms for bait, that they dug up at the edge of the woods.

Mack and Larry didn't have much luck, and only caught a few small sunfish. They were big enough to eat though, so they kept them. Sue had better luck, and caught several somewhat larger sunfish and crappies. Early on, Lisa didn't catch anything. Then something attacked her bait and ran away with her line. Even as it flowed off her reel, her rod was bent nearly in half.

Her line was only a few feet from disappearing before she gained enough control to begin reeling it in. She managed to retrieve several feet of line before she lost control again. This time it was only inches from disappearing before she managed to once again reel some in.

She and the fish managed to do battle for nearly an hour before it finally tired enough for her to bring it all the way in. It was a northern, one of the best fighting fish to be found in Minnesota lakes. It weighed close to eight pounds. Lisa took one look at it and knew she couldn't kill such a magnificent creature. Without looking at anyone, she said, "He has to go back in the lake. I think he earned the right to live another day."

Without a word, Larry removed the hook from its mouth and put it back in the lake. It didn't immediately respond, so he eased it back and forth, forcing the water through its gills. Gradually, it came to life. When he let it go, they all gave a silent cheer, hoping the life they'd given back to it would be a good one.

Larry was an expert at cleaning and filleting fish, so he took care of all of them they caught and kept. He again roasted vegetables, and when they were nearly done, Mack pan fried the fish in butter. Salt, pepper, and garlic were the only seasons used.

The meal was even more of a success than the night they ate steaks. Partly because fish from a cold Minnesota lake always make a great meal, but just as much because this time Larry was able to join in on the entire feast.

When they finished the meal and Lisa and Sue were doing the cleanup, Larry asked Mack. "I'm curious about one thing. Are you still going to let me have some time off every year to spend up in the wilds? You know I'm going to miss that part of my life."

"Personally, I doubt like hell once a year in the wilds will do it. I think you should get two trips a year there. Two weeks each time. My only request is that if she wants to go, you take Sue on one of them. She should be allowed to share that part of who you are with you."

"That's a good idea," Larry said. "What made you think of it?"

"It's part of what we've learned from Jasper. It's things like that which have kept us wanting to know more about him. He wasn't some kind of miracle man. He was just an ordinary person who lived his life the best he could. He went through some sad times and some hard times. But up to the end he tried to do what he thought was the right thing. That's why he didn't want to burden anyone."

"Like I told you before, what you were doing with him made no sense to me when you first told me about it. But now, especially since I've spent this short vacation time with you guys, I have more and more found a lot of sense in what you are doing. I think there was probably a lot more to Jasper than what he was ever given credit for. Above all, he was a lot smarter man then what his family ever gave him credit for."

Mack shook his head in agreement. "The truth is, Larry, he was very intelligent, along with being such a decent person."

Lisa and Sue joined then then. Without thinking about who she was saying it too, she said, "And I've always kind of regretted that I didn't go even farther than I did when I helped him out."

"What did you just say?" Sue asked, the tone of he voice filled with disbelief.

Lisa shook her head. "Nothing. Nothing at all important."

"It must be something," Sue argued. "You're blushing."

Lisa didn't answer. Instead she looked at Mack for help. He shrugged. "It's no big deal. Lisa just did something nice, something special for an old man who hadn't had anything special done for him for a very long time. The truth about it is, I'm proud of her for what she did. It took a lot of courage for her to do it."

"Jesus," Larry said, "you guys are talking like she did something sexual with him. I can't believe you would do that?"

That was the wrong thing to say to Lisa. She felt like she was being judged for what she did. That was the last thing she thought she had coming for doing it. A pat on the back would have been much closer to the right thing to give her. "It's like this, Larry. You shouldn't be so quick to judge people as you are. All I did was to use my hand to give that old man the kind of pleasure I'm sure he hadn't had for many years. It wasn't more than a few days before he was dead. At least once in his last days he got something good. So don't judge me for doing something decent and right. I will never have even the slightest regret for doing it. And Mack supports me a hundred percent on it."

Larry felt properly chastised for his comment. "I can't see any reason to argue with you, or in anyway disagree with you. It's just that I've never known any woman who would give of herself that way."

"Now you know two," Sue said. "Because if I would have been there at the time, I would have done whatever I could to assist Lisa. I hope you can understand that, Larry."

He tried to smile, but didn't quite make it. "I do, in my own way, understand. But you guys are going to have to give me time to adjust to your ways. 'Cause they are often different from what I'm used to."

Mack told him, "It will take some time, Larry, but if you give us a chance you'll find that even though our way of looking a life, even our way of living our life, makes sense. None of us are looking for anything more than the chance to live a decent and simple life. And a large part of doing that is sharing that life without ever trying to own each other. So yes, I am damn proud of what Lisa did that night. Too anyone else, he was just a sick old man with little to no value. She could see beyond all that, and know that he deserved a lot more than what the world was willing to give him."

Larry smile them, and said, "I damn sure hope there's people like you folks around when I get old.

CHAPTER 24

They were home for two days when Mack got a surprise visit from a pretty lady. Charlene Leaf was the postmaster of the Kingsburg postoffice. She loved flirting with Mack, and often tried to push their relationship beyond simple flirting.

Mack had forgotten that he'd promised her that he would let things go further if they found Jasper while the two of them were looking for him. Because he was sure, at the time, that they wouldn't find him that quickly, he readily agreed to go along with whatever she wanted. Now she was there to collect on their deal, and he was at a loss as too how to handle the situation. It was difficult to have a totally private conversation at the Refuge Rescuers's office, they agreed to meet at Katie's Kafe in Kingsburg in an hour to talk about the deal.

Mack knew that he'd promised to do what she wanted. He also knew that he was known as a man who kept his word. But he'd promised Lisa that other than occasional episodes with Kathy, he would never stray. The only saving grace in all of it was the fact that he did talk with Lisa about it back when it all happened.

Lisa's answer to the problem then was simple. "What you have to do, Mack, is what your conscious tells you to do. If you keep your promise to her, you won't be lying to me, because I know about it. As for me, my only hope is that you can talk her out of it. But if not, I will live with it."

Either way, he knew that no matter what he did, he needed to talk to Lisa about it again. She was out on a case, but he tried to call her on her cell phone anyway. By what seemed to Mack to be a minor miracle, there was a break in her activities when he called. She answered the phone.

"I've got a big problem," he told her. "And I need your help to figure out what to do." He explained the situation.

"I don't know whether to laugh or cry," she answered. "Only you could themselves into a position like you're in. What do you think you should do?"

"What I want to do, is too somehow keep my promise without keeping all of it."

Lisa sighed heavily enough for Mack to hear her do it. "What exactly the hell does that mean?"

"I want to do something nice for her, but I don't want to have sex with her. I don't think either one of us has any excuse for cheating."

Lisa sighed again. "Well, I think you should talk to her and try to get her to accept this. You take her out to dinner, and maybe even dancing. But end your evening there. If she insists on more, you could even neck a little. But convince her that sex would be wrong."

"About the necking part? Where the hell could we do that?"

"Go park in the refuge somewhere. You, more than anyone else, know where there are a lot of private places to park."

It was Mack's turn to sigh. "I guess that would work, if I can't talk her into going home after either the dinner or the dancing."

"Good." Lisa was quiet for a couple of minutes. Finally she said, "Mack, I really don't want to share you with anyone, but if things do get out of hand, it's not the end of the world. I will still want you to come home after it's all over. And I will definitely still love you."

"Well, I sure don't plan on letting anything serious happen. Even so, I am so thankful for your understanding. I know how stupid it was for me to end up in this position."

"At least you had a good reason for doing it. At the time, your first concern was Jasper. Finding him made however this turns out worth it. I love you, Mack. But it looks like I have to get back to work. Bye."

Mack went to Katie's then. He was somewhat nervous when he went inside. He was unsure how Charlene was going to react to what he had to say, and what she might say or do in answer.

She was in a booth located at the back of the cafe, so they couldn't be seen through windows from the street. He sat down across from her. She picked up on the concern on his face right away, and needed to struggle some to keep from smiling at it. She didn't really expect anything from Mack, but was enjoying watching him struggle with what he considered to be a serious problem. She managed to maintain a strait face while he struggled to explain why he wanted to limit what they did, and proposed an alternative. She was both surprised and delighted with what he offered. She was all smiles when she accepted it.

"And tomorrow night is perfect," she said. "It's my husbands bowling night. The best part of that is the fact that he and his bowling pals always stay out drinking. So he won't be home until late."

When Mack and Lisa talked about it that evening, as they relaxed together on their couch, she said, "From the sound of it, Char didn't expect that you two would be doing something serious. And knowing her, with her sense of humor which is seriously bent, she probably wasn't expecting anything at all."

"I guess that's possible, but I think it's best to take her out for dinner, so the issue can be settled."

"I agree. I wasn't going to suggest otherwise. I was only pointing that out about her, so you can legitimately avoid most physical contact with her."

"I will do that. Do you want me to call you during the evening and tell you how it's going?"

"Not really. When you go, I'm going to take a long, hot bath, eat a light supper, and go to be early. You can, however, wake me up when you get home. If nothing else, I can go back to sleep feeling your body close to mine."

"I will definitely do that. The best thing about nighttime is holding you."

When Mack left for his date that night, he was happy to see that Lisa didn't show any signs of being upset about his going. Char was waiting for him, and answered the door as soon as he knocked. She was wearing red dress that fit each and every curve of her body perfectly. It was low cut enough to be sexy, but not enough to be risqué. It ended just above her knees, which left just enough of her legs showing for him to see that they were perfect. Her hair was combed out and flowed down over her shoulders.

When she let him in, he took a step back from her, and shaking his head he said, "Wow! Double wow! You are beautiful. I think I'm going to enjoy tonight. All I have to do is look at you and it'll be great." On impulse, he stepped forward and gave her a kiss on the cheek.

She tipped her head to one side, then wrapped her hand around the back of his head and pulled him to her. The kiss they shared lasted far longer than Mack thought it should. The problem was, he did nothing about it until they broke it.

Then he said, "I could all too easily do that all night. But…"

"I know," she said before he could finish what he was going to say. "But it's better that we don't do anything more. The thing is though, just one more won't wreck our marriages." She kissed him again, showing him a lot of enthusiasm. He didn't argue with her.

As soon as they broke it he said, "I think we'd better go now, while we still can. We don't want to miss our dinner reservation, do we?"

She laughed. "I hope you don't believe what you just said. If I actually had that choice to make between you and food, I could go hungry for a long, long time."

Knowing he was playing with fire, Mack took her hand and they left the house. He held it until he opened the door of his pickup for her. When she got in, she pretended that she didn't notice how far her dress rode up her legs. She didn't even try to pull it down on the ride to the restaurant. It wasn't until it rode up even higher when she got out of the truck that she pulled it back down. During the entire time, she didn't show the slightest sign of embarrassment over the amount of leg Mack could see.

They ate at a restaurant out on the four lane, south of town. The service was excellent and the food was good, so they shared a more than pleasant meal. Char avoided any talk about her home life, so Mack ended up telling her about his and Lisa's fragmented vacation, and what they'd learned about Jasper. She didn't comment much. Instead she mostly listened, seeming all the time to intently study Mack as he talked. The closer to the end of their time at the restaurant got, the more her expression moved from lacking much emotion to one filled with what appeared to be love. It took Mack a while to realize the look she was now carrying was serious. He knew that if he wasn't careful, whatever it was that she was feeling could grow from wanting something to needing it. Since he too was beginning to be filled with the wrong urges and thoughts, he decided it was time to leave.

He got the waiter's attention, settled up with him, then left a good tip on the table. Char didn't say anything during the time Mack was getting ready to leave. She didn't speak until they were in the truck.

"Yes," was all she said.

"Yes what?" Mack asked.

"Yes, I want to go dancing for a while." She looked up at him. Just the hint of tears were in the corners of her eyes. "You said it was on option tonight. You said it was my choice."

"Yes, I did. Where do you want to go?"

"To the country bar on the two lane west of town. It's one place we shouldn't have any chance of running into my husband. He's always said he hates the place, ever since the one time he took me there. He doesn't like to dance either."

"If you're worried about him seeing us, Char, we probably shouldn't be out like this in the first place."

"I'm not worried that he might see us. I just don't want anything to happen that could wreck what has been such a great night so far."

"Okay. Let's go then."

It was a quiet night, so the bar was only about half full. They found a booth in the back. Char sat down first, then pulled Mack down next to her where she wanted him. Not across from her. When the waitress came, Char ordered a glass of white wine and Mack a beer. They were quiet until a slow song was played.

"Let's dance," Char said, and they went out on the dance floor.

Without hesitation, she pulled him tight against her. She made no secret of the fact that she wanted him as close as she could get him. When she looked up at him, her eyes told him a story. Even with the tears there, they were deep, dark, and a wonder to see. He had a difficult time pulling away from her look, their eyes were so tightly locked together.

When the music stopped, she kissed him. Her passion was so strong that it pulsated through him. It would soon be time, he knew, when he'd have to take her home. In another place and another time, what was happening to them would have been a wondrous thing. Now, it was unfortunately something best left where they were. Not taken with them when they left for home.

He knew for sure it was time to go when three very loud couples came into the bar. Their conversation and laughter told everyone there that they were going to raise some hell. It didn't matter who did or didn't like it.

The loudest, and most obviously drunk male of the bunch, made a big show of kissing the woman he was with. As he did, just to show his incredible manhood, he put his hand over her breast and squeezed it hard.

"Goddamn," he howled, "you sure do got nice tits."

Mack looked at Char then, to see what her reaction was. She was so pale her skin was almost white, and her hands were shaking. Mack watched her for a few moments, then asked, "What's wrong, Char?"

"That's my husband, Jim. And I thought I was being kind of unfair with him for having dinner with you. Not anymore."

"What do you want to do now. We can leave, you know?"

"Let's wait a while, Maybe they'll leave before he sees us. He can be mean sometimes. I don't want to make any trouble for you."

"Don't worry about me. I just want you to be okay."

Before she could answer, her husband finally saw her. He let go of the breast he was playing with, threw his head back, and yelled, "Well, fuck me. If it ain't my wife, here with another man. It is time, ladies and gentlemen, that I kick both their asses."

Mack left the booth to greet him. When Char tried to get out too, he put his hand on her shoulder and shook his head no. He stood calmly, with his hands hanging at his sides, waiting for Jim to get to him. He was staggering, so it took him a while.

"I don't know," he said when he finally reached Mack, "what the hell it is you think you're doing? But that's my wife who you're sitting with."

"I'm well aware of who I'm sitting with. I'm just returning a favor she did for me. We were about to leave and I was going to take her straight home."

"That's all well and good, but there's no way she should be here with you. So I'm going to kick your ass right here and right now. Then I'm going to take my lady friend home, go home myself, and teach the bitch I'm married to what happens to cheating whores."

"That's your intention then? You plan on going home and beating your wife?"

"Goddamn right I do. No man can let his wife do what she's been doing tonight."

"She hasn't been doing anything but eating a meal with an old friend, and now enjoying some decent conversation. So I suggest you back your ass off so we can leave."

"You sure as hell ain't going nowhere with her. Not now. Not no time. All you're gonna do is lay on the floor when I get done with you."

He made the drunks common mistake and took a swing at Mack. He barely had to move to duck it. Mack blocked a second blow with his left forearm. After he ducked the third and fourth blows, Char spoke up.

"You don't have to put up with anymore of his childish bullshit, Mack. So will you please just knock him on his sorry ass. I'd like to get the hell out of here. Enough is enough."

Mack blocked one more blow, then asked Jim, "Are you ready to quit now, or do I have to take you out to stop this?"

"You ain't goin' to stop nothin'. I'm gonna kill you now."

Jim's next swing and miss were so hard that he was spun around with it. It knocked him down. As he struggled to get up, Char kicked him in the ribs. "You try to move again, Jim. and I'll kick you hard enough to break some of those ribs. When you come home tomorrow, plan on packing up your shit. You and I are done."

"And," Mack added, "if you lay one hand on her, I will put you in the hospital. And if I do, you'll be there longer than you can now imagine."

They left the bar, and as she'd done every time she got in it, she let her dress ride up high. This time high enough to show more than Mack had ever expected to see.

"I've suspected him of doing a lot more than drinking with his friends on his bowling nights for a long time," she said on the way to her home. "So what happened tonight was no big shocker. I would appreciate it though, if you'd be there tomorrow when he comes to get his things. I'd hate it if I have to shoot him. I'd have to go through too much legal bullshit if I do that."

"Just let me know when you want me. I'll be there."

They were quiet again until they got her home. Before she got out of the truck she said, "Please come in with me, Mack. I don't know why, but I feel real uncomfortable going in alone."

"Okay, but I can't stay too long."

They went in together, with her holding tightly onto his hand. She closed the door behind them, then without hesitation she pulled them together in a kiss filled with all the fire inside her. She took his hand and put it on her breast.

"That's so you know just a part of what I'm more than willing to give you, if you ever get interested in taking it." She kissed him again, then moved his hand to an even more intimate place. "Thank you," she whispered. "Just being with you, Mack, has been a very special thing for me. I just hope we can do it again some day. Now go home, before I attack you."

She turned him around, opened the door and pushed him out. He heard her start to cry before the door was closed. He hated hearing her. Like it or not, he hurt her. It was something he very much regretted doing.

At the same time, he wondered what or how much he should tell Lisa when he got home. He knew he couldn't quite tell her everything. He didn't want to hurt her too. The one thing he was determined to tell her, was a warning about Char's husband, Jim. Something that proved to be a wise thing to do.

CHAPTER 25

Char's husband Jim was on his best behavior when he arrived home the next morning. He was having some trouble moving, because his ribs were extremely sore from the kick Char gave him the night before.

Mack got there shortly after he did. Char hadn't been the least bit shy about calling him and asking him to come. Especially since Jim brought a couple of his friends with him.

Nothing came of it though. The three men packed most of Jim's personal things in boxes, loaded them onto the back of the pickup they came in, and quietly left.

"Now that's a relief," Char said. "I can't thank you enough for being here for me, Mack. I have no doubt that you are the reason he didn't start any trouble."

"I'm not so sure about that," Mack answered. "He seemed pretty calm today. Either way, I'm glad it's over and you are safe. I would hate to ever see anything bad happen to you."

"Really? Even after I put you through so much crap last night and again today?"

"You didn't put me through anything, Char. All you did last night and today is allow me the pleasure of your company. I always enjoy the time I spend with you. You are a special lady. I hope we can spend some more time together again."

She hugged him, gave him a quick kiss, and said, "Anytime you want to do that, Mack, will be the right time for me."

He felt better about her when he left her this time than he did the night before. She seemed as if she was already adjusting to the changes in her life. Changes that were a lot bigger than what either she or Mack realized. And they couldn't have imagined how it would impact Lisa or Larry, a man from Canada who was a complete stranger to Char.

Mack and Lisa talked about it that evening, and she was relieved that it seemed as though all of the troubles with Char were over. "I hope now," she told him, "that she'll quit pestering you."

Mack laughed at that. "I think it's just part of Char's nature to flirt. So that will probably never stop. But I think she's learned that it'll never get past the flirting stage with me. She knows how much you matter to me."

"I can live with that. And speaking of flirting, I'll have Larry for the day tomorrow. I hope he knows I was only joking when I talked about flirting with him on the job."

"If he doesn't, I don't have any doubts about you setting him straight. I know that if you aren't in the mood for something like that, it won't happen."

"That's right, Mack. It sure won't."

Neither one of them needed to be at all concerned about how Larry would react or behave with Lisa. From the moment he got in the passenger seat of Lisa's pickup, he was a perfect gentleman.

"What are we going to be doing today?" he asked when they started out.

"The first thing I need to do is stop at the post office. I have a couple of packages to mail. Normally, the post office picks up all of our out going mail, but I want to talk to Char. So I thought I'd drop off the packages while I was there."

"Is this stop about official business with Char, whoever she is?"

"It is now, as far as I'm concerned, part of our official business for today. But it is personal for Char too, who is the postmaster, so I will probably be talking to her alone. And that's no offense against you. It's just that this is my first meeting with her about this problem, and I want her to be comfortable."

"That's considerate of you. Are you that way with all of your clients?"

"Not necessarily. This time, what we're doing for Char is as much a thank you for what she's done for us, as it is anything."

"Is it okay to ask, what it was that she did that was so helpful."

"It's okay to talk with you about it. You're part of the agency. It would not be okay to talk to an outsider about it."

"I didn't think so. The only reason I'd like to know about it is because that's part of learning what this job is about. Not because I want to poke my nose in anyone's private business."

"I didn't think you wanted to." Lisa went on to tell how Char helped them, starting with the search for Jasper. She omitted most of the flirting stuff, but did carry the story all the way to Mack taking her out for dinner and dancing.

"So her husband, who was feeling up some other woman, got pissed because she was sitting next to Mack."

"That's right. It was lucky that his two friends stayed out of it, or Mack would have had his hands full."

"He sure could have. He could have been beaten badly, having to take on three guys."

"Yes, there's a good chance he would have lost what ever fight there was. But I doubt that he'd been beaten badly. Mack's become one hell of a fighter since he became a deputy sheriff."

"That he has. The one thing about this that has me wondering though, is why you would let him go out to dinner with another woman? Especially one who you say is beautiful."

"That's easy. Because he owed her a lot. Without her, we probably would never have found Jasper. We'd still be wondering about him. And we'd all be poorer for it. And as much as anything, I trust my husband. Mack is honest to a fault. If he makes a promise, he does everything in his power to keep it. He promised nothing would happen between them. That's all I needed to hear from him to let him take her out without my having to worry about it."

"You guys continue to surprise me. You said, while we were camping, that if I took this job you were going to flirt with me if we worked together. You haven't. You let your husband go out to dinner with a beautiful woman without getting jealous. There was that thing you did with Jasper. And I'll never forget what you looked like when you opened your robe and flashed me. None of that is what I've always considered normal."

"Given how short a time you've been here, living around us and now working with us, it's about what I thought you would think. A lot of people who've known Mack and I for a long time still wonder about us. So you might never get used to the way we do things."

"You might be right. But living with Sue, I know for certain that I'm going to have to adjust to a lot of things. There's a lot more to her than what I know now. One of those things I'm most curious about, is how did she get connected with you guys? All I know is that she was already grown up when she met you."

Lisa had to chuckle some when she thought about how Roy behaved most of the time as if he adopted her. "Roy is a trader. He has been since he was a kid. He'll buy, sell, or trade nearly anything. As long as it's legal. Most of the time he makes money on his deals. He met Sue at an auction. He outbid her on a painting, and after felt bad about it. A lot happened, but he ultimately trained her to be a trader. She was a good one. She made enough money to get into electronics. She's even better at that than she is at trading. When we decided to open the agency, she was definitely someone we wanted as a partner."

"What about you, Lisa. You are sometimes about as patient with people as any one I've ever seen. But with some men, you are pure hell. I can understand hating some of them, given what they do, but you look you get when they piss you off is downright scary."

"This isn't something I want at all to talk about, but I'll give a short version of why I'm that way. I was kidnapped and raped when I was sixteen. It was the most horrible thing…" She went on to tell him her story. She finished with, "I made a vow when I got out of the hospital that I would die before I'd let any man do that to me again. So I learned how to fight. I've worked with professional trainers, but I've also learned a good part of what I know from hard ass street fighters. When I have to fight someone, there are no rules. I take them anyway I can. And some of them I hurt, whether I need to or not."

"At least you come across as someone who can live a normal life as someone's wife."

"If you're referring to a sex life, for me, it's all Mack. I was just fifteen when I met him. I fell in love with him the instant I saw him. He wouldn't come near me until I was old enough. When he did it was great. I couldn't go near any other man without panicking. With a lot of them, I'd even get sick. With Mack it was always the opposite. He has also gotten me through most of those other feelings toward men too."

"If Mack's been the only man in your life, how can you possibly so sure about not still having those feelings about other men?"

"I think it's best we leave it at this. There are reasons why I'm sure. And if you ever get the idea that you think you'd be just the right man to prove to me that I am cured, keep it to yourself. You can probably beat me in a fight, but winning it won't be worth the price you will have to pay to win."

Larry laughed. "Lisa," he said, "I don't have any intention of ever doing either one of those things. First of all, I've grown a healthy respect for you and all of your abilities. Second, I'm really very fond of you. I'd hate like hell to lose your's or Mack's friendship."

"Good," she answered. "That means if the day comes when I do flirt a little, you will understand that there's nothing to it. It's just my way of showing you that I'm fond of you too."

"I'm glad you were willing to talk to me like this, Lisa. It means that I can stop being concerned about working with you, and enjoying it."

"Me too, Larry. Me too."

When they got to the post office, Lisa asked Larry to wait in the lobby while she went into the back of the building and then Char's office. Char gave her a big smile when she went in.

"I just came to make sure everything's okay with you today," Lisa told her. "Mack told me about the trouble with your husband, and I also wanted you to know that I'm on your side. So if you ever need help with anything, you can feel free to call me."

"That's awful generous of you," a surprised Char answered her, "especially after your wonderful husband took me out for dinner and dancing. I wasn't sure how much he told you, and to tell you the truth, I'm kind of surprised that you're not pissed off at me. If things were the other way around, I probably would be a lot more than just pissed at you."

"Maybe, but maybe not. You see, I was just as concerned about Jasper as Mack was so, as much as he did, I appreciated your help in finding him. As far as the dinner and dancing goes, it was as much my idea as it was Mack's. And for me, it beat the hell out of what Mack thought he owed you. That might have upset me."

Char blushed, but smiled too. "I'm sorry about that, Lisa, but there's something about Mack that makes me want to hold him until he does everything to my body that a man could do to a women in the name of love. When I do something as simple as just talk to him, he makes me feel as though I'm the only person in the world who matters. He gives me his full attention. And those eyes of his, they seem to bore down into my very soul. I've never known anyone else quite like him. I do want you to know though, I never want to do anything that would hurt what you and Mack have. It's way too easy to see how special it is."

"I didn't think you would, Char. I was sure it would be okay for you guys to go out to dinner when you readily accepted that as an alternative to what Mack promised you when you two started the search for Jasper."

Char smiled again. "Of course I accepted the dinner. I wasn't expecting anything from Mack. I was just doing my usual flirting and teasing him. He does sometimes get a little flustered when I do it. That's kind of fun to watch."

"I can't argue with you about that. It sometimes can be fun to watch him when he gets that way. But, as much as I'd like to stay and talk a lot longer, our new detective is waiting for me, and we do have things we need to do today."

As the someone waiting, Larry was getting a little impatient. He was beginning to text Lisa to see how much longer she would be, when three men came into the post office and charged through the lobby. Larry didn't react until he saw the gun in one man's hand as they disappeared into the back. He jumped from the chair he was sitting in and followed the men. Two men were standing outside Char's office, and the third man had an arm around Char's neck and the gun pointed at Lisa.

Larry didn't hesitate. He drew his own pistol and quickly slammed it into the head of one of the men. As the man fell, he took out the second man. As he stepped into the office, he could see the man with the gun trying too steady himself to put a bullet in Lisa.

"This is what your husband is going to get for what he did with my wife," the man screamed. He took an extra second to tell Char, "This is what happens when you cheat on me. You are going to be next."

Before he could pull the trigger, Larry dove in front of Lisa. The bullet caught him in the arm. He went down. Lisa instantly knew she had to react. She slammed into the man with the gun so fast he never got the chance for a second shot. She knew it was Jim, Char's husband. A man she'd had a strong dislike for, for a very long time. As he fell back from Char, Lisa grabbed his wrist and twisted with all she had, forcing Jim to drop the gun.

She went berserk then. Her fingers reached for and found his eyes. She scratched them as deep as she could force her fingers, leaving him temporarily blind. Knowing it would cause maximum pain, she reached down and squeezed and pulled his manhood with everything she could put into it. When he opened his mouth to scream, she picked up a stapler from Char's desk and jammed it into his mouth, breaking most of his front teeth. She knocked him down, and the second he landed on the floor she kicked him in the ribs. It was in the same spot Char kicked him the night before. This time three of them broke. She looked at him for the first time then, and although she was tempted, she forced herself to stop her attack on him. That's when she heard the sirens.

It was only then that she became aware of her surroundings enough to see Larry on the floor. The young lady who worked behind the counter, waiting on customers, was leaning over him and fastening a tourniquet around his arm, just above the place where the bullet went in.

"I called 911," she said.

"Good. You're doing the right thing with Larry too."

"You were awful busy for a while there, so I thought I should at least try to help."

Lisa turned to Char then. "Are you okay? He didn't hurt you, did he?"

"Not this time. I have to thank you, Lisa. If you wouldn't have reacted so quickly, he would have killed us both."

"We both have to thank Larry. If he wouldn't have taken the bullet meant for me, we'd for sure be dead now."

Larry, who was groggy but still conscious, said, "It was both of us, Lisa. But I can't believe what you managed to do to that asshole over there in such a short time. He sure as hell isn't going to ever do anyone else any damage again. You really fucked him up."

"Do you think I was wrong, doing what I did? He was, after all, trying to kill us."

"Hell no, I don't think you were wrong. The asshole got what he had coming. I'm just surprised that you could do so much so fast. Watching you was enough to convince me you were right when you said I'd pay for it if I ever had to fight you. You are something else, Lisa. I'm damn proud to be on your side."

The cops got there then. Dale was the first one inside. He immediately called for ambulances for Larry and Jim and the two men on the floor. When he looked at Jim's condition, he didn't say anything right away. He shook his head, looked at Lisa, then shook his head some more.

Finally, he asked her as he pointed at Jim, "Is that your work?"

"Yes it is. He tried to kill me, but Larry took the bullet and saved my life. Then he said he was going to kill all three of us. He would have if he hadn't told us what he was going to do before he did it. That gave me just enough time to disarm him, then disable him. He's lucky I didn't finish what I started. I was sorely tempted."

A city cop, who arrived shortly after Dale, stuck his nose into their conversation. "I don't believe you," he told Lisa. "I think what you did to him was intentional and without cause. So I'm going to take you with me to the city jail. You'll be held there until this poor man you've so totally abused can sign a complaint against you. After that, you'll be prison bound."

Before Dale could argue with the man, Char spoke up. "It's like this," she said, getting right into his face, "what she said is exactly what happened. The son of a bitch who got his ass kicked the way it needed kicking is my husband. And the simple truth is the fact that he came here to kill me. The only reason he didn't is because Lisa here, and Larry there, with the bullet in his arm, were here. So forget about arresting anyone but my husband and those two unconscious jerks on the floor."

"But I don't think it's possible for any woman to do to him, what she did to him, without in some way surprising him."

"I suppose you can't. But that's only because you're stupid."

Dale stepped in. "That's enough. I know everyone involved in this, and I know enough about them all to know Lisa's not the one responsible for this mess. The bullet in Larry's arm is further proof of that. And finally, all the witnesses here agree with Lisa's story. So she won't be going anywhere she doesn't want to go."

"But I have jurisdiction here. And I think she's guilty."

"I don't give a good goddamn what you think you have," Dale said, loud enough for everyone in the post office to hear. "So I suggest that you shut the hell up and back out of the way. If you don't, I'm going to arrest you for interfering with a criminal investigation with the intent to abstract justice."

The city cop finally backed off then. He knew he was wrong to start with, but thought that if he used his authority to arrest Lisa, everyone would see how important he was. The only thought they had about him now was the fact that he was a real jerk.

Lisa called Mack, and waited for him to get there. She was sure he would be upset when he did. Especially with her. She was wrong. When he got there with Sue, his concern was written all over his face. The only way he was upset was his worry about Larry's wound, and that Lisa and Char were okay.

Jim was being loaded onto the ambulance as he walked by, and his only thought was, "Good for you, Lisa. You just did what I failed to do when I was at the bar with Char."

When Larry was loaded onto an ambulance after his wound had been dressed, Sue got in it with him. She didn't say anything while she was with him. She just held his hand and occasionally brushed her other hand across his forehead.

It was just before she got into the ambulance that she said, "It'll be okay, Lisa. It wasn't you who did this."

After everything at the postoffice was completed, Lisa decided to call it a day and go home. None of her plans for the day were critical, so leaving them for another day wasn't going to cause any problems.

Just before she left, she told Mack, "If Char needs anything before you leave to come home, do it for her. She's had a really bad day. I'll be there when you get there. I love you, Mack."

He knew what she meant, but knew that nothing like that was about to happen. He'd hold Char, and give her what ever comfort he could, but knew that anything more wouldn't be good for anyone. Including Char.

If he would have asked her, she would have agreed. Now was not the time. That decided, as far as the future was concerned her thought was, who knew?

CHAPTER 26

Mack and Lisa ate breakfast the next morning. They were the second ones there, only a few minutes later than Roy and Wanda. They surprised Roy enough with their early arrival, so he only said hello when they walked in. His normal teasing comment was forgotten.

Mack and Lisa said, in perfect unison, "Good morning to you."

"You two sure do sound good after all you went through yesterday. I would have thought it might have dragged you down some. I know how upset you get, Mack, when Lisa gets into serious trouble like she did yesterday."

"He couldn't this time, Roy," Lisa said. "I didn't cause or start any of it. All I did was react when I had no other choice."

"I'm sure that was the case," Roy said, "but from what Mack told us last night, there aren't many people who could have done what you did."

"That's not entirely true. All of you here, especially you Roy, would have done exactly what I did. And think about Larry. He took a bullet that was meant for me. He didn't have to do that for me."

"Yes he did," Mack said. "Any one of us would have done the same thing, no matter who the gun was pointing at. That's why I didn't get even slightly upset with you, Lisa. You and Larry just did what you had to do. There were no other choices. The thing is though, he is such a new part of us that it did make what he did special. I think he's going to be a genuine asset to Refuge Rescuers."

"I agree," Lisa said. "I think he's going to be good at the job."

"Speaking of Larry," Roy said, "have either of you talked to anyone yet today? How is he doing?"

"I talked to Sue just a little while ago," Lisa answered. "She and Emma spent the night at the hospital. They had enough empty beds so the hospital staff could let them use one. She said Larry was sitting up already, and anxious to get out of there and go home. The bullet missed the bones and major arteries, so everything considered, he's in decent shape."

"I'm curious though," Roy said, "is he going to still want to work as a private detective? Getting shot, even if it could have been much worse, sure as hell doesn't make the work we do seem all that attractive."

"Sue said they he's more excited than ever about the job. Getting shot just showed him how challenging the job can be. He likes challenges."

"That's good, because there's no way he can do the job if he doesn't."

Mack's cell phone rang then. When he answered it, the voice of the feminine sounding person calling said, "Are you the Mack Thomas who's been traveling around, asking about Jasper Klug?"

"That would be me, yes."

"If you can give me a good reason for doing it, I might be able to tell you a few things about him you might not otherwise know."

Mack did a quick search of his mind for some outstanding reason to tell her, but couldn't think of anything other than the truth. "I don't know if my reasons, no, our reasons for trying to learn about him will make sense or not." He went on to tell her everything they were doing connected to Jasper, from first finding him, up until the visit with his son. He ended with, "Like I said, I don't know if it makes sense to you or not, but we would all like to learn as much as we can about him, so it will be in his book when we finish it and then publish it."

"Do you really think he'd want his life out there for anyone to see. He was often a very private man while he was alive."

"Yes, I do. He wouldn't have written it if he didn't. He also said I should do whatever I thought was the best thing to do with it. More than that, all of us who are involved in the project now have a deep admiration for Jasper. There's not a one of us who doesn't wish that we could have found him sooner and convinced him to let us help him. He definitely would have been a big asset to our lives. He certainly never would have been a burden to any of us. And finally, if his book, his story, helps even one other older person, it will all have been worth it."

"You sound, Mister Mack Thomas, like you might actually care some about him. So if you want, you can come see me. I will tell you what I can about Jasper. He and I became friends when we were about four years old. I still remember the day he moved into the neighborhood. We were friends up until those few of us who loved him the way he should have been loved, lost him to the street."

"I definitely want to see you," Mack told her, "but I am curious as to why you aren't mentioned in his book?"

"It's simple. He always worried that if the wrong people knew about our relationship, it might in some way hurt me. If nothing else, he always said it would be an embarrassment to me. I cared too much for him for that to be true, but he always worried about it anyway. That was the way he was. He very rarely thought of himself first."

Mack talked to her for a few minutes more. She gave him her address, and they agreed to meet the next morning. He felt a bit out of sorts when shut his phone down. Lisa, who was listening, but also looking at the changes taking place on his face, took his hand shortly into the conversation. She continued to hold it when he stopped talking.

"There's something about this," he said, "that tells me that tomorrow is going to be a big learning day."

It was a long drive to the town where they were going, so they left early. They knew Minnesota well enough, so they didn't need to use GPS to guide them to the town where the person they were meeting up with lived. They thought they might need it to find her home, but it turned out to be close to the biggest building in the town. The only one bigger was the nursing home. The person they were meeting lived in a convent. She was a nun.

She was waiting in the lobby when they went in. What made them take notice of her the most wasn't the fact that she was dressed in black the way nuns almost always used to dress. It was because she was over eighty years old, but still very pretty. Mack's first thought was that she must have been an awesome looker when she was young.

She was confined to a wheel chair. Her handshake was strong, and her voice was sharp and clear. Her eyes though, said it all. They were bright and shining and full of life. To Mack, she seemed to be a person who still had a lot to offer anyone willing to accept what she had to give. Her name was Matti.

"Well, Mister Mack Thomas and Lisa," she said after their introductions, "where do you want me to start?"

"At the beginning," Lisa said. "We want to know everything you can tell us."

"We'd also like to record our conversation today," Mack added, "If you don't mind Matti. We don't want to take the chance of forgetting anything."

"No, I don't mind. My only request is that you let me see the finished book before it is published, so I can be sure you don't make any mistakes with what I tell you."

"I would like it if you would read it. You can then fact check it all the way through the book. The last thing we want to do is write anything that isn't true. We owe Jasper at least that much."

"Okay, I guess I'll just tell it the way I remember it. Jasper and I hit it off from the first time we met. We lived in what was a real neighborhood that was full of kids like us. The war was over and the depression was ending. Over all, live was good. There wasn't a lot of money. Every family lived on whatever wages dad earned. Almost all of the moms stayed home in those days. During the summer, the kids in the neighborhood got together and played games. The thing was though, more often than anyone noticed, Jasper and I would go off on our own. We had our own games. That was okay, but by the time I was thirteen and Jasper was fourteen, those games often turned into a boy-girl thing. Not that we did anything too serious. At that age, we never did anything to get me in serious trouble. But there was a lot of kissing and some way too intimate touching."

Matti paused a moment then, as her memories drifted back to that time in her life. She touched her breast, one lone tear ran down her cheek, and she continued with her story.

"All through high school, Jasper and I did everything together. Every party, movie, or get together with friends, it was the two of us. We did a lot of heavy necking back then, but he never pushed it. I let him touch me a couple of times, but when I asked him not to do that again, he didn't. We went to different colleges after high school. We both dated other people then, but when we came home, it was a just us again. The biggest problem we had was my looking for something more than what an ordinary life could give me. I got religion. When I told Jasper that I wanted to become a nun, it near broke his heart. All he said was that all his life he want nothing more than to spend his entire life with me. The closer the time came for me to go into the convent, the sadder he was. Finally, I knew I did owe him something. After all, he had been my best friend all my life. And such a good friend he was. I loved him too. I think nearly as much as he loved me. It's just that I thought I loved God more. Even so, I decided to give him something of me before we went our separate ways."

She paused again, this time dropping her head to hide the fact that she was actually blushing a little. This time, when she started talking again, several tears rolled down her cheek.

"I told him I'd give him nine days. two weekends and the full week in the middle. We went up north and stayed in a small cabin on a lake. I made all the arrangements, so he didn't have any idea about what I had planned. He thought it was only going to be some time together. Maybe doing some fishing and some short walks in the woods. He even talked about wanting to take me to some nice restaurants to eat. I hope you can imagine the look on his face when there was only a double bed inside the cabin. When he saw it, he right away volunteered to sleep on the floor. I thought he might faint when I start to undress. He definitely wasn't sure what to do. He was smart, and when I told him we only had nine days, and that I didn't want to waste any time, he quickly shed himself of his clothes. What a glorious time those few days were. I faintly remember eating a few times, and I think we went for a couple of walks, but mostly, we were in bed. Never in my life has time gone by so fast. So much of my life since them, things have forced me to ask myself why we didn't just stay there. If I could do it all over, I would gladly spend my entire life in that little cabin with that man. He cried when we said goodby. Something inside him changed at that moment. He didn't say anything about it, but he never went inside a church again, except for weddings and funerals. He even refused to take part in it when his wife had his kids baptized. He went to their confirmation, but he didn't seem to be at all proud of them for what they accomplished. He never had one good thing to say about religion or God after that. As far as he was concerned, God had cheated him out of a good part of his life when I went into the convent."

She dropped her head into her lap and sobbed. Her entire being broadcasted the fact that she was admitting that she regretted the choice she made when she left him when they got home from that cabin. It took her a while to recover enough to resume talking.

"We didn't see each other again for a few years. Then I transferred here, and I contacted him. We became friends again, but I could see right away that he had changed. All his life, until we left that cabin, he smiled a lot. When I saw him again, he almost never did. He tried to whenever I saw him, but the sadness he still felt from losing me wouldn't let him. He was still a kind man, and he would help anyone who asked him for it. But he no longer smiled when he did. Always, deep in his eyes, there was a sadness that never went away. He was married by then too. It was a bad marriage for him from the get go. I think the cheating started on their honeymoon. After he caught her a few times, she promised to never do it again. But she did. Only one man after that, but it was with his best friend. When I could get away, I would often sit with him, holding his hand. I was always filled with the temptation to break my vows. The truth is, I wish now I had. In fact, I wish I would have had the God given sense to know that my rightful place in the world was with him. I couldn't have served mankind in any better way. I was stupid and so I didn't. Everyone wondered why she stopped cheating on Jasper. She did it after her and I had a long talk one night. I explained to her that if she didn't, I was going to leave the convent and take him away from her. I also told her I would make sure everyone, especially in her church, would know what she'd been doing to him. She was catholic and belonged to the same church I was part of, so she got the message. She was a decent wife after that. I think that then, she was actually beginning to care about him. She didn't want to lose him. I would have made good my threats if she hadn't changed. I might have left the convent and taken him away from her anyway if he hadn't, in his own way, still been in love with her. More than that though, he had kids. Given my own beliefs, I didn't want to break up a family. He lost in the end anyway. He was a proud man, and truly didn't want to be a burden to anyone. He should never have died alone. If I would have known about him, about him on the street, I would have done everything I could to help him. Even if it meant living on the street with him. But I was sick for a time. The illness I had took away the use of my legs. So I didn't know he had disappeared until after I was better."

She sat there then, looking from one of their faces to the other. Back and forth.

"You know," she said, "you two are very lucky. You are together, and I can see that you are still very much in love. Don't ever throw that away. I had what you have and I threw it away for something that is no longer real to me. If it ever was. Whatever you do, stay together. You don't know it now, but when you get old and are no longer pretty or handsome, you will love each other more than you do now. And no one, no matter who they are, will matter as much to you as you do to each other. Everyone failed Jasper. Me included. If I hadn't been so blind back then, he never would have died alone, under a goddamned willow tree. It took until I learned that he was gone, that I would never see him again, to understand why he never went to church again. It's pretty easy to be angry with God when you realize how cruel it was to convince me to give up my life to live in a convent. Jasper and I both lost most of what life should have given us. And the saddest part was, nothing was gained from my doing what I did. Not for anyone or anything. And most certainly, not for either one of us."

Mack couldn't help himself. He needed to tell Matti about Lisa and Kathy and everything they did for Jasper. He wanted her to know that he'd been shown some kindness, some actual love, a short time before he died. When he finished, Mattie motioned for Lisa to come closer. She hugged her, then kissed her on both cheeks. When it was Mack's turn, she kissed him on the lips. He was pleasantly surprised to find out that kissing an old lady could feel as good as her's did.

When he moved away from her, he felt good about the time they were with her. She was smiling, and the light in her eyes was bright.

"When I called you, Mack, after I learned about Jasper, I had no idea what to expect. Now I find myself hoping that you will come and see this old lady again. If you do, maybe I'll remember more about Jasper that's worth telling you."

"We'll be back, Matti," Lisa said. "We will for sure be back. Seeing you has been the closest to Jasper we've been since that night we found him. All we can do is thank you for giving us your time. Seeing you has made what we are trying to do seem even more worthwhile."

"I'm glad that what I had to say has helped. And as long as I am alive, Lisa," she promised, "I will always have time for you and Mack."

They reluctantly left her then. It was a quiet ride home as she filled their thoughts. It was for them such a sad story that she told. It left them wondering how a man as good and decent as Jasper could be tossed aside the way he was. At the same time, it told them a lot about the character of the man, while at the same time it pointed out how easily people can be so completely misguided. Matti was a good, intelligent woman, and she'd for the most part thrown two lives away for virtually nothing. She did it because she thought that was what God wanted and expected. She knew now that if that was true, it didn't say much for God. It was only a lot of senseless hurt for a lot of senseless nothing.

Just before they got home, Mack said, "It seems like there's something missing in most of this world today. You and I are so incredibly lucky, Lisa, to have what we have. I sure don't ever want anything to happen to make us lose that."

"I don't either, Mack. So when we get home, you are going to have to hold me for a very long time. I might not ever let you go. I think I'll hold you for nine days. I might get hungry by then."

Mack finally was cheered up enough by her nine days comment to say, "Speaking of hunger, there's that part of those nine days that you've got me thinking of now. With you, I could go the whole time without eating. Food, that is."

"Good, because there's nothing I want more right now than for you to go hungry."

They didn't eat food until they went to Ben's for breakfast in the morning. They were the last to arrive. Roy noticed. He commented. They finally managed to smile then. It was good to be reminded of who they were.

CHAPTER 27

Bob and Beth had both found jobs after they auctioned off their farm, so all they could manage for part of Mack and Lisa's vacation was a long weekend. They stayed in a state park, located a little over fifty miles north of Kingsburg. It was a quiet weekend, with the most exciting thing they did was getting close to a large black bear on one of their short hikes.

It was easy for all of them to see that Bob's heart problem was having a negative effect on him. He moved much slower than he did in the past, but still managed to do all the walking anyone wanted to do. He was also in a positive mood during the whole weekend. Most of all, he followed Lisa's lead and ignored the way Beth looked at Mack when she didn't think anyone was watching her.

In spite of Beth, Lisa wasn't at all concerned about her and Mack. Since their visit with Matti, he seemed to want to be close to her, not Beth. He didn't do anything specific, but when they walked together, he always took her hand. If they sat at a table in a bar, restaurant, or anywhere like that, he always held her chair for her. There were a lot of other things, but the change in him showed up the strongest at night. He always held her as tight as he could without having any kind of negative affect on her.

Anything else they did was filled with a soft kind of love that made her feel more wanted she'd ever been before. She finally asked him why he was giving her so much extra attention.

"It's because I love you. You know that."

"I know you love me, Mack. It's just that it seems like there's something else going on. I think it has something to do with what Matti talked about."

"You're probably right. I guess what happened to Matti and Jasper is haunting me. What we have, they could have had. I don't ever want us to be what Matti and Jasper ended up being. So I guess I am holding on to you closer. But if it bothers you, I won't keep doing it. I know that holding on too tight can be a pain in the ass."

Lisa's answer started with a laugh. "No, Mack, what you've been doing with me isn't a pain in the ass. I like it. Along with everything else it is, it's flattering. To be wanted, the way you seem to be wanting me lately, is an awesome, yet comforting feeling." They were home from their weekend with Bob and Beth by then, and planning the next part of their vacation. So she asked, "What are you going to do about Kathy? We'll be with them for the next week or more. You know she's going to want some of your attention. And the odds are, Dale will want some of mine."

"Play it by ear? Take it as it comes? I don't know. Maybe cancel the trip?"

"I don't think we should cancel the trip, Mack. If we are going to have some photos in the book, we need to visit all the places Jasper wrote about where he stayed while he was homeless. He wouldn't have written so much about them if he didn't want them to be part of the book."

"You're right. We do have to go, and it's only fair that Dale and Kathy come with when we do it. They were there when we found him. I do have one favor to ask though."

"Okay. The way I feel toward you right now, I'm willing to grant you almost anything."

"If anything happens on this trip, I would like it if you weren't the one to start it. It's okay if we somehow get into something, but I'd feel better about it if this time, we were the followers, not the leaders."

"I promise not to start anything, Mack. Like you, right now I mostly want it to be only you and I. I just don't want to leave anyone feeling rejected. Especially since that's not what we're not trying to do."

"I don't either. So I guess the best thing we can do is not be the ones who start anything."

Lisa did him one better. When they started out their first day, she asked to be allowed to drive one of the RVs this one time. She asked Kathy to ride with her. On the way to their first stop, she explained to Kathy about Jasper and Matti, and asked Kathy to pretty much hold back from doing anything with Mack the first couple of days of their vacation. After hearing Lisa's explanation, she readily agreed.

The first stop they made was a bridge over the four lane, several miles south. They took pictures of it up close where Jasper spent two nights. They only took a couple of pictures of the bridge itself. It was almost identical to hundreds of other road bridges in Minnesota. From there, it was a series of abandoned buildings, a couple of campgrounds, and even a few barns. At one of them, they had to talk to the owner who lived on the same property as the barn, to get permission to go inside for the pictures. They even searched for and found a couple of almost ancient motels that had been abandoned for years before Jasper used the them for a short term home.

They visited a lot of other miscellaneous locations, but the ones that had a profound affect on them were the places where he slept outside in the cold of winter, with only a somewhat ragged sleeping bag for warmth.

He wrote about trying homeless shelters a couple of times, but only said he didn't care for staying in them at all. But he never wrote about why. When they asked for permission to take some pictures inside them, they were denied it. Privacy was always the excuse given for the denial.

Mack took over driving one of the RVs again after the first stop, and Dale continued to drive the other one. They were active enough those first two days. so all four of them were more then happy to quit early both nights, and skip the usual end of the day visiting. They slowed down considerably the third day, so after a leisurely supper that Lisa and Kathy cooked, they relaxed in front of a small, but friendly feeling campfire.

The conversation didn't go on very long before Kathy didn't want to wait any longer. She sat down in Mack's lap, kissed him, and said, "Lisa told me how you're feeling right now, and why. So if we don't do anything more than my sitting here tonight, I'd like to do that. If it's okay with you, Mack."

"It's okay. I love you too, Kathy. It's just that right now, I'd kind of like to just share what you and I have, what we all have, without taking it any further than this."

"That's fine. As long as you're willing to hold me, I know everything's good with us."

"I don't se any reason why things shouldn't always be okay with us, Kathy."

"What about you and me?" Dale asked Lisa. "Is everything okay with us."

"It is, Dale. It most definitely is. But with you and me, you have to admit it is different from Mack and Kathy. Our needs are different. We are mostly just good friends and hopefully we will always share what good friends do. With, of course, the occasional benefits. Benefits which I'd like to skip tonight. For them it's more, at least in some ways, more like Jasper and Matti's nine days. If you and I ended, Dale, it would be one hell of a big hurt. If they did, it would be a lot more. In a while, a couple of months or so, we can maybe go back to what it was. Just not tonight."

Kathy and Lisa stayed where they were until they all were ready for bed. Mack held Lisa when they got there, like he was afraid he was about to lose her. She finally had to tell him to loosen up some, so she could at least take a deep breath.

They continued to travel and take pictures, but at a much more leisurely pace. The nights around the campfire were always filled with talk the only way it can come from friends as close as the four of them. The last night out, Lisa relented and sat on Dale's lap. But she stayed true to her word and spent the night snuggled close to Mack.

After they were home for a couple of days, Mack and Sue started organizing the materials for the book. Lisa started to help, but then she and Mack got busy with work when they got a rush of different cases to deal with.

Kathy went on a short concert tour, so Mack and Lisa didn't see much of her or Dale for the next couple of months. Larry's wound healed and he proved to be a quick learner. He often could handle some of the more minor cases on his own, and proved to be a definite asset when he assisted anyone on the more serious cases. They were so busy that time seemed to fly by. All too quickly it seemed, fall was upon them and the leaves were turning. Kathy was done with her concerts for a while, and she insisted that she and Mack take a Saturday for a walk in the refuge.

They planned on only the two of them going, but the Lisa and Dale decided they would like to come along too. Mack and Lisa were talking about the day they were going to have while they were in the Refuge Rescuers office one day, and Sue over heard them. She thought that what they planned sounded like a lot of fun.

"Would I be out of line," she asked, "if I wanted to go with you? I think I'd love a day like that, and it might be good for Larry to do something with you guys."

"You'd be more than welcome to come," Mack told her. "But be warned, we might not always act the way you and Larry are used to seeing us." He made no effort to explain further. And she didn't ask any questions.

The only one who minded at all that they were going together as a group was Kathy. She treasured her time alone with Mack. An all day with him, doing nothing but walking the refuge while holding his hand, and stopping occasionally to talk, was for her a great way to spend her extra time. Either way though, she wasn't going to let having people along during what she considered her time with him change the way she did it. She was going to make the walk the same way they always did it.

As soon as they got to the trail head she took Mack's hand. As they always did with other people along, they took the lead. Dale shocked Sue when he took her hand and followed behind them. Larry just looked confused when Lisa held out her hand for him to take.

"What is this all about?" he asked. "I came here with Sue."

"And I came with Mack and Kathy came with Dale. But we are all friends, and in our group friends hold hands. Sometimes we even kiss each other. So take my hand and hold it. While you do, think of all the times in your life when you didn't have a hand to hold.

He did, and she pulled him close and kissed him. When she saw the shocked look on his face she said, "That was just my way of telling you that we are friends. So you don't have to be shocked. You are a part of us now, and we all want you to know we are happy about it. So get used to it. On days like this, you'll be kissed again. Even if it isn't me doing it."

"Will anyone be kissing Sue?"

"More than likely."

"What about holding hands? Will Mack and Dale both be holding her hand?"

"No, today it will only be you and Dale. Mack won't be kissing her either. He's with Kathy today. Saturdays spent walking the refuge with Mack is something Kathy treasures. She'll be dominating his time today."

"Don't you mind that. A beautiful woman like her, holding on to your husband that way?"

"Not really. They're in love, so it's hard to get upset with them."

"Jesus, Lisa, how can you say something like that so casually. Mack is supposed to love only you. Not someone else."

"It's easy to say and to live with. Their love isn't doing anyone any harm. It's just something they have in their lives to share that most people can't dream of. And as far as what it does to me, well, I can get a little jealous now and then. It never lasts though. Mack loves me more than anyone or anything. Even life itself. I couldn't ask for a better husband."

"Like I've told you before, Lisa, you people do live life differently. How long is it going to be before I get Sue back?"

"Anytime. But you haven't lost her at all. Her and Dale are only friends. The same as you and I. They have been for a long time. So relax and walk with me. And when Mack stops to tell Kathy something, we'll want to listen. I'd be willing to bet that even a man who's spent as much time outdoors as you have, can learn something from him. This is his refuge. He owns it."

"What about you. Isn't this your refuge too."

"I suppose it is, in a way. But not my real refuge. I tried seeking refuge another way once. It didn't work. You see, I have my own special refuge. Mack is my refuge. He is my comfort and my joy. He makes me feel safe while he lets me be me. At the same time he protects me, I'm allowed to be free."

EPILOGUE

Jamie Foster was on his way to the general store to see if he could find a new video game. As he always did since he showed Mack where the body of the old man named Jasper was, he stopped at the willow tree. He couldn't help wondering each time he was there, what it was like for him to be alone under that tree. He was sure it had to be scary. He knew that he would be afraid if he was alone and dying.

The hardest thing for Jamie to understand was why the man was alone. He seemed to have friends. The man, Mack, looked like he cared a lot when he found out the old man was dead. And the lady named Lisa looked real sad and turned white when they brought his body out. If he had friends like that, why was he alone?

He then thought about his grandpa, who lived close by. It made him remember that he hadn't seen him for a long time. Mom asked him to come along every time she went to see him. But he didn't like to go, so she let him stay home. She always told him when she came home from her once a week visit to him, that he had seemed awful lonely. He wasn't so sure now, that staying home instead of going with mom to grandpa's was what he should keep on doing.

He pushed those thoughts out of his mind and walked the rest of the way to the general store. None of the new video games interested him, but he bought a cheap digital camera while he was there. Compared to the money Mack gave him, it didn't cost much. Someone, he couldn't remember who, told him once that if he carried a camera with him when he walked the country roads around his home that he hated, he might learn to see them differently. The effort it took to take good pictures, he was told, made a person see things differently.

Jamie didn't really believe that, but like most people his age he was easily bored, and today he was very bored. He still didn't see anything he thought was worth taking a picture of until he was once again near the willow tree. He jumped from the shock of it, when a large coyote walked out from under the tree.

She ignored him as she stalked a young, unwary rabbit who was enjoying the patch of clover it was chewing on at the edge of the road. I took him a moment to realize that he now had a picture worth taking. He pointed his new camera at the coyote, and snapped the picture at the moment it went after the rabbit. It was just a bit slow, so he got a great picture of a rabbit escaping the jaws of a hungry coyote.

After viewing the picture on the camera's display, it excited him enough to slice away his boredom. He right away looked for more pictures to take. Once he put some effort into it, he found picture after picture to snap. Almost all of them were of animals and birds, but he also found several trees and plants that were worthwhile subjects to be photographed. It took a while for him to discover that the landscape could provide him with a wealth of photos too.

He became so lost in what he was doing, that he didn't notice that he'd walked passed his own house. I wasn't until he walked all the way to his grandpa's that he realized where he was. It was seeing him working in his garden that did it. On impulse, he took a picture. That's when he noticed how bent the old man looked. For the first time, he looked at the old man with concern. Was he as old as Jasper was? And was he going to die too? If he did, would he be alone, the way Jasper was?"

Jamie wasn't sure whether or not he wanted to say anything to him, but then grandpa noticed him. He immediately waved, and big smiled formed on his face. "Jamie," he called out, "what brings you here today?"

Not at all sure how to answer that, Jamie thought about all the things he could say. He thought about saying something about taking pictures, and that made him think about the coyote. From there his memory took him to another coyote coming out from under the willow tree. That took him to Jasper and how lonely he must of been. Lonely like mom said grandpa was. So he lied to him, hoping it would make him feel better.

"I just came to see you, grandpa. I want to show you my new camera. I took a bunch of pictures today."

"Well bring it over here. I'd love to see your pictures."

Jamie brought him the camera, showed grandpa how to view the pictures, and looked around at the garden while he waited. It didn't take him long to realize that the garden would make some good pictures too. It wasn't very big, but what there was of it was perfect. All the plants were thriving, the rows were perfectly straight, and the few weeds were in the row where grandpa was working when Jamie got there. It was the last of the weeding he had left to do.

"You took some pretty good pictures," grandpa told him when he finished looking at them. "The coyote picture was more than good. It was special. I hope you keep on taking pictures. It's something you can be proud of. A lot more than playing video games. Maybe you can print the coyote picture for me. I can make a frame for it. I'd like to hang it in my living room."

"Sure, Grandpa, I can print it for you. It was my first picture."

"It wouldn't have mattered how many you took before or after that one, you would be hard put to take a better one."

They talked about photography for a while, then Jamie asked if it was okay to take some pictures of the garden. It was, of course, just fine with grandpa. So were the pictures he took of grandpa in the garden. After while of picture taking grandpa invited him to sit on the deck with him and have a glass of iced tea. Grandpa added some lemon juice and a couple of scoops of sugar to Jamie's, so he actually enjoyed it.

He also found himself enjoying the stories he was told. Grandpa talked a lot about the past. He knew and understood it far better than the modern world they now lived in. The world so full of hate and greed and the lust for power. Those weren't the only things that left him feeling out of it, like he could never fit into it. All the electronics he had to put up with, were also a constant source of frustration.

It had never before occurred to Jamie that life was so different before he was born. At first, when he was told about the way life was for his great grandparents, he found it awful hard to believe. Especially the parts about what they didn't have. It didn't seem possible that anyone could live without electric lights and running water. And what did anyone do at night if they needed to go to the bathroom and the toilet was outside in the backyard. And how could it be that such a short time ago, none of the modern day electronics even existed. How could people stand it without TVs, computers, and video games? What did they do with their time?

When grandpa explained that they didn't have any problem with their time, he was surprised by his explanations. They talked through the afternoon then. It was grandpa, who missed his normal afternoon nap and was now very tired, who called it a day. Jamie reluctantly left him then. When he got home, he was surprised to find a very upset mom. He was gone a good part of the day, and she was worried sick about him.

"So where were you all day?" she demanded. "You scared me when you were gone so long."

"I'm sorry, Mom. I was at grandpa's. We were talking, and I forgot how long I was there. Tomorrow when I go see him, I will call you if I'm going to be that late."

"Jamie, you shouldn't tell me something that isn't true. I want to know where you were today, and where you are going to go tomorrow."

"But it is true. I was at grandpa's. I went there accidentally, but when I showed him the pictures I took, we started talking. You can look at my new camera. There are some pictures of grandpa on it. And did you know, Mom, that there didn't used to be TVs or computers or video games? And a long time ago, the toilet people used was outside?"

She laughed then. When she looked at the pictures on Jamie's new camera, she was surprised at how good they were. He seemed to have a natural talent for photography. She could see the care Jamie put into the pictures of grandpa that he took. They were dominated by a show of respect that Jamie gave him. She never again had to worry about him on those days he seemed to disappear. If he wasn't visiting with his grandpa, he was wandering world he no longer hated, but now loved, taking pictures.

Often, he thought of the man he found under the willow tree. He felt bad that he died alone, yet was in his own way thankful to him. If he hadn't have been there for Jamie to discover, he would probably still be spending his free time playing video games instead of taking pictures and spending time with his grandpa. He knew that missing the time he spent with grandpa would be the biggest loss he could have growing up. He also knew that after he did grow up, as long as grandpa was alive, he needed to be there for him. Letting something happen to grandpa, like what happened to Jasper Klug, would be unforgivable.

*****

Mack wrote the first draft of Jasper's book. Lisa and Kathy followed his work with it and did a thorough job of editing. It was next passed around among everyone at Refuge Rescuers for comment. Even Larry, who was close to completely recovered from his gunshot wound, read every word carefully. He even made a few suggestions that Mack liked and incorporated into the next draft.

Everyone involved was so serious about the book, that they went through that same process five times before they did anything with the manuscript. It took submissions to ten agents before they found one. She loved the book, and managed to sell it to one of the largest publishers in the country.

Sales started slow when it was first published, but word of mouth did wonders for it. It never reached the best seller lists, but did sell far better than they'd expected. A lot of money from the sales of it went to places that helped seniors who needed it. So in the end, Jasper managed to do one more very big thing in his life. The book, now titled Jasper's Story, was about to do even more. It was about to lead to events none of them could have imagined before they started.

*****

When the three men who tried to kidnap Emma so they could keep her to rape were killed in a crash, all of the hard copy information the Canadien officials had about Emma was destroyed. All of it was then on their computer system.

While the information was being moved from one file to another, it somehow disappeared out to somewhere in cyber space. The only person who knew where it went was Sue Sartor. And she wasn't about to tell anyone.

Once that information was lost forever for official use, Sue went work creating a new life for Emma. She quickly had a birth certificate, which was filed in the computer in Hennepin County in Minnesota. She also created and filed in the proper place, a Social Security number for her. She searched until she found information about a couple, that were the right age, who were killed when they drove off a cliff out west. Their bodies were never recovered. Sue made them the parents of Emma, since they had lived in Minnesota. She also created a document saying that the parents requested that if anything ever happened to them, Sue should adopt Emma. Sue then created the adoption papers and properly filed them. She also set things up for Larry to actually adopt her, should he choose to.

All in all, those three useless rapists who met a fitting death, did one thing in their life that turned out good. They gave Emma a whole new life, free from a lot of legal hassle which in the end would have done nobody any good.

*****

Shortly after the book, Jasper's Story, was published, someone from PBS read it. She contacted Mack, and convinced him that a documentary should be made about Jasper, using the book as the base for it. Mack agreed, as long as neither he nor any of the rest of the Refuge Rescuers people were given credit for it.

They all wanted Jasper to be the famous one, if there was going to be anyone famous. The film that was created was done extremely well, and got better ratings during the reruns than it did for the original broadcast.

They were in fact good enough to raise hopes that the serious problem of homelessness, along with the shoddy treatment of senior citizens would be improved.

There were scattered improvements on a local level in several places, but nationally nothing of any significance changed. The Republicans still controlled the federal government, and nothing ever changes for the better when they have control.

*****

Mack and Lisa visited Matti several more times. She absolutely loved the book, and especially the careful way they wrote about the nine days she spent with Jasper. She cried through the entire PBS video about Jasper, but there were also some smiles in between the tears.

The last time Lisa and Mack went to visit her, she wasn't there. She died peacefully during the night. They found her in the morning, lying on her back. Her eyes were closed and under her hands on her stomach, she held Jasper's book and a photo of her and Jasper. They were only around ten years old when it was taken.

Mack and Lisa realized then that Matti was Jasper's real story. He was a good man, with not enough ups and more downs than what he should have had. And the biggest, most important event in in his life was the one he didn't have. The fulfillment of his love for Matti. The one thing he deserved the most.

*****

Char personally delivered the mail to Refuge Rescuers. There were three packages along with the regular mail, but the main reason for doing it was to find Mack there. It was her lucky day and she did. She took him outside so they could have a private conversation.

"I have a favor to ask of you, Mack," she said to start it.

"Ask away, Char. I still feel like I owe you, so there aren't too many things I wouldn't do for you."

"Good. I don't know how big a deal this would be for you, but for me it's a real big one. It'll only be your time that I want. I know how busy you always are, so I might be asking too much."

"I doubt it, Char. The least I can do for you is give you some of my time."

"Good. I've heard about that you sometimes give to the most special people in your life a day with you in the refuge. I want one of those days with you, and you alone, walking the refuge you love so much. I want to be able to hold your hand and listen when you tell me all about whatever it is that we see. Do you think we can do that?

"What day do you want to do that?"

"On the first day you can get free."

"Will tomorrow work for you?"

"Oh god yes." She gave him a big smile. "Tomorrow is perfect."

They met early the next morning at the trailhead of Mack's favorite hike. The trail wandered through a hilly part of the refuge, and was a mixture of new growth woods and meadow. Its recovery from the fire was remarkable. For a short ways it followed the St. Catherine river, then traveled along the shores of several small ponds.

As they walked near the ponds, Mack often stopped to point out the ducks and geese in the water, or the numerous different shore birds. She did impress him when she listened with a rapt attention to what he told her. She was very much interested in everything he said, which was very different from what he had expected when she made her request. All he initially expected from her was a day of flirting. Instead, it was a contented walk in the refuge. The closest she came to any kind of flirting was constantly holding his hand and kissing him once, each time they stopped to rest.

They did make a full day of it though, and managed to see all manner of wildlife. When their day was over, she held him tight when she kissed him goodbye.

"All I ask from you, Mack," she said, "is that now and then you give me a day like this, in this place that is so much you. I love you Mack Thomas, but I don't ever want to do anything to hurt you. So I'll never again try to take what belongs to Lisa."

"I love you too, Char. You've always been more than just a good friend. As far as walks for the two of us, you only have to do is ask. I'll always make the time for you."

*****

Larry left for his first sabbatical from life with Sue and work with Refuge Rescuers. When he got on the plane, he wasn't sure he would ever return. He was deeply in love with Sue and felt as if he was Emma's real father. But his love of the wild and his time alone there was a strong calling for him.

His first three days wandering the forest that was a big part of his life before he left Canada, took a strong hold on him. Strong enough so by the time he bedded down that night, he didn't think he would go back. His love of this life and what it gave him was too strong.

Before going to sleep, he read part of Jasper's book on his cell phone. It was about Matti, and when she talked about the strong calling she got from God, and how she felt God needed her to dedicate her life to him. Thinking of what it did to her and Jasper, and of how much they lost, his sleep was limited that night. His major thought through the night was why? How could God's need for her be more important than what she and Jasper should have had?

He wondered the whole time why she would think God needed her more than Jasper did. He remembered what Lisa told him about seeking refuge somewhere else. Was that what Matti had been looking for? God could do anything, have anything, or create anything. What did he need Matti for? That led him to thoughts about where he was. Sue filled his mind. Her face covered any picture he could create of the wild place where he was. That place certainly didn't need him for anything any more than God could have needed Matti.

Sue did need him. As important, he needed her. He could always return to these wild places. But he could easily lose Sue the same way Matti lost Jasper. He knew, if he walked away from the wilds, they'd be there when he returned. In the same way, he knew that if he lost Sue, she would be gone forever. And he could never replace her. He lost her once because of walking away, and the wilds weren't all that great while he was missing her. He was extremely fortunate that she accepted him back. She wouldn't do it again. So he knew then that he would return. He didn't want to be a Matti and give it all up for virtually nothing the way she did. And he didn't want to hurt Sue the way Matti hurt Jasper. And as much as anything, he didn't want to die alone under a willow tree.

When Sue asked him why he came back three days early from his sabbatical, he said, "Because not even God or any wild place matters as much to me as you do. I love you Sue." She knew then that he would stay with her. She also was once again thankful for all that they'd gained from an old man named Jasper. A man that she now loved dearly, even though she never knew him.

*****

Mack woke up an hour before sunrise. Lisa was lying with her back tight against him. He gently moved his left arm out from under her head, and carefully got out of bed. He walked out into the kitchen, turned on a light, and the coffee pot he'd put together the night before. As he took his first sip of coffee, he heard the shower. Lisa was up.

When she joined him in the kitchen, her head was wrapped in a towel and her body was covered with an old, terrycloth bathrobe that was held closed with one tie. He tipped his head to one side, his eyes focused on her face. He couldn't control the smile he had.

"No matter how many times I look at you and know that you are my wife, I will never know how I can be this lucky. You are so beautiful, Lisa, that every time I look at you I doubt that my life is real."

She gave him the same look he was giving her. "I ask myself the same question, Mack. You know that I fell in love with you the very first time I ever saw you. I've told you that enough times. Seeing you so early in the morning makes me want to ask you. Do you want to go back to bed?"

"Yes, but we have commitments today. Sue and Emma are coming with us to the refuge this morning, and Jamie and his mom are meeting us there."

"I know, but I thought I'd ask anyway."

"And you know that if we could, I would take you there in a second. We've been married long enough now, so this should be wearing off. It isn't. It often seems as though I want you more now than I ever did. So I'm going to take my shower and get dressed, before we end up disappointing those people. Two of them are kids, so we definitely don't want to do that today."

"I know. You are right." But just to tease, she took off her robe and carried it into the bedroom to get dressed. Mack started his shower with cold water.

Jamie's mom told Mack, during one of their conversations about Jamie, about how he'd changed from an unhappy, dissatisfied teenager, to a young man wanting to learn as much about life as he could. So Mack and Lisa were both aware of how much Jasper's death, and the fact that he died alone the way he did, had such a big affect on him.

When they came to the spot on the trail they were hiking, where Mack found Jasper, he hesitated for a moment. He looked to Lisa to see if she had an answer for what was the best thing to do.

She just nodded her head yes, so Mack told Jamie, "See how the ground dips down some on the edge of the trail. That's where I found Jasper. He was pretty well worn down, and too tired to move. So we took him home with us."

"I know about that, but you should have kept him there at your house."

"That's what we tried to do. But sometime in the night, he left us. If it wasn't for you, we never would have known what happened to him."

"Why did he leave though. It doesn't make any sense."

"He said he didn't want to be a burden to anyone. I think that by then, he was homeless so long that he genuinely believed that that's all he was or ever could be."

"My grandpa says that stuff about not being a burden too. I sure hope I can keep him from ever going away like Jasper did. I sure don't want him to die alone."

"My daddy didn't die alone," Emma said then. "Wanda shot him so he can't hurt me anymore."

Jamie's mom looked at Sue. "Where did she get a story in her head like that?"

Sue rolled her eyes up in her head, shrugged her shoulders, and answered, "Probably from something on television I shouldn't have let her watch."

Mack knew then, that it was time for him to start talking about the refuge. He pointed out then, how far its recovery had come since the fire that destroyed most of it years before. The trail was moving closer to the river at that point, so they were lucky enough to see a pair of otters play as they moved in and out of the water. A short time later, they watched a raccoon pull a crayfish out of a stagnant pool of water. It carried it to the river, washed it, then proceeded to tear it apart and eat it. At first Sue and Jamie's mom wanted to pull their kids away from the sight of what the raccoon was doing.

Mack told them, "I know that it is in some ways hard for them to watch, but it is part of nature, part of life. They should know what nature really is, and watching that is as good a place to start as any."

"But it's so harsh," Jamie's mom complained. "I'm not convinced that it is the right thing for them to see."

"I guess it's possible that it's not, but it's a lesson we all have to learn. In our world, for life on this planet to exist, there's one rule we can't change. For anything to live, something has to die. And there's nothing we can do to change that."

"But you still believe that nature's beautiful?"

"I do. Just like I know that we humans are, for the most part, destroying it. That raccoon didn't do anything wrong when it killed and ate that crayfish. It only did what it needed to do to survive. We, on the other hand, are more than happy to kill anything, even each other, to get what we want. Even when we don't do it directly, we do it through neglect. Witness Jasper and how his life ended. People who are aware of that neglect are becoming fewer all the time. That's why you should be proud of Jamie. He is aware."

"I know that. The one thing about all this though, is how one old man who was pushed to the side, and from what I read in his book, kind of neglected his whole life, could have so much affect on all of us."

"It is. And if I was a much better writer, I might try to write a book about all of us who were affected by him." He stopped for a moment and looked at Lisa. He thought about how close they came, for a while, to not making it together, and how the conversation they had with Jasper had changed so much for them.

Lisa, who was listening to Mack's every word, said, "That's a project I think you need to tackle, Mack. And I'll be by your side every step of the way."

"As will I," Sue added.

"Even I will try to help if you'll let me?" Jamie's mom said.

"I'll take pictures for you, if you want any?" Jamie added.

"You can even tell about how mean my daddy was," Emma told him.

Other than Jamie's mom, they all tried to ignore Emma's comment. If it would have only been something she imagined, it wouldn't have mattered. The problem was, what happened to him was true. Wanda did shoot him. Sue knew then that she had to try to teach Emma not to talk about it.

"Well, maybe I can give that book a try," Mack agreed. "Just don't anyone get their hopes up too high. Doing Jasper's book was a damn hard thing for me to do. Writing the book all of you want might be impossible."

They moved on with their walk then, and for some reason they had a day filled with the sights and sounds and signs of a large variety of wildlife. Jamie had a great day of photography, and had thought ahead enough to bring plenty of memory along with him. By days end, he'd taken over two hundred pictures.

That night, Lisa asked Mack, "If you do write that book, will you write about us? Will you write about you and Kathy and Dale and I?"

"I don't know. Do you think I should?"

"Yes, but if you do, you should write it like it is someone else. Make them up."

"Is there a reason why you want any of that in the book at all?"

"Yes, there is. I think that people should be able to see another side of life. A side that isn't necessarily bad, only because it's different."

"I know that none of that has any negative effect on our relationship," Mack said, but what would you say about it if I told you I want to stop doing it. That I want you only for me."

"I would say, okay, I love you, Mack, and if that's what you want, that's what we'll do. Everything that isn't you and me is okay and even really special sometimes. But the truth is, for me, it's us together that matters far and away the most. We are together now, and that's what I want as long as you and I are both alive. And I'm selfish enough, Mack, to hope when the time comes I die first. Because I don't know that I'd want to continue very long without you."

"I think there's only two possible good solutions to all that for you and I, Lisa. Either we'll have to die together, or both of us will have to live a very long life. Personally, I prefer we have the long life."

Lisa took his hand and led him to the bedroom. "Just in case we don't live as long a life as we want, we should continue, as much as possible, to do what I want to do right now. Especially if it's just you and me forever."

"Don't worry, Lisa, whatever it is, it will always be you and me. You are the love of my life, so even if we do live it a bit different from what most of the rest of the world does, it will always be in the end, you and me."

They were in bed by then, and she moved over him. As he felt the magic her body gave him, he for one quick moment thanked Jasper for the words he spoke to them that helped keep them together. Quickly though, he was lost in the world they only shared with each other. For them in that moment, there was no other world.